Pussy, King of the Pirates

Pussy, King of the Pirates

Kathy Acker

GROVE PRESS
New York

Printed in the United States of America
Published simultaneously in Canada

The musical companion, *Pussy, King of the Pirates* by The Mekons and Kathy Acker (Q536), is available from Quarterstick / Touch and Go Records.

Library of Congress Cataloging-in-Publication Data

Acker, Kathy, 1948–1997.
    Pussy, king of the pirates / Kathy Acker.
    ISBN 0-8021-3484-X (pbk.)
    I. Title.
    PS3551.C44P87   1996   813'.54—dc20   9521012

DESIGN BY LAURA HAMMOND HOUGH

Grove Press
an imprint of Grove/Atlantic, Inc.
841 Broadway
New York, NY 10003

05 06 07 08 09   10 9 8 7 6 5 4 3

Contents

Preface:
Once upon a Time, Not Long Ago, ☼ . . .

Artaud Speaks:

When O was a young girl, above all she wanted a man to take care of her.

In her dream, the city was the repository of all dreams.

A city that was always decaying. In the center of this city, her father had hung himself.

This can't be true, O thought, because I've never had a father.

In her dream, she searched for her father.

She knew that it was a dumb thing for her to do because he was dead.

Since she wasn't dumb, O thought, she must be trying to find him so that she could escape from the house in which she was living, which was run by a woman.

O went to a private detective. He called O a dame.

"I'm looking for my father."

The private eye, who in one reality was a friend of O's, replied that the case was an easy one.

O liked that she was easy.

And so they began. First, according to his instructions, O told him all that she knew about the mystery. It took her several days to recount all the details.

At that time it was summertime in Dallas. All yellow.

O didn't remember anything in or about the first period. Of her childhood.

After not remembering, she remembered the jewels. When her mother had died, a jewel case had been opened. The case, consisting of one tray, had insides of red velvet. O knew that this was also her mother's cunt.

O was given a jewel which was green.

O didn't know where that jewel was now. What had happened to it. Here was the mystery of which she had spoken.

The private eye pursued the matter. A couple of days later, he came up with her father's name.

"Oli."

The name meant nothing to her.

"Your father's name is Oli. Furthermore, your father killed your mother."

That's possible, O thought, as if thinking was dismissing.

The detective continued to give her details about her father: he was from Iowa and of Danish blood.

All of this could be true because what could she in all possibility know?

When O woke up out of her insane dream, she remembered that her mother had died eight days before Christmas. Despite the note lying beside the dead body in which the location of the family's white poodle was revealed, the cops were convinced that the mother had been murdered. By a man unknown. Since it was now Christmas, these cops had no intention of investigating a murder when they could be returning to their families, Christmas warmth, and holiday.

O realized, for the first time in her life, that her father could have murdered her mother. According to the only member of her father's family she had ever met, a roly-poly first cousin whose daughter picked up Bowery bums for sexual purposes (according to him), her father had murdered someone who had been trespassing on his yacht.

Then, her father had disappeared.

O became scared. If her father had killed her mother, he could slaughter her. Perhaps that's what her life had been about.

During this period of time, O lived and stayed alive by dreaming. One of the reveries concerned the most evil man in the world.

It was at a fancy resort that was located in the country, far from the city: O stood on one of the stony platforms or giant records that jutted out of a huge cliff. Shrubbery was growing out of parts of the rock. Each record lay directly over and under another record, except for *the top* and *the bottom*. The one on which O perched thrust farther than the others into a sky that was empty, for this record was a stage.

In the first act of this play, O learned that evil had entered the land. That the father, who was equivalent to *evil*, was successfully stealing or appropriating his son's possessions. Both of them were standing behind O. Then, the father began to torture his son. He inflicted pain physically. O actually saw this older man point three different machine guns at her. Each of them was different. O understood that he wanted to scare, rather than shoot, her.

He laughed. And then disappeared.

O hated him more than it was possible to hate anyone.

Either the next day or some days later, the young woman began to search for the older man. She and his son were partners, co-mercenaries, in this venture; in fact, it was the son who taught O that to be a successful detective, one has to get rid of fear.

For some reason unknown to O, she was always frightened of people.

The father left one clue to his whereabouts. *DN*.

Nobody seemed to know whether *DN* was the initials of someone, of something, whether the letters were part of a language no human could understand. O and the son believed that *DN* was the name of a coffee joint . . . .
. . . .

They entered a deserted western town. The coffee joint they found in the loneliness, whose name was *a street*, within all the yellow, didn't have a name . . . .
. . . .

They traveled to a ranch. The main building, which at first they didn't notice because it wasn't noticeable, was one-story, white peeling paint. In its right side, a cafe-in-the-wall.

A girl was feeding her dog-horse, 'cause it was as large as a large horse, a plate of raw hamburger. She used to be married to the son; now she was living on this ranch and happy.

This is the second clue.

One didn't need to find any more because the man for whom she had been looking walked right up to her. In all that openness, there was no one but those two. O realized that all that had happened to her had happened only because she was attracted to this man. To this father. And she hated him because he was violent.

It was at this point that O began to teach him how to change violence into pleasure.

Now O decided that she wanted to go where she had never been before:

O Speaks:

The revolution had yet to begin in China. At that time, the word *revolution* meant nothing to us because the same governments owned everything. There seemed nowhere left to go. All of my friends, including me, before we reached old age, were dying and, until we died, living in ways that were unbearable because that's what living was. Unbearable.

I had no interest in politics.

I had come to China as I usually came: I had been following a guy.

I had believed we were in love.

It didn't matter, the name of this unknown city to which I came. All the unknown cities, in China, held slums that looked exactly like each other: each one a labyrinth, a dream, in which streets wound into streets which disappeared in more streets and every street went nowhere. For every sign had disappeared.

The poor ate whatever they could put their hands on.

Right before the revolution, the Chinese government told its people that the recession was over. This lie made the poor unable to distinguish between economic viability and disability. Some of them walked around with needles sticking out of their bodies.

Many of the women were whoring for money.

W, my boyfriend, said that if I loved him, I would whore for him. I knew that W got off on women who were prostitutes. I didn't know whether or not he had deep feelings for me and, if so, what those feelings were. I used to wonder, again and again, why I ran after men who didn't care for me.

It was my mother, not my father, who dominated my waking life. When she was alive, my mother didn't notice or, if she had to, hated me. She wanted me to be nothing, or something worse, because my appearance in her womb, not yet in the world, caused her husband to leave her. So my mother, who was ravishingly beautiful, charming, and a liar, had told me. While she was alive.

Absence isn't the name of the father only.

Every whorehouse is childhood.

The one in which W placed me was named *Ange*.

Outside the whorehouse, men fear women who are beautiful and run away from them; a ravishing woman who's with a man must bear a scar that isn't physical. My mother was weak in this way; her weakness turned into my fate.

Inside the brothel, the women, however they actually look, are always beautiful to men. Because they fulfill their fantasies. In this way, what was known as *the male regime*, in the territory named *women's bodies*, separated its reason from its fantasy.

Since I was the only white girl in this brothel, the others there, including the Madam, who had once been a male, hated me. They sneered at my characteristics, such as my politeness. What they really detested was that economic necessity hadn't driven me into prostitution. To them, the word *love* had no meaning. But I didn't become a whore because I loved W so much I'd do anything for him. Anything to convince him to love me. A love I was beginning to know I would never receive. I entered the brothel of my own free will, so that I could become nothing, because, I believed, only when I was nothing would I begin to see.

I had no idea what I was doing.

When I entered the house, Madam took away all of my possessions, even my tiny black reading glasses. It was as if she was a prison matron. She said that, because I was white, I thought that I deserved to possess commodities. Such as happiness. That I was too pale, too delicate to be able to bear living in this place.

The other girls thought that I could leave the cathouse whenever I wanted.

But I couldn't walk away, because inside the whorehouse I was nobody. There was nobody to walk away.

I was now a child: if I ridded myself of childhood, there would be nothing left of me.

Later on, the girls would accept me as a whore. Then I would start to wish that I loved a man who loved me.

There were many prescients in the slum. The whores, in their spare hours, visited these fortune-tellers. Though I soon started accompanying my friends, I was too scared to say anything to these women, most of whom had once been in the business. I would stand in the shadows and rarely ask anything, for I didn't want to confess anything about myself. When I, at last, did inquire about a future, I asked as if there were no such thing. I felt safe knowing only the details of daily life, johns and defecations, all that was a dream.

As if dreams couldn't be real.

Fortune-tellers wandered around the streets outside Ange.

The one fortune, *mine*, which I remember, was based on the card of the Hanged Man:

The woman who was reading the cards still took tricks.

"Does that mean that I'm going to suicide?" I asked.

"Oh, no, O. This card says that you're a dead person who's alive. You're a zombie."

But I knew better. I knew that the Hanged Man, or Gérard de Nerval, was my father and every man I fucked was him.

My father was the owner of Death, of the cathouse. Sitting in his realm of absence, he surveyed all that wasn't.

The cards showed me clearly that I hated him. When a message travels from the invisible to the visible world, that messenger is emotion. My anger, a messenger, would lead to revolution. Revolutions are dangerous to everyone.

But the cards said worse. They told us, the whores, that the revolution, which was just about to happen, had to fail, due to its own nature or origin. As soon as it failed, as soon as sovereignty, be it reigning or revolutionary, disappeared, as soon as sovereignty ate its own head as if it were a snake, when the streets turned to poverty and decay, but a different poverty and decay, all my dreams, which were me, would be shattered.

"And then," the fortune-teller said, "you'll find yourself on a pirate ship."

The cards that I remember told me that my future is freedom.

"But what'll I do when there's no one in the world who loves me? When all existence is only freedom?"

The cards proceeded to show images of stress, illness, disease . . .

I had been in the cathouse for a month. W hadn't once visited me, for he had never cared about me.

I was a whore because I was alone.

The fortune-teller had told me that I would be free after I journeyed into the land of the dead.

I was trying to get rid of loneliness and nothing would ever rid me of loneliness until I got rid of myself.

Artaud Speaks:

O said, "I want to go where I've never been before."

I was living in a room that was in the slum. I was still sane.

I was just a boy. All I saw was the poverty of those slums. In order to counteract the poverty that was without and within me, I ran to poetry. Especially to the poetry of Gérard de Nerval, who wanted to stop his own suffering, to transform himself, but instead hanged himself from a rusty picture nail.

I had no life. I only loved those poets who were criminals. I began to write letters to people I didn't know, to those poets, not in order to communicate with them. To do something else.

Dear Georges, I wrote.

I have just read, in Fontane *magazine, two articles by you on Gérard de Nerval which made a strange impression on me.*

I am a limitless series of natural disasters and all of these disasters have been unnaturally repressed. For this

reason I am kin to Gérard de Nerval who hanged himself in a
street alley during the hours of a night.
    Suicide is only a protest against control.

Artaud

The alleyways were lying all around me. They ran every
which way, so haphazardly that they stopped. There was the
brothel.

I would watch man after man walk through its doors.
Men went to this brothel, not in order to have the sexual in-
tercourse they could have on the outside, but to enact elaborate and tortuous fantasies which, one day, I'll be able to
describe to you.

I'll be able when there's human pleasure in this world.

Day after day I would look through one of my windows
into one of theirs. There I first saw O, who was naked. My eye
would follow her, as much as it could, trying to clear away for
her everything that was before and behind her.

I would die for her. Whenever a man hangs himself, his
cock becomes so immense that for the first time he knows that
he has a cock.

One day O came out of the brothel. I saw her stand on
the edge of its doorway and look away. Obviously she was
terrified. Finally, one of her feet peeped over the door-
frame's bottom. I had no idea what was mirrored in those
eyes. Three times her feet darted back and forth across that
doorstep.

As soon as she was fully outside, she began to turn in the
same ways the winds do through the sky. Perhaps she was

meeting the outside, the sky, for the first time. Perhaps, in the staleness of the brothel, O had been a *she* and now she was another *she* who wasn't distinct from air. I watched this girl begin to breathe. I watched her encounter poverty for the first time, the streets that my body was daily touching. The streets whose inhabitants ate whatever they could and, when they no longer could eat, died.

These streets reminded O of her childhood. For when she was a child she had always been alone. Even though she'd a half-sister, who was now married to a European armaments millionaire. Every summer O's mother, so she would never have to see her, sent O to a posh summer camp. A camp of girls.

There the girls passed through the latest dances in each other's arms in the hour before they were ordered in to dinner while O watched them. She knew that she couldn't dance. For the first time in her life, in the whorehouse, O was safe because, here, there were no humans.

In the whorehouse she had become naked.

Now that O felt safe, she had the strength to return to her childhood. To poverty. I watched O walk down street after street, searching for who she would be. I knew that when she had found what she had to find she would belong to me.

O Speaks:

The first time W and I slept together I knew that he didn't love me. But I didn't know why. The nausea and confusion that resulted left me shreds of belief to which I could cling: I clung to belief that in the future W might start to love me.

Like a child who's not able to believe that her mother doesn't care about her.

I remained in that brothel. One day W came back to tell me that he wanted me to meet the woman he adored even more than his own life. To meet her, he was going to take me out of the brothel for the day.

They had been together many years before he met me. He said. That she had left him. It had been his fault: he wasn't good to her. She returned to him in China, and now he wanted to be as good to her as it was possible for a human to be.

Though she had come back to him, she still wasn't sure whether she wanted to be with him, and this made him love her more.

I didn't know who I was to W, why he was telling me about the woman he worshiped.

I could cling to my nausea. Maybe nausea, then, is something. A man's body. I followed him out of the brothel. Into those streets which I had started to explore by myself.

A bird was flying through the sky.

His girlfriend was as white as me. But she was beautiful and rich. As soon as I met her, I knew that I didn't exist for her, in the same way that I didn't exist for W, that she didn't know how to love. She was one of those owners. She was somebody.

I could love W, which she never could, but what did he want? Did he want all that I would be able to give him?

After dinner, he brought his girlfriend and me back to the brothel and he tied me to my bed. Needles inserted into the flesh just below the lower lashes kept the eyes open. In front of me, W made love to her. First with his fingers. Delicately playing with her outer labia. They turned from pale pink to blood-red. Opened to my eyes as his fingers disappeared. Some were in her mouth. He was bending her over and then he turned around, her cunt juice dripping so much that I could see it on his fingertips, and put his cock, which was in my mind, into that cunt that must have been open, wanting, screaming for pleasure, whether she loved him or not, she was being fucked inserted thrust into pummeled bruised and all that comes out is pleasure, the body is pleasure, I have known pleasure, and I am watching the endless pleasure, as it comes again again again, that I have known and now I am being refused.

Rich, she could never know what my pleasure was, and so I changed.

Throughout all of the dinner and the sex I was forced, also by myself, to watch, I was wearing the red lipstick that my mother had worn. My mother always walked around her house naked, touching her own body. She wore her menstrual blood on her mouth. In her house there were no men, for my father had left her before I was born.

Since I never knew you, every man I fuck is you. Daddy. Every cock goes into my cunt which, since I never knew you, is a river named Cocytus. I said that I'm only going to tell the truth: When you, Cock of all Cocks, you, the only lay in the world, and I know for I'm supposed to live, not die, for sex, when you took a leave of absence ejaculated disappeared skipped out and vanished before I was born, you threw me, and I hadn't yet been born, into even another world.

The name of that world was China.

Who can understand China's teeming populaces, its children, its marching student soldiers?

Artaud Rewrites His First Letter to Georges Le Breton:
*I am a violent being, full of fiery storms and other
catastrophic phenomena. As yet I can't do more than begin
this letter, begin it again and again, because I have to eat
myself, my own body is my only food, in order to write. But
I don't want to talk about myself. I want to discuss Gérard
de Nerval. He made living: a living world. He made a living
world out of myth and magic. The realm of myth and magic
that he contacted was that of a Funeral. His own death and
funeral.*

> *I'll talk about death, my death, later.*

> *The Tarot card in the realm of Nerval is the Hanged
Man. Heidegger, under the same sign, reversed himself and
turned away from Hitler. Trying "to come to terms with his
. . . past in the Nazi movement," he explained that "the
very possibility of taking action" or "the will to rule and
dominate" was "a kind of original sin, of which he found
himself guilty." Instead of* Dasein, *he placed emphasis on*
Sein, *or an essentially reverent contemplativeness, one that
might open and keep open the possibility of a new paganism
in which no sovereignty could arise, no sovereignty out of the
ashes of Hitler's aborted revolution.*

> *Reverent contemplativeness is the Hanged Man in the
realm of Nerval. Contemplativeness is the act of turning
inside out, reversing, traveling the road into the land of the
dead while being and remaining alive. Contemplativeness is
seeming to do nothing. In other words, the Hanged Man
card, to me, represents the slight possibility that this society in
which human identity depends upon possessing rather than on*

being possessed, that this society in which I'm living, could change.

Gérard de Nerval was a sailor who descended into oblivion and, as he did, wrote against oblivion. He hated his own cockhead and so he descended into the Cocytus, into oblivion, three times, until his cockhead floated bloody on those waters. In other words, he hung himself.

O Speaks:

I spent day after day walking the streets, looking for W, whom I would never again find.

The Letter Continues:

I am Gérard de Nerval who hung himself 12:00 P.M. on a Thursday by his own hands. The other one died in Paris or announced that his death was going to happen, he announced that he was going to die from loneliness.

I, Gérard de Nerval, who write in the teeth of the utilitarian concept of the universe, will hang myself from an apron string tied to a grating. There will be nothing left.

At this moment, I, Gérard de Nerval, want to talk about the difference between hanging and the Hanged Man:

I, Antonin Artaud, hung myself and I haven't died.

I'm living in a slum in China and I'm going to become sexual.

O Speaks:

If W's not around, I don't want to be a whore.

Artaud Speaks:
I entered the brothel so that I could meet O. The Madam stopped me to ask where I was going. I said that I was going to serve O.

She told me that I had to give her money before I could be with O. Because I didn't have any money I was thrown out of the whorehouse.

I found myself in a marketplace where everything was being sold for everything else. Some of the poor who were there didn't have any limbs. Others were willing to do anything sexually for money. The children said that a third of them would die, the next harvest, if there weren't enough beans. I decided that I had to stop the hell in which I was living.

I knew that they had thrown me out of the whorehouse because I refused to give O money.

I wanted O to love me.

Their denial of my sexuality planted in me the seeds of rebellion. There would be other women and men like me in that slum. Ones who would do whatever had to be done in order to change everything.

O Speaks:
I no longer want to be a whore.

Artaud Speaks:
It was at this time that the revolutionaries, both male and female, met in what light came from the quarter-moon.

"We're poor," they said. "We need to get our hands on weapons."

"A white man just gave us some money for weapons, probably just to save his own neck."

Though I had no interest in such tools, I agreed to undertake the machine-gun delivery, dangerous at the least, in return for the exact amount of cash I needed to buy O so that I could give her her freedom.

In this way, I cut my cockhead off, and blood from a heart I had never known started to flow.

O Speaks:

How long will this reign of masochism continue?

Artaud Addresses This Version of His Letter to O:

Everywhere he went, Nerval would take with him a scummy apron string that had once belonged to the Queen of Sheba. Nerval told me this. Or it was one of the corset laces of Madame de Maintenon. Or of Marguerite de Valois.

From this apron string, which was tied to a grating, he hung himself. The grating, black, partly broken, and stained by hound excretion, was located at the bottom of the stone stairs which lead to the rue de la Tuerie. There's a straight drop from that stair platform downward.

As Nerval swung there, a raven hovered over, as if it were sitting on his head, and cawed repeatedly, "I'm thirsty."

They were probably the only words the old bird knew.

I, Antonin Artaud, am now an owner, for I own the language of suicide.

Why did Gérard de Nerval hang himself from an open string? Why is this society which is China insane?

To learn why Gérard madly offed himself, I shall enter his soul:

Gérard was a man like me. He wrote this:

. . . le dernier, vaincu par ton génie, (Jehovah)
Qui, du fond des enfers, criait: "O tyrannie!"

Gérard was le dernier because, when he wrote that, he was just about to suicide, he was writing his own suicide note to God the Tyrant, whose very existence was putting Gérard in hell. That is, Gérard suicided because of the existence of God: Gérard opposed the tyrant God by cutting off his own head. For God is the head, le génie. Gérard cut off his own head with a woman's apron string, so now he is a woman, so now he has a hole between his arms. Every soul is nothing. The soul of Gérard de Nerval has taught me that nothingness is the abyss of horror out of which consciousness always awakes in order to go out into something in order to exist.

A hole of the body, which every man but not woman including Gérard de Nerval and myself has to make, is the abyss of the mouth.

I have found this language, which is why I can write this letter to you, O. You see, Gérard, who was naked like you are, gave me a language that doesn't lie, for it spurted out of the hole of his body.

You're naked so I know you've got a body.

When Gérard cut off his head, he made all that was interior in him exterior: today all that's interior is becoming exterior and this is what I call revolution, and those humans who are holes are the leaders of this revolution.

I have gotten to know Gérard de Nerval, and he was a revolutionary both before and after he hung himself from an

*apron string. He hung himself from a woman's string in
order to protest against political control. Suicide is only a
protest against control. I repeat that. After he castrated
himself, language came pouring out of him.*

I am evidence that this is true.

*Now I am Gérard de Nerval after he castrated himself
because consciousness in the form of language is now pouring
out of me and hurting me and so I can be with you. I shall
own you, O.*

O Speaks:

Now I knew W would never come back to me and take me out
of the brothel.

Being aware that he would never love me was equal to
knowing that he never had.

I was no longer safe, so I became sick. I hovered at death.

It was at this time that the student revolutionaries, more
professionally armed than any of the cops around them, burst
into the English Embassy, which was located next to the slum.
Though paying in serious injury and death, they successfully
demolished the government building.

When my health returned, I learned that W was a part
owner of the cathouse. I had known that he was rich. I no longer cared what W felt about me: all I wanted was for him to be
absent from me.

I wanted W to remain absent from me: I didn't want anything to change.

It was W who had first given the terrorists the money to
buy weapons. Perhaps he hadn't known why. Perhaps there
was a need in him to disrupt and destroy. I didn't know W and

I don't. When the revolutionary raid on the English had suc-
ceeded, probably he had become frightened. *For the first time in
his life* he had realized that to be rich and white is to be vulnerable. So when the revolutionaries returned to him to ask for
more funds he refused.

They started to beat him up. They almost killed him.

As soon as I learned what had taken place, I stopped hat-
ing W for not returning my love.

In a skirmish prior to the explosion of the English Embassy, a young boy who had run guns for the revolutionaries
had one of his arms severely injured.

With the other hand holding the money that he had
earned by working for the terrorists, he walked into the
brothel. He found the Madam and gave her the amount she
had requested as the price of my purchase.

I knew nothing about the purchase of my freedom.

Behind my bedroom door, Artaud told me that he had
come back for me.

"I'm still sick. I don't want to see anyone."

He forced himself into my room, so I hit him. He fell
down to the floor on the arm that had been broken. When he
cried out, I was surprised.

"You're just a boy, so how could you be hurting so badly?"

His arm was bent the wrong way for a human.

Now I understood that someone could hurt more than
me. Reaching down, I lifted up his body, on to my thigh, as
much as I was able. I only wanted to fuck with him. Pain, for
him at that moment, was the same as sexual pleasure. For me,
every area of my skin was an orifice; therefore, each part of his
body could do and did everything to mine.

We wondered at our bodies.

Artaud Rewrites His Letter:

When I saw O, I wanted to protect her because she worships her cunt.

O Speaks:

I never saw Artaud again.

Weakened not only by the beating but also by the desertion of his rich girlfriend, W began to go mad.

He learned that the young boy and I had fallen in love. He began to follow Artaud through the slum's streets, which now reeked of more and more revolutionaries, and into alleyways which were blind. In one of those, he shot the young poet and left him for dead.

In those days, there were too many bodies for there to be such a thing as murder.

When I heard this, I no longer cared what happened to W. I quit that whorehouse. For me, there were no more men left in the world.

I had been searching for my father, in a dream, and found a young and insane boy, who was then killed.

I stood on the edge of a new world.

In the Days of Dreaming

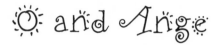

O and Ange

BEFORE THE DAYS OF DREAMING

O, a woman and a Jew. Her father's family, originally in Spain, first emigrated to Morocco, then on to Algeria.

It was the days when women were economically either wives or whores . . .

O: "How can I do this? Begin.
   "Begin what?
   "The only thing in the world that's worth beginning: the end of the world."

O, being a whore, had to find the origin of whoredom:
   Alexandra, one of Cleopatra's friends, had loved Cleo-

patra so deeply that she had tried to persuade Anthony to be both kind and gentle to his paramour's children.

In order to please Alexandra, the first princess, Herod the Great had made her seventeen-year-old son into a priest. The boy was beautiful. Herod drowned him.

Of this Alexandria, no longer anything remains.

O remembered the poet saying that Alexandria is replete with men who are sick, solitary, prophetic. All those who have been deeply wounded in their sex. When O came to Alexandria, the air was as dry as the wings of insects. There were neither male solitaries nor male prophets. For such men were found only in the white world and that world had died.

Here, O thought, lies the center of all prostitution.

O began to dream that she was in the whorehouse for which she had been looking. She wasn't anywhere yet. She had already passed by "The Brothel of the Virgins."

O:

"I entered the most famous whorehouse in Alexandria.

"These are the names of some of the whores:

"Whore #1, Ange, twenty-one years old, politically mature, a professional imagination, a sweetheart only when she comes into contact with children, or with anyone (men, women, or other categories, sedentary, semisedentary, and nomadic) uninterested in money. Ange lucidly believes in the progress of this country.

"I HAVE NEVER FORGOTTEN HER.

"Two years ago, Ange was put into the prison of M——.

There, though still lucid and generous, she was broken. I saw her bruises.

"Thus, in shit begins the new world.

"Whore #2, Barbara, in older days left Egypt for France in order to continue her studies. Classical ones. Some days off the ship in the harbor of Marseilles, to her consternation she learned that she would have to do whatever she would have to do in order to survive there, and so she returned to her activities of the night. What I am saying is that in order to earn the right to education in the Western world, it was necessary for the whores who were not from the Western world to be at war and to continue teaching themselves.

" 'You fuckers,' said Barbara. Finally sick of whoring, every morning, to earn her right to education, she got up at four, in order, for the rest of the day, to work her ass off in the shipyards of Midnight-by-the-Sea. A machine cut off her right foot; despite that, or in despite, whenever possible from then on, she came to the aid, effectively and materially, of those whose social origin was named *Misery*. Misery due to exile. Exile, whose other name is *Delayed Death*, is the fate of all those who live in the realm of racism.

"Barbara, now known as St. Barbara, again inhabits an Alexandrian whorehouse.

"Whore #3. She sleeps all the time. Her name is Louise Vanaen de Voringhem. While she's sleeping, her record player blares. Not that she's got anything against music. But she has to sleep because she's been so worn down by work.

"Some day Louise Vanaen will have to get up, and one day she did. Because her body wanted to wake. Immediately she walked toward the source of her music. Suddenly she was thrown to the ground and cut in her left eye. A neighbor, one of the many Algerians Armenians Bedouins Egyptians Vietnamese surrounding the brothel, hearing screams which he recognized as unusual, ran over to the house, gun in hand. *In order to defend herself*, with this neighbor's help, she mortally wounded her attacker by cutting off his balls.

"For this reason, Sister Louise was convicted of voluntary homicide. For this reason: she was Arab and her rapist was white. Since only her natal family was allowed to visit her, there, in jail, and they lived far away, Louise Vanaen dwelled in solitary for many years.

"Her family was poor.

"In her prison, the whore Louise Vanaen began to dream of a revolution, *a revolution of whores*, a revolution defined by all methods that exist as distant, as far as is possible, from profit.

"Among other things, Louise wrote this to her sisters:

" 'These pages smell of women.

" 'I perceive more clearly during sex. All the lips, all the fists: it's necessary to have the deepest discipline so that all these, so that everything, can be seen. In the brothel, where women are talking, where the women are cooking, lips on lips, hands on hands: all the world is at peace.'

" 'In these rooms of sleep and of dream,' she continued in another of her letters which will become famous after history has gone to sleep, 'we will walk around, brushing by each other, touching each other without actually touching. There we shall affirm everyone, even flesh that is bourgeois, the flesh that likes to be done but not to do, the flesh that is the object of desires.'

"From these letters, St. Barbara developed her political theory of religion: Every revolution starts in a church or in the place of the church because churches and brothels do not have windows that lead to what lies outside. And so are refuges to all the shipwrecked of the world.

"To you, Barbara, courage. Courage for all of you, the generosity that inhabits prostitution."

Ange, St. Barbara, Louise Vanaen de Voringhem, and the rest of the whores learned that if language or words whose meanings seem definite are dissolved into a substance of multiple gestures and cries, a substance which has a more direct, a more visceral capacity for expression, then all the weight that the current social, political, and religious hegemonic forms of expression carry will be questioned. Become questionable. Finally, lost.

The weight of culture: questioned and lost.

"I've been so tired lately," Lulu, another prostitute, complained, "that nothing's turning me on."

Ange replied, "That's the fate of us who are prostitutes."

Lulu and Ange decided to masturbate so they could find a reason to live.

Lulu, starting to masturbate: "My mind's all over the place so I can't do this right now." After some time had passed, "No. Not now."

Ange, who was doing the same thing, muttered, "Me too."

Lulu: "Now we're entering the night."

Entering the night resembled entering a room. Entering

through those narrow doorways, the room could be glimpsed. The halls' walls were pale green. A lighter green than the color of the walls of most of childhood.

Lulu: "Here's a toilet. No, I don't want a toilet. Now, turn the door's handle and walk in. It's necessary to sidle in sideways . . . Why did I just stop feeling anything?"

In order to live, Lulu needed to be in the realm of sex.

Lulu: "Body, talk.

"While I masturbate, my body says: Here's a rise. The whole surface, ocean, is rippling, a sheet that's metal, wave after wave. As *it* (what's this *it*?) moves toward the top, as if toward the neck of a vase, *it* crushes against *itself* moving inward and simultaneously *it* increases in sensitivity. The top of the vase, circular, is so sensitive that all feelings, now circling around and around, all that's moving, are now music.

"Music is my landscape.

"Deep down, at the bottom. Whatever is bottom is so deep that it's spreading away from its center . . . Toward what? Opening up to whom? Opening up only to *sensitive*. Sensation is the lover.

"If I could move down there, down the rabbit's hole, I would never stop coming . . .

"Never never . . .

"And I want to come and come and come . . .

". . . why? . . .

"The middle ring, or the ring around the middle of the shaft, is doing most of the feeling, but now it's slipping downward. If this tunnel, which the ring's slipping down, becomes rigid, there won't be any more sensation. *No sensation is nothing*. If this tunnel becomes rigid, there'll be nothing. I must make my world out of nothing. Relaxation's opening the field, but I don't dare—I'm holding back—open to being a rose; a rose unfolds again and again until the nerves drive the flesh into pure nerves; they are—I'm closing again (becoming rigid)—these are the rhythms of the labyrinth.

"The vibrations (pleasure) are taking over. Now any desire to stop . . . . oh yes, there *it* goes; this disappearance of *it* causes laughter; laughter's a threshold that's soon reached.

"As soon as I went over this threshold, for the first time I began to play; I was opening and opening to the point that I could touch being pure nerves.

"In the realm of being pure nerves, to touch is to be touched: every part of mind, body and feeling is relaxing so much that sensation has domain. When I came, the spasms traveled all the way down the funnel, to its bottom, where there was an opening. Then or there, everything disappeared; the world or everything became more sexual.

"My hole opened up into only opening: the vibrations intensified.

"Soon this world will be nothing but pleasure, the world in which we live and are nothing but desires for more intense and more intense joy.

"I want more now, I want every rose, all the major rows down there, but something is always going over. Again again. An animal. It would always come again: the animal claw."

Thus Lulu entered the labyrinth.

She taught the whores to do this and all of them began to masturbate regularly.

Lulu: "I want to talk about being a criminal because that's the only thing that makes sense to me now."

* * *

Ange said to Lulu:

"Today I had to come by reading pornography.

"First, I took any book and just opened it. I was only going to read a few sentences until I became wet enough for my dildo to slip easily into my cunt. But the first sentence I read was about a woman who was beautiful and older seducing a very young boy who was just so hot for her that he would have come even if she had done nothing. This sentence turned me on to such an extent that I couldn't remain at the edge of the text, I had to enter into those words, and this entering, as I sat there with a dildo up my cunt—I think that must look ugly—was a moving into the halls, with all their walls, there, of my rising sexual energies. I don't think this space which I was now in was my body . . .

"I wasn't in a body, but in a place.

"In my cunt, there's a little animal, a type of fish, but it's a mammal. A weasel-cat. The weasel-cat, who's hungry, is sticking out its tongue . . .

"And so I came without language.

"My whole cunt is now this animal who's becoming hungrier: mouth opens more widely, the clit is a tongue that licks, laps, is tapping like a foot, tapping what's outside as if a floor. Eyes lie above this tongue. All my sensations are a sky. I could no longer talk. As soon as I stopped talking, everything turned white and the waves that were approaching, slowly, steadily, and very strongly, solid, solid, transformed into my blood, then into my bones; whatever had been the rhythms of my body inside my body were now rhythms outside. This is the meaning of *mantra*. The final orgasm will occur when my brains are making mantra."

Lulu said to Ange: "I would smear the whole world with sperm."

*   *   *

Here finally were the days of the beginning of happiness, when the heat and the yellow were dry. When the spine's bottom rose up from its body:

"No," exclaimed one whore, "I'm not going to mastur-bate today because, inside my cunt, the well where all is bot-tomless has come out so far, as if an animal is moving out of the hole, that I'm turning inside out. I'm scared. I'm scared . . . that if the animal gets out . . . god knows what might happen . . . I'll never be able to stop coming, so it'll have to be a new kind of world.

"But I don't know if I can give up the pleasure of mastur-bating even for a day."

St. Barbara was the first call-girl to tell a client to go get fucked so she could continue masturbating:

"Old-Filthy-Husband-Who-Kills-Off-Wives—this was a common term for 'husband' in Alexandria—Old-Scum-Tongue-Who-Can-Only-Lick-Off-Wives, Azzefonian, you're just about to depart for the seas of Europe, right?"

"Right," Azzefonian answered.

"Well, those waters stink of the cunts of women who don't masturbate and other strange fish that cause diarrhea, whereas our cunts, O Legba, Eleggua La Flambeau, La Sirène, O Legba You Who Are Truly Us, our cunts are made from the sun and out of rubies. Cunts to whom we gave birth in the foyer of the end of the world. Our cunts are knives in our fists and the insides of our thighs are becoming darker.

"Come inside, come inside."

Azzefonian, in love with white, went off to Europe.

*   *   *

Finally free of johns, the whores, now alone, spewed out bits of ink, words in ink, sexual or filthy words, words that were formed by the scars and wounds, especially those of sexual abuse, those out of childhood. All the women bore their wounds as childhoods. Therefore, words apocalyptic and apostrophic, punctuations only as disjunctions, disjunctions or cuts into the different parts of the body or of the world, everything priced and priced until, finally, all the numbers disappeared and were displaced by the winds:

Ventre, vente, vent.

These were only some of the elements of whore writing: all will never be named, for both word and self, whore, are always being lost because it is the winds who screw them.

(END OF THE FIRST WHORE-SONG)

Secret Contracts   Type. no.(2)   General Security
  General Index Card
    Curriculum Vitae
Tripartite name: Aziz Salih Ahmad
Date of Birth: (left blank)
Profession: Fighter in the Popular Army
Activity: Violation of Women's Honor

Journalist's report:

> Every major prison seems to have had its own specially equipped rape room (replete in one case with soft-porn pictures stuck on the wall opposite the surface being used).
>   . . . in the woman's section of the Juweideh

Prison, a section is called "adultery room." Police roaming the streets outside apparently have the power to detain young and unmarried women in the company of men unrelated to them. The couple are taken to a medical officer who tests the girl's virginity. If she is not virgin, the police immediately inform both families. The families negotiate the feasibility of marriage. Should the man refuse to marry the woman he was with, both are charged. Within two months, the man is released. But the woman is compelled to stay in prison beyond the period of her sentence.

Half the women in the adultery room of this prison had no sentences to serve. Some had been there five years; they had stayed because they needed protection from their families. The police did not take responsibility for a girl being shot or stabbed to death by a family member on the day of her release from prison.

In order to alleviate this situation, the police hunted for men who would marry the women in their custody. They found either old men looking for a new lease on life before they died or pimps.

Of this ancient world, very little will remain.

O now began to masturbate full-time, imagining every sailor, cock, hairs dripping from cock when wet, cats . . .

O:
". . . all this while masturbating. There's farther to travel.
"Sailors, who're pirates, journey into nonexistence or *the world of the unfurling rose*:

"I'm a man. I hold her head in my hands. Her finger, rotating inside my asshole, makes all the liquids move. All the liquors flow into the centers or my balls, two spheres which hang black down there.

"As her finger travels, the pressures of the liquids build. They're going to shoot up through me into her hole."

"Now it's starting again the sensation's deep down have to keep it there, deep down open, or else it, or all, or I, will stop. The problem's the rigidity of everything and, above all, this must be prevented."

"A *map of rigidities:* the world's stopped. All feeling's gone. What did I do wrong? Or what went wrong?"

"Feeling or sensation evaporates whenever the feeler—the subject here is the object—tries to perceive and understand a particular feeling or sensation.

"This doesn't make sense anymore because I'm feeling too much. Any feeling is feeling too much."

"It's all over. The world's stopped. Then, another round of feeling, like a wave, rises under the most recent, retreating wave. Each new wave's bigger and stronger."

"I think about him. Any thought or agitation which lies outside feeling, outside the space in which subject and object are the same, causes cessation."

"oh yes baby starting to come too excited shaking eyes fading regular spasms contraction mouth is smiling going yes yes wants no open stay open I didn't expect to come and I am now squeezing all legs and thighs around wrist while inside, in there, all the shakes

"I'm going to come harder now, in there, no end in sight"

"sailing, each series, starting with a high rise then swoop downward, each one more violent, direct"

"where is there an end to these convulsions?"

"Being with someone would be more violent."

"I will turn again to dreams"

"the ocean; all the fish go crazy; see them all orange"

"now this final orgasm all stirred up: the walls become rigid and in between, there's burning"

"today there's no end"

"now I have to use my fingers to masturbate."

"Later, the convulsions increased."

"After this, the whores accepted me, O, as one of them."
          (END OF THE SECOND WHORE-SONG)

Even before this, O would say that she never wanted to be a master.

The Entrance of the Punk Boys

Among a hundred brothers him I greet
Who ate my heart and I his heart did eat.

According to the first of the dirty, filthy boys, the body is still in a process of being forged.

Especially his body—his name was Antonin Artaud—which was thin nasty sick mangled distorted ravaged by drugs and by desires which had been repressed by thinking.

The body, the kid said further, when not being robbed blind by family and religion, has an infinite capacity for self-transformation.

He had actually talked in a much more disgusting manner. Before he had died.

The punk boys were the ones who followed him. After his death.

All of them had fucked their mothers and were no longer colonized.

The growth of private property, one characteristic of the bourgeois industrial world, ceased; private property, in the form of multinational and extranational capital, returned to the hands of the few. Economic, therefore political, power seemed to be centralizing.

This decrease of the separation between private and public property, finally this disappearance, was directly related to a movement away from, and then to the passing away of the memory of, patriarchy.

In other words, the punks were one beginning of a new world.

Though these brats were at the edges of a new world, they had no idea how to relate to each other. For them, language just wasn't a problem.

Though he had been the protopunk boy, Artaud was the one the punk boys publicly disavowed. Like him, they wanted to destroy.

They disavowed history, but they were the direct descendants of Heliogabalus of Alexandria, who had been made emperor at fourteen years of age. Heliogabalus despised his own government and was anarchistic. His reign was replete with murder, incest, and a lack of values.

The Alexandrian police cut Heliogabalus apart when he was eighteen years old, in the toilets of his own palace, and then threw his corpse outside on the dirt where two dogs happened to be pissing.

To be kissed by a punk boy was to be drawn to insanity or toward death. The last of the race of white men.

And to fuck one of them, said a girl who was doing just that, is to be drawn into murder.

Perhaps this was what happened to the prostitutes. They didn't commence their violent actions because they had started masturbating. As O had thought. They began because the punk boys came to town and the whores got touched by these boys.

It was the days before the boys who came after the punk boys landed in England.

The boys taught the whores: "We're not free because at any moment the sky could explode into shreds of flesh . . .

"Europe is far away . . . farther because the civilized West has disappeared . . . already shreds of flesh . . . without any explosion."

The punks said further, "Terror is the answer for our times because we, whores and punks, cannot liberate ourselves by running away from horror, a horror that's nameless."

"But," O replied, "I've already lived through horror. I won't know where prostitution came from until I get rid of it.

"My mother's inside me. She wants me to suicide because she suicided. I could try to find a father so there would be no more mother, but there are no fathers around."

All of the whores agreed with O: it was the end of the white world.

It was at this time that O became friendly with a girl who also worked in the brothel, who had black hair and green eyes.

In order to figure out how to stop being a prostitute, O told her friend, Ange, this story about St. Gall Bladder:

"Until the world of water, earth, air, and light begins, all there can be is desire for water, earth, air, and light.

"St. Gall Bladder was running in the mountains. He was traveling through forests. In the woods, the dew dripped out of the cedars; hard, stiff stalks vibrated in the scintillating light. St. Gall Bladder stood up to his knees in dead spiders, mosses, saliva; soon all was a clarity: gold light and liquid. The gold of the air was that of the water.

"Below the cedars, bits of insect wings were lying on the high-tension cables; around the poles, the grass was virgin.

"St. Gall Bladder fell asleep on what was virgin . . .

"When St. Gall Bladder woke out of his dream of loneliness, he decided that it was time for him to return to the human world. He felt that now it was time for him to become nothing, to give everything away, and to go down into blackness, that blackness which is called *the world that is under.*

" 'When I'm nothing,' he said out loud, 'I'll become human.'

"St. Gall Bladder went down and met some whores who were spread out on the ground. He walked up to them. During the Algerian war a bullet had blown a hole in his left thigh, so when one of the two prostitutes raised her eyes to him, she just as quickly lowered them.

"He seated himself between the two. 'I entreat you, my sisters, be true to the earth. Do not believe those who speak to you of superterrestrial hopes.

" 'In times that were past, the soul looked contemptuously down at the body. This contempt was the supreme virtue. All the soul wanted was to escape . . .'

" 'Take some if you're hungry,' the slender whore replied.

"St. Gall Bladder grabbed a banana; he was just about to put the fruit to his lips; he glanced at this girl who was the younger of the prostitutes; his eyes were gleaming with wet dreams.

"The young girl took up one of the hands of her lover, whose name was Ange, and held it. Fingers that trembled while held down in that valley which felt like sand, where the sea began, then explosion after explosion, made the world tremble.

"St. Gall Bladder watched everything carefully.

"The whores explained to the saint that they were voyaging to the end of the night.

"One of them placed her swollen membranes over the saint's face and the other licked his cock. For there was no way to be a whore anymore.

"Then they told him about the origin of prostitution: 'We, and all the other prostitutes, come from the city of KaWeDe, where mothers eat their own children and afterwards fuck dogs. Now, it's time for us to go back, for all whores to go back, for whores to return to their origins.

" 'Go to KaWeDe and tell them that hell is coming to them. Inform them that we are coming. That we're going back to the source of prostitution and that only a saint who has had his day can be our messenger.' "

St. Gall Bladder became the messenger of revolution and the women set the brothel on fire. Flames leapt from this building to nearby buildings, to edifice after edifice. When there was nothing left that could burn in the city, the flames shifted toward the forest. Turning trees and air into black smoke, the fire touched the doves in their flight, and the vultures, and threw them, as they lacked breath, against the sun. Fire ate at the feet of the animals, who were racing, nostrils as wide open as mouths stuffed with living coals: the whole mountain was blazing.

Aware that he was beginning to suffocate, for he was now journeying through this forest, Bladder retired into the bathroom of the hut that had formerly been his hermitage. He picked up his own shit, rubbed it into his face, for he was a saint. Then Gall Bladder threw himself into the source of the river that ran through the woods. A gun, which had been left by a murderer, to his own eye.

"Enough blood. Enough hatred," he said. "Turn to water. Turn cocks into water."

The moment that his face touched the water, the saint shot himself. Blood spurted out of the skin, reddening the river burning under the smoke; his head rolled ball-like through the underwater billows while above, lions, serpents, pigs, even vultures, all chased by heat and smoke, passed and were passed by each other.

The corpse of the father was turning into water.

The crayfish hid under the dead man's armpits and orange fish nibbled at his lips . . .

The whores were drunk.

O didn't know whether she should leave with the other prostitutes. She began to dream about women.

She saw that she was in the room of a witch. It was colored pink-red. In its middle, there was a tweed couch. To the side of that, a Christmas tree.

The older woman proceeded to show O objects that scared her. O had to decide whether she would go through something more terrifying, a particular ceremony: if she went through it, she'd be allowed to enter the other world.

The other world lay in the upstairs of that apartment.

O felt two opposite emotions: her desire, her need to be in the other world accentuated her fright.

It was in the upstairs room that the witch showed O her crystal gun. O tossed it away. As soon as she had done this, she knew she shouldn't have. That it was against rules which hadn't yet been spoken. O also understood that the purpose of the ceremony, through which she still had to pass, was to scare her out of her mind.

"I don't want to lose my mind."

The ceremony began when O opened white business envelopes. O's Visa slips sat in the first one. O had to see them. She had to realize that she always spent more money than she earned or would ever be able to. By overspending, O was placing herself in the position of her mother before her mother had suicided.

O wasn't scared enough.

The second envelope held those plastic dolls made for the tops of birthday cakes. They were either cowboys or Indians. All of these carried insects in their mouths, under their chins, and inside their palms. The most horrible possible insects, such as scorpions. They had something to do with sex, but O didn't understand what.

O wasn't scared, because she was holding herself back because she was most scared of being scared, and yet she wanted to. She wanted to become scared out of her mind so she could cross into the unknown.

It was here, in the city that had burnt down, that O dreamed her last dream about herself and her friend:

"John, fingerfuck O." Said Ange. Ange was directing her first play, perhaps in what had been the brothel's theater. And John was the boyfriend of O's only male friend in Alexandria.

The boy slowly inserted one of his middle fingers between O's thick outer labia. "Is this okay?"

"Okay," said O.

She was wearing a Kotex pad and the black cotton panties that she always had on whenever she had her period. These were the only underpants O owned that didn't disappear into the crack of her ass.

John screwed his finger in as far as he could. He knew how to do this so that a woman felt pleasure, pleasure as if every type of pleasure was coexisting yet separate from every other type in the same space.

Neither John nor O was upset by her blood.

John ordered O to suck his fingers, which, having been up her cunt, were now soaked in blood. O couldn't tell if these fingers were still up there. She didn't mind licking them over and over again.

O drew away from John. Now she was conscious—if her mind was eyes, a veil had been drawn away from them—that she was experiencing sexual delight in a public space and that this was wrong. One shouldn't open up sexually in public to a man one didn't know when one was bleeding. Nevertheless she was doing this. And adoring this. In other words: what was clearly happening, with her, couldn't possibly be happening.

Everything was happening, as it always does, sexually.

John bit down hard on the tips of her nipples, and bit down hard again. O felt joy. She knew he was on the verge of fucking her. She didn't want him to fuck her because she was in a classroom and exposed to all the students and blood was showing everywhere but the outer strips of her thighs.

It was the beginning of the night when Ange asked her why she hadn't let herself be fucked. She knew that O wanted desperately to fuck.

O thought about this question. She decided that she must be a victim, though she had never before thought she was a victim, a victim of her society's definition of women her age. These women, no longer children, according to the society were no longer sexually desirable to men, except perhaps as prostitutes; more important, according to her society they no longer possessed sexuality.

O realized that the women who were younger than her were far more intelligent about these issues than the women her age.

Now night had come to the dead city and lay everywhere.

O found herself in the middle of one of its great streets. She was walking down this middle, as if she were a car or a motorcycle.

Somewhere in her, O knew that it was dangerous for her to act like a motorcycle. She believed that the middle lane, the middle of which she was in, was going to disappear, so just as it did, just as it became one of the other lanes, O swerved into the right lane.

In safety, she reached the bottom of the great thoroughfare. There Ange was waiting for her, though O hadn't expected to see her friend ever again. In the deserted city.

"Stay with me, O. Here."

There had been a previous arrangement between O and a man whose name she didn't know, to meet, at this very hour, in the tenderloin district. O remained with Ange.

The two women were already walking. O was upset that she was missing her appointment with the older man, but she couldn't be worried about that because she had to do something about the blood. She wasn't wearing anything so, at any moment, blood was going to seep through her clothes into the outside.

She remembered that there was a pharmacy on the corner, down the street from the department store where she had planned to meet————.

Instead of walking toward this department store, Ange and O moved in the other direction, across the principal street that crossed the one down which O had been running. Into the darkest and most deserted part of the burnt-down city.

This was where the artists lived.

In the gigantic pharmacy that was situated in this district, O was looking up toward a glass countertop far above her. She saw a pile of Tampax. The Tampax, she realized, was Eastern, because it hadn't been boxed, because it was wrapped in only the thinnest, the cheapest colorless paper. Its covering, in spots, was torn.

Since O couldn't buy the Tampax because she thought that it might be diseased, she asked the woman behind the glass counter if the pharmacy had anything else for periods.

An emaciated blonde pointed to wooden shelves which were so high that their tops and bottoms had disappeared. They stood behind O. On one of the higher shelves lay a jumbo box of Kotex. Pads so huge they must have been designed for elephants.

"You see, O," the salesgirl said, "you could have gotten fucked even though you had your period."

Everything about the restaurant to which the older man brought O spoke of wealth and the upper classes. The man turned out to be a professor O had once met, one of the most respected teachers in the country, and a novelist. Unlike the other ones who had fucked O in the recent past, the men she could remember, this one treated her gently and with respect.

It was toward the end of their meal that he pulled her toward him, across the red leather couch on which they were still sitting.

So he does want to get to know me, O told herself.

The hands that were holding her head pushed her head down to where she saw a cock that wasn't human. That was small, very pointed at the end, a ring of flesh around its middle, white rather than red. Like a cat's. O put her mouth around it.

She didn't think anyone in the restaurant, certainly not their waiter, was noticing her disappearance, or the head, beneath the white-cloth-covered tabletop, down in the realm that lay under.

When everything was over, she raised her head and saw that the man had changed: he was smiling angelically; the hair on his head, once scanty and white, was now very thick, black, an Afro, like what white liberals had once worn.

O was feeling sick. She realized that having this sex, during which she never lost consciousness, made her queasy. Such sex was immoral. Whereas the sex during the sex show had sent her over the edge, over every edge, over her self, flying, until all that was left was sky and endless blackness. During the loss of herself, "she" had become scared. O realized that she wanted this sex, that she needed it, this sexuality that she had known when she was a whore.

(END OF THE THIRD WHORE-SONG)

O, the Jew, told herself, I have to go back to my roots.

IN A WORLD WITHOUT MEN, IN A WORLD PUNCTURED BY DREAMS

Later, Ange told O that she had had a dream about her father. O hadn't known that she'd had a father.

"I was back in my childhood. It was a large room. Below that room lay an even grander hotel.

"As spacious and majestic as possible, for it had been designed for spectacles. Theatrical. Medical.

"We were all alone in this room. Daddy and I. Since

there was no door out of there and its only phone wasn't working, we had only each other.

"I watched him slip to the floor. As he lay on that wood,
he gasped. Gasped again.

"Then I knew Daddy was a businessman.

"I don't know how the doctors found out what had happened. Nevertheless, they arrived and carted him away to a
hospital that was equally gigantic, underground. The whole
time while he was being rolled into that hospital, I held on to
one of his hands.

"The doctors took my parent away from me.

"I waited for him to come back. Until I met you, O, I'd
never known how to do anything but wait.

"The times of waiting were when there was no time.

"Now there was no time . . .

"The doctors informed me that Daddy was going to live.
'But'—my heart sat in my mouth—'he's blind.'

" 'Oh.'

" 'If you want,' said this doctor who was kind, 'you can see
your father now.'

"I entered a small room where I saw long, thin tubes, a
differently colored liquid filling each one, connected to longer,
thinner tubes connected to Daddy. I think they were feeding
him. I must have banged my funny bone against the corner of a
chair or something because I started to scream.

"The crowd around me, all of whom were my friends, told
me to shut up. My father had a bad heart and now he didn't
have any eyes and he wasn't screaming.

"Daddy didn't say anything.

"I was young. Just like Antigone, I didn't want to spend
the rest of my life with an old, dying man. To be shut up with a

father. I looked for a phone. There were some outside my father's room, but they were dead. Every phone in the hospital, dead.

"I left my father only 'cause I was looking for a working phone. I came to what I thought was a hotel.

"The building, which could have been a hotel, was a theater whose insides mirrored the hotel's outside.

"Like a mole, a small store hung off of the building's skin.

"Its back was full of books. Its front was crowded with wooden shelves weighted down by porn mags. The bottom two shelves, each stand, held comics.

"Louise Vanaen was standing next to me in that store. Her eyes were greener than mine because she knew more about comic books. So I wanted to turn to her, but instead I secretly watched the huge eyes, where they journeyed, how long, where they lingered. I saw each comic the hands touched."

O was getting jealous.

"When I could no longer see, a man explained that two other men had just questioned him.

"Though he hadn't been talking to me, he stopped speaking and two jocks came up to me. One of them placed a piece of paper in my mouth.

" 'What're you doing to me?'

" 'This paper is litmus. We use it to take fingerprints.'

"I was the only one they were doing this to. 'Why me?'

" 'We just want to ask you some questions.'

"They shot liquid—it was either pale yellow or pale orange—into my flesh. I didn't understand why they were doing it. It couldn't be to find out my secrets because I tell everybody everything. I turned to Louise Vanaen and begged her not to leave me. 'I feel funny. Maybe it's 'cause there's this liquid in me.' "

O and Ange were standing next to a lake of stagnant gray water which had once been part of the wealthy and exclusive spa of the port.

"What does this dream have to do with your father?"

"I don't know." But she knew. Since her father no longer had any eyes, Ange could begin to see. She saw the green and gray water, the gulls, and beyond the birds, where there might be other seas whose roads led to treasure.

"I've never dreamt about a father," O said.

"I've dreamt about cities. Last night, you and I walked through a dead one.

"We came to the city's heart. In its center was a monastery.

"Monks crawled over the floor.

"Below were the pits. Sand mounds looking like cutoff breasts rose upward.

"O, you couldn't understand the meaning of any of the words you read in the dense, illuminated manuscripts, found elsewhere in that edifice."

The two ex-whores were standing in their favorite spot in Alexandria; unordered clusters of broken walls; pools too fetid for the filthiest of birds; substances between the sand and mud which reeked of the strangest of excrements. Once the foundation of a spa so magnificent that teenage boys had traveled from all parts of the known to hide in its shadows. O, more than Ange, loved decay. At times, the stench, more pungent than sweat, under her own armpits.

They huddled against one of the structures, for sharp winds were now moving off of the salt-drenched sea.

"My dreams're no longer telling me what to do. There's nothing in this place, Ange. We can't stay here."

"Where are we going to go?"

They watched a gull fly from one point of a rock covered with gull turd to another.

"We got rid of our johns. Now our dreams don't mean anything."

A storm burst. The air transformed to charcoal, grew into itself until it became so thick that it was material. It was like the creation of the world.

In full day, the sky broke into two.

"Myths mean something," said the green-eyed girl.

"They do?"

The former tried to disappear into the part of the wall against which she was leaning but couldn't and curled into O. "Let me recite a myth. Anyway, I think it's a myth. It's one of the stories the punk boys told me."

The brats had disappeared from the city.

"There was this girl who had a boyfriend. She had black skin and he had white."

O kissed Ange. "I told you there's no more meaning."

"He lived in burial grounds."

"Oh," said O.

"He and his girlfriend were always fighting: that's how they remained together.

"One day she yelled, 'You're always naked except for that bunch of skulls around your neck. In which maggots're living. That you never take off. And you're odoriferous. In a bad way. You think that death's sexy, that's why you stink most of the time; of rot and foul, fetid fur, but you smell worst when you're about to come.'

"The boy was always about to come because he never came. Sometimes the girl wasn't sure whether she liked this.

" 'What're you talking about?' asked the boy. 'You're not white.'

"To win their argument, the girl decided to get white skin.

"In solitude so complete that it approached nothingness, she'd meditate on whiteness. Which is nothingness.

"She went away.

"Abandoned by love, the boy was vulnerable.

"A demon, because demons're always hanging around skulls and graveyards, saw that the boy was vulnerable. Open to demon attack. 'Yum,' uttered the demon and turned itself into a snake. Now it was a male. Demons, being without any gender, can become whoever and whatever they want.

"As snake, he slithered up to the mausoleum of the boy and girl. At that threshold, he turned himself into a replica of the girl, and crossed the threshold.

"The boy thought that his girlfriend was coming back to beg him to take her back. He wasn't going to make it hard for her.

" 'Darling,' he said. He was naked. 'All that I've done since you've been away from me is smell you. The wood and moss that sleep in your pussy. The liquids that drip in pools out of your cunt. From now on I'll do anything to be able to smell you beyond the end of time.'

" 'I've come back because I love you.'

"The snake into whom the demon had changed itself had been poisonous. And the demon took those poisonous fangs, when it metamorphosed again, and placed them high, hidden, in the fake girl's cunt.

"From her words the boy recognized that this wasn't his girlfriend, so he attached a bomb to the tip of his cock. Just in the slit. With this explosive cock, he conquered his sexual loneliness and the vulnerability that rises out of such loneliness.

"Having been subdued, the demon, in snake form, wound around the erect cock."

Ange finished the story she had gotten from the boys. "I want to be like that."

The winds that were coming off of the sea were turning fiercer.

"I want that serpent power."

"We can't stay here," O said. "We need to do more than be whores and masturbate."

"I agree."

"Let's go to Europe."

"No way. I don't want to go to Europe. Europe's dead."

"We'll just go back to Europe to steal."

"Okay."

This was the first significant decision that the girls had made since they'd helped burn down the brothel, since the subsequent conflagration of the city.

Ange: "How're we going to get there? There's no money."

"Once I tried to go to Europe," said O. "I went to an airport. I had my ticket in my hand.

"In those days, I was earning money.

"My hand was clammy. It was holding only the top half of

the ticket because the woman behind the desk had taken away the rest. Now there was no one in the airport.

"I knew I'd never get back to Europe.

"I stood in those cavernous passageways. It must have been evening, for there was no longer any weather. I searched for the woman who had taken the bottom half of my ticket away from me.

"There was no one.

"It was as if there was no more time.

"Time had died and anxiety mounted. The higher it climbed up my body, as if it wanted to sit around my neck, the more I wanted to reach Europe. Until desperation or need was so intense that I didn't know whether I could keep on living.

"I thought, where I am in this world which is no world, there's nobody."

Ange knew O was describing loneliness, which she had also felt in the brothel.

"I had to find another human. Someone who would help me." O continued.

"Time began when I saw a girl standing behind a desk. I walked up to her to explain all that had just happened.

"She disappeared.

"Beyond my range of vision lay numerous sections of the airport. In some of those areas, the passengers who had obtained tickets were able to pass through the gate.

"A shrunken man whose face was like a goat's sat in one of those areas at a folding table. He was staring down at the white part of a Visa slip. It was the bottom of my ticket.

"I handed it to the girl who had disappeared.

"Now I was allowed to return to Europe, where people still read books.

"I had arrived at this airport long before the travel agency told me to come. Long before any airplane was due to depart. It had taken me so much time to repossess the whole ticket that, as soon as I had obtained it, my plane was due to leave.

"There was only one more gate to pass through before I boarded the airplane: the one where all possessions were checked.

"The checker, who was male, inserted his middle finger into the stuffed zebra my last boyfriend had given me as a good-bye present. The tip of the finger encountered something hard. Up there. This tip curved, scraped, then brought out with it a number of large coins. Nazi war money."

"We're going to go to Europe, O."

"Yes? . . ."

"We're beginning to travel."

The winds were sinking with the sun: all the gold that's hidden treasure on the ocean, which changes from day to day, started to become visible. Ange sat down on a small, flat rock; O sat on top of her.

"Shh. Calm down. Until you calm down, we can't begin traveling."

O didn't say anything.

"We're traveling now."

O hid her eyes in the safety of the chest in front of her body because she could vacation only when she didn't have any eyes.

"Tell me what you're seeing, O."

"I don't know. I've got to come out of hiding, Ange. It's very scared down here."

"It?"

"It doesn't think that anyone likes it. It doesn't know it can come out and play and it desperately wants to come out and play. And I'm scared it's going to take me over, Ange."

"You've got to stay with me." She smoothed down her friend's hair.

"There's a spot," the slender girl announced.

"Where, honey?"

"In the ocean. The ocean of drudge, of gook. Brown, dirty water."

For a while, there was silence.

"Now the spot's beginning to send out arms. Its eyes open.

" 'This is nice,' is the first thing that the spot says."

Ange's mouth opened like her friend's name as she listened and watched what she couldn't see.

"It began to play," O reported as if everything, or the world, had already taken place. "By turning, then by moving under itself. It somersaulted; it sent out rays again.

"Now I think it's gone. I think it became this circle of swirling water. My center just shivered."

"This is what traveling is," said Ange when O could no longer hear her.

"The animal awakes, shivering," O said.

"The vibrations want to move downward. 'Nothing,' they are telling me, 'will happen until all of us go down there. The only way you can wake up, O, is by going down there.'

" 'I'm lonely,' I cried.

" 'Come down here, you motherfucking bitch,' they said to me.

"I said, 'Thank you.' "

"Let's go inside. Inside somewhere," Ange corrected herself when the world was over.

"I want to go down again."

The two girls had started to walk away from the dead fish. "We've others to fry, O. We've the future."

There were no men, so dead fish lay everywhere. Ange remembered a former girlfriend, a nurse, who had advertised hers on a male nude beach.

Some odors never go away, for they are never forgotten.

That night, Ange dreamed that her father visited her. She was lying with her stuffed animal. Her father wanted to tell her that there would again be men in the world, but instead he started discussing Ange's mother.

"Your mother's waiting for you, A. She wants you to go to her."

"Come in her, more likely."

"A. We're your parents. She wants you to go to her apartment. In the bathroom sink there'll be a layer of leftover rice and peas mixed with brown shit. In its bottom half, as if a circle had been drawn. You'll have to clean everything up. Your mother has placed all your cosmetics and oils inside her washing machine."

"I've never heard it called a 'washing machine' before."

As if childhood had relevance to anything.

The next morning, Ange told O her dead father had visited her. He had explained to her how to get to Europe.

"Okay," O replied, "let's crawl through all the houses of the rich who once fucked in this city and see if we can find anything to enable us to reach Europe."

It was early morning, not yet yellow, and they began to scramble through the homes of the rich. These buildings were broken; some without doors or a wall; sometimes so shattered that they were no longer edifices. They resembled sets of Dario Argento movies. Though a few of the upper class had remained in this city, O and Ange met only nonhumans who, like them, were on their hands and knees.

O thought, it's not that we've become animals, it's that the animals accept us. Now.

It was as if a world was beginning in which a sun knew no misery and all that was appearing was alive and moving.

Ange began to tell her friend about childhood because, at this time, it was hard for her to talk: "All money . . . my mother's side . . . she insane . . . totally insane . . . the freedom, that is, the isolation of the rich due to money." She was repeating herself. "My father had a son who died, so he brought me up as a boy. 'Your mother loves you,' he would say, because he protected her.

"When I was a child, I never spoke. I was a boy."

All that Ange and O found in these houses were boxes of condoms.

"If we keep on crawling, we're bound to stumble over something."

"Something other?"

The house they were inside had no more walls. Ange wriggled to the outside, where she found a road. Rather, a path that was egotistic. When she realized that she was moving over dead dogs, she ran into the first shelter she saw.

Here was only half a front door. Ange knew everything about this house. Though there was no light inside, she stepped quickly through a mélange of planks and shattered objects until she came to a stair.

She found a second stair.

O had followed her friend. She was thinking about her coming period.

"Draw down the blind, O." The one blind wasn't attached to a window. In this bottom room.

O let down the blind.

"Now the stairs. Follow me."

She reached the top of the stairs and walked forward until her knee hit the doubling of a body and a bed.

Ange: "I'm following my father's instructions."

She hadn't been able to fall asleep, when a child, until she was safe. Safe on a ship which an ocean surrounded. She became even safer when, as she fell into sleep, monsters emerged out of those emerald waters. No two monsters were the same.

Ange knew that the body was her mother, and dead.

"Mommy."

She didn't answer Ange. She had never answered Ange because she was on the phone with her friends.

Ange kicked her.

She had been stubborn, only concerned with herself. All that she had noticed was her incredible beauty and her friends. She had green eyes and hair blacker than Chinese pussy. A mouth that was always red covered by red lipstick. Red, black, and green. Ange didn't know what color her skin was because the girl could no longer see.

Ange began to feel her mother up.

"O, come over here."

When O realized that Ange was doing what she was doing, though O knew nothing about mothers, she asked Ange why she was doing what she was doing.

"There's the key, O," Ange answered.

"The key?"

"The key to the box that contains treasure. We're going to search for buried treasure, aren't we?"

O began to remember. She decided, without having to decide, to help Ange locate the key.

As soon as they opened this box, they'd be able to journey to Europe.

Ange had come upon this box only once when she was young. She had been all alone in her parents' house. Which was unusual. In her mother's green clothes closet, three rows of two-inch, high-heeled shoes. Below was the box. Locked.

Ange ordered O to feel around the breasts, for the key might be on a chain.

O couldn't feel anything with her hands.

Ange was searching down below. Nothing was there to which a key could be tied. "O, help me."

"What am I supposed to do?"

"Keep on looking. I've become lost."

And Sailing toward her India, in that way
Shall at her fair Atlantick Navell stay;
Though thence the current be thy Pilot made,
Yet ere thou be where thou wouldst be embay'd,
Though shalt upon another Forest set,
Where many shipwrack, and no further get.

O was disgusted. But since Ange was her friend, she'd do anything for her. Perhaps that's what friendship is. So O tried to convince herself that any dead body's only a dead body.

She remembered a North African writer's words. "Source or transformer of meaning and sense, forever relativizing the right, the left, and the earth whence these directions spring, you have fused your compass into the liquid body."

These words gave O the courage to begin searching this body more profoundly. Not only the surfaces that were the breasts, but those that lay in between. In there, she found a bit of string. She followed this string, as if tracking an animal, until she came to a hard object.

It was about to get away from her.

"Give it to me, O." Ange, grabbing, fell on top of O, who tumbled onto the dead body.

All of them lay still for a moment. Ange took the strange object away from O. The dead mother didn't say anything.

"Now we have to find your mother's box."

They started to search for that object, which was as yet imaginary.

The two girls abandoned the dead body and arrived at another flight of stairs. The top of these steps, resembling an arch, immediately presented a room that was smaller. A room like a window looking out over an ocean larger than the window. The room had a desk and a large black box.

The top of the container was embossed with letters from an alphabet unknown to the girls.

While O sniffed, Ange turned the key in its lock.

"I smell something," whispered O.

"What're you sniffing?"

"I don't know." She started to investigate herself.

The green-eyed girl opened the box. "There's nothing here."

"I agree."

At the edge of the threshold of the unknown, O was about to give up.

Ange reached into the box as deeply as she could and touched paper.

"Heave ho!" she announced.

And placed what appeared to be a number of papers, wrapped in a piece of oilcloth a dog must have pissed on, in an area of her sweater; then, O did the same with whatever money she could find in that bottom. They groped their way downstairs, removed the half of the door still standing, and walked into the night. Where fog so thick that it absorbed both the visible and audible concealed the burnt city.

This was the last time that either Ange or O were to return to a parent's home.

The fog gave them the sensation that they had arrived at the end of the world. There were only fish and birds, none of whom could be seen or heard and so were only sensed: here and there, where the fog broke, a band of clouds.

Ange knew that the roads that they were about to follow, those made of seaweed and the bone that line the ocean, mirrored the pathways of these birds.

O: "My final dream of Alexandria was about my last boyfriend. The last time I was with a man.

"I was in a city which was located at the end of the world. I was waiting outside a diner-like restaurant for my boyfriend, who was much younger than me and worked in that joint.

"As for me, I was working in the film business. Sometime later, the director of the film I was on informed me that he was into strange sex. I accompanied him to a hotel, into a room with an enormous bed.

"Even though he looked like Steven Spielberg, he didn't mind when he discovered that I was having my period. But I didn't want to take off my white cotton underpants.

"While we were on that bed, a number of well-dressed New Yorkers walked around us.

"The sex between us was negligible, so we started to gossip. In an attempt to be polite—such endeavors always fail—I mentioned some semifamous New Yorkers whom we both knew.

"But I wanted to return to that gray street. The one outside the diner-like restaurant. Waiting for my boyfriend to return.

"Out of that low building he walked, all tall and gangly, until he reached me.

" 'Do you want to be with me?' he bluntly asked me. 'You're hungry, so I'm going to feed you.'

"I went away with him. I didn't know where.

"He asked if I wanted to see him again.

"I told him, the boy I loved, that I couldn't see him again because I was a whore. While I was saying this, I knew that whoring had nothing to do with loving. 'I guess we're never going to see each other again.'

" 'Of course we're going to, O.'

"Now I knew, even more than it was possible for me to know anything, that I was going to go away from him and never return."

After Ange had listened to O's dream, the two of them abandoned the now almost deserted city.

Manuscript Found Next to Map:
The Beginning of the World of Pirates
(In Our Scummy Pirate Language)

Incest begins this world. Incest begins the beginning of this world:

A father's fucking his daughter. Night's fucking with morning. Night's black; morning, red. There's nothing else.

In this area between timeless and time, a father, realizing that maybe he shouldn't come in his daughter or maybe just that he shouldn't come, pulls his cock out of her box. His timing must be off because his cock spurts white liquid out. Out into the future, what will be time. In this arena between timelessness and time, the most dangerous thing or being that can come into being is time.

Sperm is explosive.

The night's black.

The moment that the white drops fall on what will be ground, down, time or this world begins.

Sperm is lying everywhere, in the world of time, on its ground. Lying in viscous pools. Since there's time now, the sun, the first being in the world, not yet quite being, cooks away all the sperm; black char and red earth are left.

The first animals are colored red or black.

Night's black; morning, red.

This is how we name the terror of our primordial dawn.

The only person who doesn't approve of incest is a boy who inhabits graveyards. It's his own father who's been fooling around with his sibling. What isn't bearable is that his father wanted to make the kid pregnant.

In other words, that his father is a father.

In order to stop the incest that's going on, and all the incest that will ever be, therefore all that's already taken place in the world, the boy snips off the father's head with a fingernail. Separated, the head falls down, into the boy's hand. There, sticks to that palm.

But the boy isn't into possessions. He likes not death but all that lies outside life and death. The brat hasn't owned anything in years and years, though he's been stealing—that's why he steals—and now, here he is with a head. As soon as it's happy in his palm, the head turns into a skull. Into a skull-bowl. Because it loves the boy so much that it wants the boy to use it.

The brat does. For now he's able both to steal and beg. This is how he comes to love skulls and graveyards.

Play or delight will be endless.

The father, headless, is pissed that he doesn't have a head. He's determined to punish this brat severely. The brat's related to him. Moreover, the brat's an immoral brat because he doesn't want a family. Because he doesn't want to be a man. He'll teach the boy what it is to be a man. To be responsible. To want to reproduce oneself, to keep one's seed alive in the world.

Not that the brat's been celibate. In fact, this child's continually screwing a girl who's as scummy as he is and looks like a rat. One of her names is Rat-Brat because she's the rat of the brat. The brat never comes in his girlfriend, which is even worse 'cause this means that the boy's into sex only for the sake of sex.

Continually.

And what makes everything even more reprehensible is that the girl, who looks like some rat, loves the parricidal boy more than anyone and anything else in the world, and beyond the world, 'cause, since he doesn't come in her, he fucks and fucks her and she comes and comes and so, then, keeps on coming and then there's no more time.

Those who live in graveyards don't know time.

They don't think about love 'cause they think about sex and skulls. They're perverts.

Thinks the father. The girl's his granddaughter.

And since the boy never comes and the girl never stops coming, he comes in the same way that she does. That's the most perverted or criminal thing of all.

"Those two'll have to marry each other," the father without a head declares. "That's all there is to it."

It was the only way to solve everything.

The girl's been coming for twenty-five years. She's so full of coming, she decides she wants to feel something else.

She wants to be married so she can live in a house that isn't full of half-rotted corpses and prowling animals who smell dead things and smell like dead things. It's at this very moment that her grandfather, entering the graveyard, orders his bad son to get married.

"No way. As for babies, I'd rather be dead."

The girl's upset that the boy's not going to wed her. For the first time, she questions his love.

Thus, the father gets his revenge.

Instead of marrying her, the brat fucks her even more often. The more he makes this girl who looks like a boy come, the more she doubts he loves her.

As soon as he realizes she's questioning his love or him, he wants to be free from her. He makes her come even harder.

So she knows he no longer wants her. "What's the use of this sexual body," she cries out loud, "which desires and at the same time fears? What's the use of this sexual body which alienates what it desires? How can I bear to be conscious? Better not to be." She attempts to run away from herself and burns herself up.

The boy, of course, is the last to learn that the girl has done herself in. That, burnt up, she's gone away from him forever. He goes over to her body. He rubs whatever is black char into his skin. He touches her blood. His hands pick up the rest of the material that's her and hold it high above his head. Holding her there, delicately and precisely, he begins to circle, faster, more rapidly and more rapidly, now that he's reunited with the rat, whirling twirling. Limbs flail at branches, at the rocks that have thrust themselves into the universe. Neither he nor she feels anything.

What remains of her is hanging like crabs' legs around his neck.

His sperm flows through the world.

As long as she has any hairs left, they lash the stars.

Irritated by the smell of his own sperm, the boy rotates at such a speed that what limbs there are, then the other parts of her body, fall off. The pupils pop out.

There's nothing and no one left. Of this world. Except for the cunt. Of a girl. On a nearby tree, a bird hangs and leaves its heart.

With the eyes he has left, he watches her cunt fall into a crevice. It's the end of the world. There are no more eyes. It's as if the head has fallen away.

The world has to begin again.

He dreams without a head. Dreams only one dream: He begs the girl to come back to him because he can't live without her. It's at this moment that he begins to search for her.

For the treasure of the world.

The Pirate Girls

KING PUSSY'S STORY

Pussy, Who Always Lives Inside Her Own Head . . .

Childhood ended when Pussy learned that she was pregnant. It didn't matter to her, at that point, who the man was. Or it did.

Naming:
All that she knew was that he had come from across an ocean. After she had fucked with him twice, he had mentioned to her that he was on methadone. But he had run out, or else he was kicking it, therefore he couldn't fuck her anymore.

Since Pussy was a nice girl, she offered him her apartment, or hole, as a refuge; she offered herself as a friend. Three days later, she asked him to get out of her home . . .

In those days, Pussy made meager amounts of money by being a performance artist. That's what it was called. After the flight of the stranger, she went on the road.

It was during the second week of road work that she remembered that her period was a day late. It was the first time in her life that it ever occurred to her that she could become pregnant.

The possibility had never before been a possibility. As soon as it was possible for her to be pregnant, Pussy was sure that she was. She was definite that she must get an abortion as soon as she got off this road, and even sooner.

Before this time it hadn't been possible for her to be pregnant, because she hadn't wanted a child. She had no idea why she didn't want a child, because all women want to bear children.

Pussy got off the road.

She ran to see a gynecologist whose name she had found in the telephone directory and then she informed him that she was pregnant.

The clinic in which she had found herself seemed to be devoted to abortions. The gynecologist, who was actually a nurse-practitioner, informed Pussy that she had to be pregnant for a full six weeks and then her baby could be aborted.

Pussy *waited*, as if *waded*, rather than lived, through the remainder of the full six weeks. During this *period*, according to Pussy, her body became alien to whatever was her, because her breasts turned so painfully swollen that she could no longer sleep in her usual positions, because she was simultaneously and continuously hungry and nauseous, because she wanted the child to remain alive.

She didn't know whether or not to tell the stranger that she and he could now have a baby; she decided not to bother him, because by not disturbing him she was being polite.

"I can't have a baby," she told herself. Since she could, she made up reasons why she couldn't. She couldn't bear her child because she had no money, because there was no way in the future for her to earn money. Because the child wouldn't have a father.

A week lay between this conversation with herself and the abortion. Her only hope, though she didn't know what *hope* could mean, was to stop being pregnant naturally. Her immune system had never operated in regard to pelvic inflammations and abortions lead to such infections. Pussy drank cup after cup of pennyroyal tea until she almost puked. She waited a few hours, then began the process again.

After three days of pennyroyal tea, nightmares rather than swollen breasts kept her awake. The final nightmare, she murdered her daughter.

Upon waking or leaving the nightmare, she realized this was true. Her doctor who wasn't a gynecologist agreed with her. "After your abortion," he said, "you are going to have to pay."

Since Pussy never had thought, nor would she think, that women shouldn't have abortions, she had to come to terms with the realization that to be human, and woman, includes the possibility and even the act of murder.

Nothing but abortion was going to work.

The night prior to the suction, the stranger phoned her. He hadn't contacted her since she had been on the road. "You're going to be a father." These words fell out of Pussy's mouth before she knew about them. She was out of her mind.

He wanted her to bear his child. He replied. He began to talk. She was the fourth woman he had made pregnant. For the

first time, he wanted one of his children to become alive. Perhaps this desire was a sign that, now, he was adult.

"I can't afford to bring up a child."

"I'll help you out financially if you need it."

"You can't 'help me out financially.'" For the moment
Pussy forgot his name. "Since you're the child's father, you're
as responsible as I am in every possible way.

"But you can't be the father, because we don't have a relationship. We knew each other only for a week."

"I agree with what you're saying."

"The question of responsibility's complicated. I never
knew my father and look how fucked-up I am. Not knowing
my father fucked me up my whole life. Because I never let people get close to me. I won't do that to a child; I won't give my
child my childhood."

Pussy didn't tell the stranger that she was going to have
the abortion the next morning.

Now I Tell This Story the Way I Say It

That night, because after I got pregnant it was always night,
one of my girlfriends led me through whatever city I was living
in.

To an antique store. I didn't want to go *there* because antique stores are graveyards for all those who are dead.

This one was located behind a street. When we found it,
it was shivering like a dying animal behind iron bars. Dead
clothes filled it up. Dead clothes, the parts of the skin that
have been used and used until they're flaky and yellow.

For weeks I needed new clothes. The city had been turning colder. Holes had crept into all of my wool clothing. I had

searched for sweaters. Here, in this store, for the first time, were the sweaters I craved, sexual ones, the kind that aren't manufactured anymore. I tried one on. Two of them. Sweater after sweater. Each one softer, more developed than the last. No two were ever the same.

My guide must have been a guy because he was trying on men's clothes.

I hate it when I can't fuck, for whatever reason, someone I want to fuck. I went back to whatever stood for a dressing room. In the back of the store, in a corner.

A red velvet curtain, rather than a door, obscured whatever lay inside.

In there, I looked at myself in a green sweater whose hairs were so long that they curled around each other. Green glass jewels hid in this hair. Its huge collar didn't imprison me, like most collars. Watching myself in a mirror that was older and taller than me, a mirror that was also outside, I realized I was beautiful.

The second sweater I put on, though black, was so thin that I could still see my own breasts. They had no nipples. The more naked that I became, the more beautiful.

Sweater after sweater.

I wanted to own every single one. I couldn't afford this. I arbitrarily decided on number four. Abandoning the four I had chosen, all of the sweaters I had tried on, heaped in turds upon the floor, I went back into the dressing room, which I thought was empty.

My boyfriend was in there.

When we were inside, he told me and the girl who was with me what I had never known, that he was going to abandon me.

Right then, everything, or the world, stopped.

This was how MD, who was my girlfriend, and I started our journey through this forgotten city.

Its streets were more crowded than I remembered. I don't know who was driving that car we were in.

. . . As yet I didn't understand that I was in the city's heart . . .

. . . I saw women, dressed in black, standing on a sidewalk. They were milling, that is, not yet in a line, around, under, a bright pink movie marquee . . .

. . . The color of all the streets was brown . . .

. . . The street down which we were driving connected the two ends of the city . . .

. . . I saw a poster on a wall that was the color of the streets. It read "Maya Angelou." Then I looked down an alley: all of the buildings down that tube were brownstones. In that street, the sky was that gray which is perpetual and never devoid of light. When I looked again, the women under "Maya Angelou," now even more of them, dressed in black, stood in a line.

I didn't understand what I was seeing. But I couldn't have been hallucinating because my girlfriend was seeing what I was.

"Why are so many women wearing black waiting for Maya Angelou?" I asked her.

We were driven the same distance we had been driven. Again, I looked down an alley. Here the perspective reminded me of a world in a Renaissance painting: the condition of the space, especially in regard to infinity, depended on its perceiver's seeing.

I saw a line of women which extended down that alley as

far as I could see, turned the corner, beyond my sight. All of the women I saw wore nun's habits.

"They're imitating Coffee," remarked MD.

"Coffee?"

As soon as I responded to her, in my mind's eye I saw a novel by Chester Himes. I had no idea what Chester Himes had to do with Coffee.

"Coffee's a huge draw," Marguerite explained to me, "because the people who live in this neighborhood hate PG&E." PG&E was the local gas and electric company.

Though I detest every gas and electric company I've ever encountered, I didn't rationally understand how Coffee connected to hatred for PG&E. But nonrationally I understood.

MD explained further: "When Angela Davis appeared downtown her audience was tiny."

I agreed. "And, unlike Maya Angelou's audience, none of the women in the former's audience wanted to be her." Then I began my analysis of mass and media culture: "There are far more women who want to be Coffee than there are Angela or Maya Angelou wanna-bes, but we don't know who Coffee is."

MD remarked that Angela read downtown and that downtown is where the art venues and rich whites reside. "No one goes there anymore."

Instead of saying this, she actually said, "No one goes down now."

We went down to where it was no longer poor.

Here streets were dark from the color of rain. The same color I saw fall in Berlin.

"Pussy, pussy," I called.

We were walking away from the antique store filled with dead clothes, and a little cat was prancing ahead of us over the light gray concrete. She darted between my legs, raced around behind me, leapt ahead of me. Until she no longer could be seen.

In all that half-light and half-dark, I said out loud, "Pussy."

Every time I called her, she returned to me. Then scooted even faster between mine and my girlfriend's legs, around and around our feet, until the world was a tangle. Just at that moment, she extended one of her paws. As if she was going to bat.

It was the only way that she could touch me. She was just like me.

The cat said to me, so that I could understand her, "I'll never leave you." As if I had been instructed in a more secret language, I then understood that, according to her nature, she goes wherever she wants whenever and at whatever speed, often disappears for days, and that if I welcome this, she'll never abandon me.

I liked this.

This was how I got my name.

Turning into a Criminal

Pussy met her gynecologist for the first time on the day of the abortion. Since he was sporting a ponytail, she decided that he must have once been a hippy. She was high on the pills that they had fed her.

They blabbed for an unknown amount of time about the nature of poetry and then Pussy asked when her abortion was going to begin.

The hippy answered that it would soon be over. She felt a twinge which was almost painful.

The abortion was over. Just before the end of this world, Pussy hadn't known a thing.

There is no master narrative nor realist perspective to provide a background of social and historical facts.

Two weeks after the abortion, Pussy returned to the clinic for her routine checkup. A nurse-practitioner, who might have been the first one, informed her that she was still pregnant.

"I don't feel pregnant."

"Some women even bear a child after they've had a termination. But we're not sure you're pregnant."

Pussy asked when they might know positively what she was. She, or her body, was confused.

"Why don't you relax for two weeks? Forget that any of this happened. You'll probably get your period before the end of two weeks and then you'll know for sure that you're not pregnant."

The Time of Possibilities was the name of these two weeks. Sometime during this time, the nurse-practitioners and the doctors—there seemed to be two of each—speculated that Pussy might have a tubal pregnancy.

Two weeks had passed. No period was anywhere to be found. So they decided to test her to find out if anyone or part of anyone was living inside her.

They photographed the insides of her uterus. The photos showed uterine insides. There was nothing else. But the quality of the photos was poor.

They, and in this world *they* always means *medical people*, then extracted blood from Pussy. The blood told *them* that Pussy was pregnant.

"This means," one of the nurse-practitioners explained to

the female, "that you might be pregnant and you might not be. If you are pregnant, we don't know where . . ." she hesitated, ". . . it's . . . hiding." She consulted a calendar. "If it's hiding inside a tube, that tube by now should be broken, so the tube must be about to break."

"What're you saying?" Pussy was in that state in which anger resembles stupidity.

"Tonight or at any other time after this, if you faint, go directly to the nearest hospital."

Do not pass Go. Instead of adding this, Pussy explained that she didn't know anything about the hospitals in the city, that she thought all of them were sites in which people were murdered. She didn't have any medical insurance.

"Go to a hospital for children."

They discussed that point.

Later in the night, Pussy phoned one of the doctors.

He was in his car, or one of his cars; the static from the car phone was louder than his voice.

"Is there any way that you, that anyone in the world, can learn whether or not I have a tubal? I have lots of money," Pussy explained.

"We'll learn whether or not when one of your tubes bursts open."

Later Pussy would remember that it was at this very moment that she forgot to be moral, especially to be moral about abortion.

For the next few days, she kept phoning the doctors.

Finally, it happened. "We've decided how we're going to know whether or not you have an ectopic pregnancy. We'll give you a second abortion. If that abortion works, you won't have an ectopic pregnancy."

The logic made as much sense to Pussy as anything else in the world.

Pussy ate their painkillers; she had what seemed to her to be the same abortion as she had the first time; again, she asked whether she was still pregnant.

The doctor who did the suction replied that this time something had come out, but he didn't know what it was.

In order to find out what it was, *they* were going to extract more blood from Pussy. In a few days, the new blood would be able to talk to them.

The blood announced to everyone that Pussy was no longer pregnant.

Now I Tell This Story the Way I Say It

Since I was poor, I had to prove to myself that I was rich, so I began to haunt clothing stores.

What I wanted was a black dress.

Two pools sat in the middle of the store *where I had once seen a black dress.* One of them was smaller than the other.

A man who was tall and thin was spooning black liquid into small vials, which he then gave to people to drink.

Like ink, the liquid tainted whomever it entered.

One of those who were infected was a girl with ebony hair.

Inside the store, there was no natural time. One day, or night, the tall thin man saw a girl who resembled the ebony-haired one, whom he had infected, to a T. For this reason, he fell in love with the black-haired girl. He fell so thoroughly in love that he stopped feeding people liquid, he left the store, he desired to go off with her for all that would remain of time.

I was in that store. I didn't have any money nor any capability for earning money in the urban society and I wanted that black dress badly, so I walked off with it. I didn't run; I didn't want to make a spectacle of myself, of my guilt. Walked out of that store.

This was how I began the occupation that I would later become.

Stealing was part of the city. Every city is born, continually being born, out of configurations of minds and desires: every city is alive. This city was patriarchal, that which allows the existence of none but itself, for it had arisen and was arising only out of the rational, moralistic bends of minds.

Patriarchal, it expressed its unbearability: for years, the economic power had lain in white liberal hands. The money was now coming from the Hong Kong immigrant community. Many of the children of these close-knit families clustered themselves into street gangs. In the lowest loins of the city, these boys engaged Hispanic and black gangs in more violence than any could handle. The white liberals who hadn't as yet abandoned the city knew nothing of this because they didn't wish to know all, in the city, that lay outside their control. They pretended that they could control gang warfare: passed laws which, they claimed, would put an end to all violence. Protect the kids. The laws defined the children who were members of gangs as hardened murderers and so turned them into lifelong criminals. The search for all those who had been tainted began.

Even though the urban arena was becoming more nonwhite than white, liberals and other whites decided that those who had been infected must be destroyed as efficaciously as possible.

Lest evil spread her wings. The evil of those who have drunk black.

The search narrowed. Soon the identities of all those who have been polluted will come to be known. Soon we'll know where all the evil in this world resides. I realized that I hadn't been touched. I was clean. Then I knew that a speck inside me, something as much like a trace as a memory, a memory of my lips brushing the black liquor, was tainted.

Immediately I thought: It really isn't anything. I'm not a sick one. I'm not one of the monsters. I thought: I'm passing for normal; I'm as normal as any moral person.

Their search narrowed further. I returned to the store where I had stolen the black dress.

It was here that the creation of the world had begun.

When I was finally inside the store, I saw that the ebony-haired girl who had escaped from here hadn't died even though she had drunk some of the black liquid. Perhaps instead of dying she had given birth to three freaks. I saw this. Three children, or things, scampering around a room now so large that it was the back of a clothes store, where its designers work and live. No longer the actual clothes store.

Everything in this room was messy. Heaps of clothes and cloths in no possible order.

Chaos had once been a clothes store.

One of these children was so tall that the body below his head was a stilt. The head was falling off, almost separated from his neck. A midget sat around the neck. Tiny legs hugged a beanpole of flesh, as if they were fucking it.

The existence and appearance of these freaks announced the revelation of the mystery. Thus of all mysteries. As if *to find out* was simply *to see*, I found out that I'm one of the tainted.

To see equaled *to accept,* because the object of my sight was exactly what I was now forced to accept. That I'm going to die.

Now I realized that no one and nothing will ever escape the chains of cause and effect: I'd stolen a dress; I had to endure the consequences of my act. I'm going to die.

I knew I couldn't escape my death.

I looked around at everyone in the room. At the man who had spooned liquid out of the pools. At the ebony-haired woman. At the half-human half-stilt. At the mongoloid midget. At all who were stranger or more monstrous. I couldn't tell which one I was. I kept looking and looking, but I could no longer find myself.

I realized that I'd escaped my death because I no longer knew who I was.

NOW I TELL EVERYTHING IN MY OWN LANGUAGE
Ending the Memory of Childhood

"There will be no more abortions. Criminality will no longer be connected to unfortunate consequence," I said.

I had just left the hospital; I was still in those environs. I looked down and into my underpants.

The underpants resembled the white cotton ones schoolgirls used to wear. Now they don't wear anything. I saw blood flowing over one of the white sides.

In order to handle this situation, I fashioned the following plan: First, I'd leave my boyfriend. Prior to the plan, I didn't know that I had a boyfriend. Second, since the pads, once as white as the panties, that were sitting one on top of the other upon the cloth crotch, were holding more blood than they were capable of storing, I'd find a place where I could be alone. There I would change.

I began looking for the place where I would change my blood.

Within the city of dusk, the only house that was real was hidden. It was wood.

Inside this house, I found the room I was looking for. The place for change. It was partly open, partly closed, like all the other areas in the house. If it had been normal, it would have had a door. There was no wall where a door should have been.

Despite all the openness and vulnerability, everywhere was dark.

The decor of this room pirated that of a 1950s New York City apartment: roses papered its walls. All the antiques were green.

As if I were outside the room and looking in, I remarked, "The lamps are especially beautiful this time of year."

And as if that sentence had just carved out a space in which something could take place, a man stood in front of the wall that wasn't there. His hair was punked up.

I couldn't change my bloody rags while a strange guy was watching me so I told him that he had to go away now. "Go away. Shoo."

I couldn't explain myself.

When he replied that he would go, I felt guilty.

As soon as he left the room, I moved left, around the bit of wall that jutted out of one of the principal ones. Within the recess that was there, I found a bathroom. The room must have been designed and decorated at the same time as the one of roses. A charming bathroom, for all of its furniture—toilet in white, white bathtub with rose-streaked curtain—its very space, were slightly too small to accommodate an adult human.

Nevertheless I managed to throw my used Kotex wrapped in toilet paper and the plastic wrapping of the new pad into the miniature wastepaper basket that was sitting under the sink . . .

. . . It was time for me again to change my pad. As if I had never before changed, I no longer knew where I could go.

Free from abortions, I had nowhere to go in the world.

I wandered, without knowing where, through that house whose insides were lightless. I came to a bedroom. Its huge door was open. I looked into the openness and saw a man. I knew him, he used to be my best friend before I had gotten a name.

I believe he was still a poet. He was sitting on a bed and talking on the phone. He used to talk on the phone so much, when we had been friends, that I would have to tell the operator that I was making an emergency call whenever I wanted to contact him. Since he was on the phone, I knew that he wouldn't catch sight of me. I didn't want him to because the fight that he had picked with me and that had ended our friendship had wounded me.

During this quarrel which had taken place just prior to my abortions, he had told me that he was one of the few men who understands what it is to be a woman.

I still had to change my Kotex. So I walked into the next bedroom.

Two men were sleeping inside there. Two narrow beds which didn't touch each other.

I couldn't change my pad because there were men every-where. But if I didn't throw away the old blood, something dreadful, like rot or disease, was going to touch my body.

I just stood there, in front of all those men. I no longer cared whether they saw me. And changed the pad in the hallway.

Childhood was officially over.

How I Tried to Become Part of Society

As soon as I was clean, again I started haunting clothes stores.

I went back to the store in which the strange people had lived. In amazement, I saw upwardly mobile heterosexuals, coupled.

I no longer belonged in that store where I had found the black dress. Black, androgynous.

But all the clothes I was seeing belonged on the bodies of secretaries or security guards, men in offices or officers.

All I wanted to do was escape what had once felt like home. The only possible home during the days of abortions.

But if I didn't buy something, I would have nothing. I thought: I have to buy something, I do, I do, even though I've almost no money.

I've to find that one object I might want to own.

Thus, I defined the word *clothing* for myself.

The only thing I came upon I wanted even a little bit was a gray catsuit. I didn't really want it. The breast said, "Gaul-tier." I looked at the rest. A white tag said, "$300."

My eyes sat on it, stroked it, even though I didn't want it. I knew I had to want something.

In order to make myself want that which I couldn't have

because I was poor, I began feeling up clothes I would never wear, clothes I would never go near if they paid me.

Short wool coats that my grandmother had forced me to wear when I was a child.

A salesgirl, doing her job, started telling me what I desired. I knew that she was trying to brainwash me by talking me into wearing a straight-woman outfit.

I was so disgusted that I was about to leave, but instead, I went the other way. Backwards. Into a dressing room. Back there where I had left all my clothes.

There wasn't anything anymore.

"Where are my clothes?" I asked the salesgirl who despised me because I wasn't like everybody else.

Bitch informed me, with as much brevity as she could get up, that she had stuffed my "things" into a plastic bag. "Other people have to use this dressing room."

"A plastic bag" means "a body bag."

She handed me a brown paper container.

Inside, a pair of wet shoes.

I was now so poor that I no longer knew what to do, so I did the only thing I knew. I went back to my mother.

She wasn't as poor as she used to be. Now she was living in a large house in the suburbs. When I was a child, she never let me near her. Perhaps it was because she was living in affluence that she let me come into her house and stay.

I was surprised. By this time I had accepted, though with agony, that she hated me.

Living in her house with her, I felt safe for the first time in my life. So safe that if the world, which lay outside the house, was going to die, I would be in that house and nothing would change.

In the days before the beginning of sexuality.

I was inside, separate from what was outside, so I looked out one of the picture windows. When I stuck out my head, I saw that a man was standing on the ledge.

I knew that he was about to break in. As if I had never seen any man before. There had been no men when I was a child. My skin was prickling; my nose smelling my own sweat: all that my mother feared, which I had learned to take inside, was now outside the window. This man or image formed by the meeting of interior and exterior fear was about to shatter the clear glass.

Thus, the image had two names: *criminal* and *mother-fucker*. The motherfucker—that's what men were in those days before the pirates again came—was doing whatever he was doing so that he could break into me. I knew it. *To know is to cause*. Knowing he was about to come in me, I screeched.

After that, there was something evil inside my mother's body. For her house no longer was safe. It had become open to every fucking stranger, to anyone who just wanted to enter for any reason at all. This is how the world really is. I screeched. Everyone's penetrating and coming. I was all alone. Inside. There would never be anyone to help me.

No one's going to help me.

Mommy's always been gone. She never wanted anything to do with me. I'm alone for the rest of time and after that. As soon as I realized as completely as it's possible to realize that I was alone, I knew that I could no longer survive on my own. I have to be with another. Because of all this openness.

As if the walls were coming down, then it started to rain. Rain seemed to be coming through those windowpanes, it was seeping through the cracks. Of my mother's fucking body. My mother's body fucking. There were no longer any differences between inside and outside. There were no curtains over the windows, so everybody could see everything.

I didn't know how to be a woman. I couldn't make a curtain. A curtain or shroud for the body of my mother.

She hadn't been there.

In all the growing terror, I looked through the window and saw people walking on a gravel path. This sight, this act of seeing, was the clue to how I could escape the house of fear. If I could reverse inside and outside, then I'd be outside, on the black gravel path down which people were walking safely to a river.

The man I'd seen on the ledge and a boy were in the house, stealing. I reversed interior and exterior: I joined them. We began to steal from my mother.

They didn't steal because they wanted anything. They wanted to trash.

Me too. I'm going to trash the house of childhood. Which had been unbearable.

I wanted to remain forever with that man and boy.

That's how I got outside.

We lounged next to her house. We kicked over some dead grass. There weren't any dogs. My mother drove by us in a car. She took a potshot at us from the car window. I saw it was my mother though she was a man.

A bullet entered the chest of the Mexican, the boy.

I went away from my mother forever. I lived with the boy. He was the only one I had ever had and all that I would love.

The bullet that was sitting in his chest made him sicker,

so I took care of him. Even though it wasn't in my nature to care for anyone. Since he was sick, we were two children together.

One day he said, "Pussy, we're going to go shopping."

I was so excited that I jumped up and down.

We decided we were going to find underwear. I would try this underwear on in a dressing room whose curtain would be open, just enough, so that everyone who was outside the curtain could watch his hands pinch my nipples, then the tips of his fingers in my crack, partly obscured in black hairs. They could watch me come. Or else I'd take off as many clothes as I could just so I could try on underwear, in the center of the store, so everyone would see everything that is me.

The store would be an antique store full of dead clothes.

Despite all our fantasies, we found ourselves in a department store. Fluorescents overlit a large room. The kid—that's what I called him—rather than me, was trying on shorts, boxers so bright blue-green that fish were swimming in them.

I wanted two other pairs of boxers and planned to buy them for myself. Because I was a selfish bitch. Okay, one of them would be for him. I told the kid that one of them was for him.

Then, I looked at him more closely. Now I was frightened.

"How do you feel?"

He was becoming thinner and thinner.

My boyfriend went downhill. All the way. During this period, we moved back into my apartment. There we lived as if we were never going anywhere again. The bed where we lay was against a wall. A small, square window hung over the mattress.

The boy phoned someone and asked whoever it was to come to our house because he didn't want me to be by myself. His request terrified me. For being lonely is what scares me most in the world.

I attempted to analyze why I was frightened. *To be lonely in the world*, it seemed to me, *is to be solely with my mother.*

After that, I wanted my boyfriend to touch me and never to stop. To do what I believed he was always doing. To slither his cock between my legs. Which was to stick his fingers into my skin. I knew that he would never do this because he was only becoming weaker.

We would no longer have sex together, but we could lie in bed.

As if a bed was a sky. All that was inside us was lying outside.

On the bed I told the Mexican boy, "I have never loved anyone but you."

I Go to the Bottom of the World

After the boy left me alone, I got on my motorcycle.

I had already placed my stuffed white cat in one of its saddlebags and made sure that she'd be comfortable.

Together, we took off. We wanted to go to the country.

I was traveling down what appeared to be a country road: a thin layer of snow, hard and dirty, almost completely covered rich brown dirt; thick white stripes separated the whole into four tracks. On each side of these four tracks, but only here and there, one- and two-story suburban houses half-sunk below the snow.

Looking down below my front wheel, which was rotating, I saw there was no more road under the hard snow.

I was aware I wasn't going to crash.

In this manner, the country ended. I was at a big, black tunnel. I had no choice but to enter it.

All light was black. Walls began to curve left while floor descended; walls were now curving so sharply that when I looked ahead, I thought I was going to slide. Turning was easier than seeing.

At the bottom of these turns, still in the tunnel, orange-and-white barriers stood in a jagged row across the black floor. Here my journey ended. The barriers forced me to make a U too sharp for my bike's turning capacity, but I turned without falling.

And parked by one of the orange-and-white barriers. Opposite the only parking lot, there was a street scene: a concrete sidewalk. A building wall. Behind windows in that wall, movie posters. As if I myself were in a film.

I wanted to attend the fun fair that took place behind this facade, but in this dead time of the year it had been shut down.

All there was was time. Face-to-face with time, I had to act: the only thing there was to do, in this dead town, was go to a movie.

I returned to those windows and looked inside them. The only movie playing was Hollywood. Too stupid to see.

There wasn't anything for me. Here, in the total bottom of the world.

I must have walked away from that entrance, for I found myself climbing up the stairs of a huge red-brick school building. Inside, a movie was about to be shown.

It wouldn't cost anything.

Wooden folding chairs had been strung across a room.

The movie began in the dark.

In the film, some of the homeless went about their lives. Watching the nonsensationalized, or non-Hollywood, details made me realize that I was like that. Never before had I known that I was homeless.

The film ended: again it was dark.

At one point during the playing of the movie I learned that this was its first screening, for government officials had been keeping it from the public.

A strange girl asked me where everyone had gone.

While it had been running, I hadn't noticed that any-one had left the room, so the only answer I could come up with was that her mind must have stopped for several minutes while the film had been playing.

And then I couldn't tell the difference between her and me. Between the disappearance of her mind and of mine.

And then, since to understand is to learn, I understood that consciousness isn't the mind and that it's consciousness, not the mind, which dies.

There was no more movie. It was time to go.

My new girl and I walked down one of those long halls.

I don't know how long it was before I realized that I was in a world dominated by the visual.

Paintings covered as much as possible of the walls of the hall I was in or of the room so open to that hall that I thought it was a hall.

Either these paintings had been made by children or they were in a naïf style. I could take anything I wanted. For it was the world of the visual.

I walked up to each painting, peered at it closely. I didn't want any. This was when I began to want.

In the room next to the front door, streamers hovered in the air. Between these party objects, I saw, through an open doorway, a smaller room:

Racks of clothes occupied its center. Everything was hung for sale. Just as I had walked as far up as I could to the canvases, I now approached the clothes the same way. I looked at them. But I didn't want any rags, simulacra of the ones sold on Haight St. Haight St. in Hippyville. The only half-bearable one was a replica of a blouse I already owned.

Paintings crammed the walls of the room of streamers as much as they had the hall down which I had journeyed with my girlfriend. That strange girl. Paintings were no longer on canvas, but were comic books, books hung on the walls. Books I had never before seen, entrances into wonder.

Into the geographical wonders of the world known only to sailors.

It was here, in wonder, in this bottom, that I met the punk boys.

I had learned how to travel through my dreams.

OSTRACISM'S STORY

PUSSYCAT FEVER
Before I Was Eight Years Old
I don't have a father.

I thought that the man who married my mother was my father. As soon as she married him, she died. I was eight years old when I found out that he wasn't my real father.

I continued to call him "Dad," this man who was kind to me, gentle and stupid.

My real father is the taker-away of dreams.

I was brought up in a lonely, primitive place. Until I left that portion of the world, I didn't have any friends. Except for a dog so old he looked dead, and dead people. The dead people lived in a cemetery. The church, remaining roofless, which sat like a dead dog in its middle, was the only building neighboring on our house. The family who had owned this cemetery and its immediate environs were now dead.

Their name was Karnstein.

The cemetery was my favorite place in the world. There I saw that the angels and the dead bed together. I wanted to live there for the rest of my life.

As if I were on an ocean.

Dad brought me up to be a boy. He had broken up a marriage to be with my mother; the child of that marriage was a son whom my father could no longer see. So he taught me baseball, and especially football, for he had been a football hero at his college. He never read books and had no other interest in culture.

Like him, I was good at sports; unlike him, I read book after book. I liked pornography best though I couldn't have defined the word *sex*, much less any dirty term. During the time of innocence, the tale which was my favorite had nothing to do with sex: it was about a bad girl:

A boy who doesn't have any parents is sitting on a snake, a snake who's wider than a human cock and longer than the path that's connecting the living to the dead.

The boy never washes his hair. His hair's so stiff and tangled that it's as good as a dead person's, not because it's never been washed but because the vermin who are living inside its labyrinths are having sex with each other. Anyone the hair touches becomes dirtier.

The boy is always dirtier. His only possessions are skulls. Not actually possessions: the boy and the skulls just live together. The snakes who wind around all the dead people that show up curl through the holes in the skulls, then through openings in the boy's hair, until they reach his ears. There, they crawl inside. They forget to turn around and leave; instead, they fall asleep and dream whatever snakes dream. If there was anyone around, she would see that when the snakes were dreaming, the boy looked as if he were wearing precious jewels.

The father of all these snakes, of all snakes, lived before the creation of creation. After creation, he turned into a cock hood.

The boy enjoys playing with his cock hood as much as he does skulls.

A girl who resembled me desired to fuck this boy and wanted him to fuck her. She wanted this so badly that she wanted time to end as soon as they started fucking so that fucking would never stop. This was how she wanted him: she wanted him to want her so wildly that if he didn't get her and get her and get her . . . he'd die and die and die and, at the same time, he'd be, and is, the one who is the beginning of everyone and everything and who can't die. Because he isn't human. Also, she wanted them to have nothing to do with each other after they had fucked each other so that fucking would be everything. After fucking, there should be nothing.

As yet, there wasn't anything.

This girl wants to want. She looks like me; like me, she thinks in two ways: she smells and she has ideas. She thought: How can I get him to want me how I want him to want me? But no one wants me. She thought: He's a baby because he's never had a relationship with another person.

She changed her mind. He has had relationships with dead people.

Being educated, the girl thought that the history of this world had taught her two lessons. Lesson #1: Human sexual desire is never reciprocal. Moreover, humans are cruel. Lesson #2: Since a human who sexually desires another human automatically loses power over the desired one, the desirer can return to a, any, position of power only by pretending not to desire. In regard to her special case: the only way that she could get this brat to want her the ways she wanted him to want her, totally in heat, would be to show him clearly that she didn't want him.

She could no longer want him. As yet there was no world.

Whoever wrote this story said that history is philosophy, therefore, sexual history is the philosophy of religion.

Because he was so dirty and evil, this girl who looked like me didn't know how to stop wanting the boy. So she fucked every animal who wanted to do it to her until she had enough confidence to walk over to the one who didn't want her. Before she did anything else, she had to talk to him, so she placed her tongue inside his ear. As if it really was a living snake, this tongue traveled until it reached the other side of the mind. Through the realms of the dead. It became hard. The boy remembered that he wasn't into sex.

Girls used to kill themselves because of him.

But the girl who looked like me was as bad as he was: when

she realized that his tongue was no longer hard, she got angry. Since she was being physically and emotionally rejected, she was more turned on than she had been. If such a thing can be possible.

History also teaches that a clit's like a knife. Just as she was about to stick her clit into him, the boy saved her from doing this dreadful act by setting her on fire.

She turned into a mare so she could reach the nearest body of water as quickly as possible. Smoke flew out of her black nostrils as she raced through the unbearable sands.

Within the water, she drank up the water she saw, and then, all the water there was in the world, for the sexual thirsts of girls are never satisfied.

Was this girl right when she tried to penetrate the boy? Should she have played with herself instead?

There was no one who could answer me.

The girl still wanted the boy who was bad to want her, so she tried another tactic. No longer would she fight him. So now he couldn't defeat her; so now he couldn't reject her.

She told him she was his slave.

Before this story had even started, the boy had hated procreation. Because his father, the horniest father in the world, though there wasn't yet a world, was doing it to his sister. There wasn't yet any procreation so there was no difference between father and son. The kid was appalled, not that his father was doing it to his sister, but rather that an act of procreation was just about to happen, an act that would destroy that perfection that exists prior to procreation. So the boy shot one of his toy arrows into his father to stop him from coming in his sibling. The arrow missed.

Nevertheless, the father was surprised, pulled his cock out of his daughter. He had already started to come. His sperm spurted everywhere. Down to where there wasn't yet a world in this time that wasn't. Fell, and in its falling, made the beginning of being born and dying.

It's not adequate to say that the boy hated procreation because, prior to procreation or creation, there was neither boy nor sister nor father and there was all three. When the boy shot his father, he set him on fire, the fire of lust, 'cause all the boy ever thought about was lust; all the boy ever wanted was for lust to go and go and never come; to come is to stop.

The boy decided that he'd fuck all the time, he'd never come. Such a boy's bad. Bad boys want to fuck girls and they don't like girls. They always do everything they can to keep their cocks hard.

Long before he had met the girl who resembled me, the brat learned that he could masturbate inside as well as outside himself and that, in this way, he would never have to come.

Just like a snake.

All the bad boys do this.

The girl wanted him to want her how she wanted him to want her even more wildly than before. Being his slave had nothing to do with this matter. She stopped pretending she was his slave. Began to fight him all over again. This time, by placing her tongue in one of his ears and whispering to him he needed to come as much as she did, that if he came like her, he would never have to stop coming and coming.

This is how the boy started to fuck the girl.

Only one other thing happened to me before I became eight years old.

I was lying in my bed. I can only sleep when I'm on my right side, my hands tucked as high as they can travel between my legs. For in this position I'm safe.

Though I was safe, for the first time in my life I wasn't able to fall asleep. On my journey to find sleep, I hunted for an image that would protect me. I couldn't find anything.

What was that saying about my life?

Then I became anxious: I was walking into a forest. All of me that was down below was thrashing: I might never again know sleep.

At the same time, I was frightened. I tried to do what I had never before done, fall asleep by feigning sleep, but now I no longer knew what sleep might be.

The forest I was entering was dark, tangled in wood. When I turned again, I was lying next to a girl who looked exactly like me. I wasn't surprised that she was next to me, so I guessed I was expecting her.

Her hands took hold of my thighs, then they crossed half-way around my stomach and held on. My back was curling into her front. I was able, now, to fall asleep.

To a sleep that was dreamless. A sharp, burning sensation woke me up. I cried aloud words I couldn't understand.

It was as if I was in a dream. I looked at the child; I saw she was looking at me. She disappeared under the bed covers. I never saw her again.

My cry must have woke me up. When I stood up, I saw that I was wet. I put my hand on my forehead. My burning was now there. I had no way of knowing if I was actually feverish; I turned more confused; I looked down to see what was wrong there.

My cunt lips and the parts of the thighs to the sides and

the front above the lips were puffed because they were retaining liquid.

Though I was aware that liquid retention isn't a problem unless it's extreme, I ran to my father. I told him that I was in trouble. He wanted me to consult a doctor. But I didn't trust them except for one acupuncturist who was a teacher of others.

My kind father brought me to see him.

Within his office, after he had examined my condition, the strange doctor announced that he was going to make three incisions into my upper thighs and cut a square of flesh out of my front. It was as if I would no longer have genitalia. Then there would be no extra liquid. He added that he wasn't going to use any anesthetic.

The images that were in my mind while he was speaking his words terrified me. I protested against this plan.

So he became more precise: if this operation didn't take place as soon as possible, my life would be in jeopardy. I am in jeopardy. For this reason, there can't be an anesthetic.

The words "I can't" sit in my mind. Then they repeat themselves because, if they occur enough times, they might have the power to change all that is taking place in my body. In me. To me.

Each "I can't" increases fear and anxiety. Fear and anxiety grow over all the world until they rush, in the form of the words "I can't," out of my mouth.

The doctor replied, "You have to."

I tried to crawl away from what had to be: "Why don't you cut into my body after I've been anesthetized? I can't bear being cut up any other way. I can't bear being hurt." This was the first time I ever explained this.

At the time I didn't see how I could become another person, a person who wasn't scared of pain, because becoming another person means dying and being hurt.

"My cutting will take only three minutes, O_2." O_2 is short for Ostracism.

To calm me down even more, the older man analyzed the nature of pain for me. *Pain* is not *being cut to the nerve*; rather, *pain* is *like being cut into, right up to, an edge of a nerve*. Then the razor will slice away all the surface of that nerve.

"If what has to happen—to me—in me—me—won't happen, I'll do anything, I'll never take a sip of red wine again, I'll stay away from all drugs," I pleaded.

My acupuncturist yielded. He agreed to drug me before he cut me open. But as minimally as possible.

I think that it took all of this which happened to make me realize who I am: I'm someone who finds that any pain is always physical pain and that physical pain isn't bearable. Just as I was about to understand why pain to the body isn't bearable, thought disappeared in me.

I don't remember anything that happened to me before I found the girl who looked like me in my bed.

As if arising out of a dark wood, I then came to this memory: during my early childhood I had been tortured, physically, with razor blades.

Another dream followed: I was in a whorehouse. I had followed something, perhaps in a dream, into a whorehouse. Even though I was a girl who had no friends, my friends and I were standing in the center of the house's central room, a reception room. All of my friends were women.

A voice, which was coming out of me, announced, not only to these women, "First I have to get away from Daddy."

I don't know who my real father is.

I Became Eight Years Old When Reality Turned Violet

I turned eight years old and my father announced that young girls were dying everywhere.

He had asked me to walk with him through the forest. It was an early summer evening whose skin was turning violet.

Frost was supposed to arrive late that very night. Frost, a dilapidated poet and my father's oldest friend. With a young girl who was meant to be my companion.

As yet I didn't have a friend because I was lonely.

They were no longer coming . . . my father was awkward to the point of being unable to explain even the simplest thing . . . he said, "I'm happy you never met her."

He further explained that the girl, who was my age, had died. Her father didn't know the cause.

He pulled a letter out of his pocket.

The poet, in this letter, told of his daughter's death only by relating her account of a dream she had had on the night before she died:

> "There was a gang of us.
>
> "It was as if I were still going to school. I detest opera above all, and there I was, about to attend an opera in a gang. As if we were going to a university, 'Bard' was the name of the opera house.
>
> "To reach Bard we had to separate ourselves into three groups. For this purpose, all of the girls in my class were selecting men as rapidly as they could. I watched them do it. I knew that I should do it too; I even tried, but I couldn't find anyone I wanted.
>
> "All of the men I saw were skinny.

"I asked myself, very honestly, 'Bad Dog, why aren't you attracted to a man?' I really wanted to be because I was supposed to be.

"But since I was stupid and mean, I didn't do what I was supposed to do. Instead I remained with my friend Heathcliff, who was hanging out with her group of two girls.

"Outside, it was night. Windows were lining only one side of the long, narrow corridor. The opera house. All of us, the whole gang, were sitting on a narrow, deep couch.

"Then we began to ascend, climbed up a staircase whose stairs were so wide that they must have been constructed only so that royalty could rise.

"I was in the middle of these stairs when I remembered about the separation. One of my friends, who was a good, gray poet, and I had fought. I never saw him again. Now he was ahead of me, on the stairs. To avoid seeing him and, worse, having him see me, I turned around, and then I saw dogs humping each other.

"As if I were now running away, I continued climbing those stairs meant only for royalty . . .

"I was fleeing all that lay below. I reached the top.

"At the highest point I realized that I had lost my black leather gloves. It must have happened while I was climbing up those stairs. Though I loved the gloves, I didn't want to return to my past, to all that lay below.

"I thought I was now free.

"So I walked the other way, into a perfectly round hall. A coatroom lay at my left. I checked my floor-length fake leopard which was every bit as elegant as my black leather gloves had been.

"But those were lost.

"Somewhat denuded, I was able to enter a room that was almost large enough to be a ballroom. In each section, a group of musicians was performing. None of their musics had anything to do with any of the others. All the musicians were dressed formally; none of them looked alike.

"An adjoining and smaller room housed an exhibit of automata. The machine that interested me the most, and so seemed the biggest, was composed of two sections. Each section was a German male punk who, like a giant plastic bird, dunked his head repeatedly into an equally giant plastic glass filled with water.

"The metaphor made sense to me.

"It was only after I had journeyed through the room of automata that I knew that, despite my fear of my past, I would have to regain my black leather gloves. Despite dread powerful enough to be loathing, I would have to descend into that world that lay under . . .

" 'Dead Dog,' I lectured myself, 'you're stupid because you gnaw at, and then throw away, everyone whom you most love. You're dead and you've got to live. It's living dogs who can search for treasure.

" 'I, Dead Dog, am promising myself that, from now on, I will actively go after all buried treasure.'

"To fulfill my only promise to myself, I began carefully walking down the black carpet that was now covering the narrow stairs . . .

"In the middle of the blackness, a pair of black leather gloves sat on a step. I bent down to retrieve them; down there, I realized they weren't mine because the black leather was covered in black silk. I stole them because mine had been stolen, though they might not have been.

"I arrived at the bottom of the stairs. The couch hadn't moved. Nor had the imprints, in the pillows and large cushions scattered here and there, of my classmates' bodies. The only difference between this present and the present in my memory was three pairs of black leather gloves. The first weren't mine because they were unlined. The third were almost mine: the only difference between them and the gloves in my memory was a slight change in the color of the lining.

"I now existed in total blackness. It was the outside. I was outside of everything. There were only girls, Heathcliff and her two girlfriends. I knew that I didn't belong in this society of only girls; I was strange; I tried to hide my strangeness, even from myself, in fake drunkenness.

"The girls couldn't ostracize me because I wasn't one of them.

"All of us were going away, I wasn't questioning where, in an extra-long black limo.

"Inside the blackness, I pulled down one of its windows. Heathcliff's cock appeared through the hole and I sucked her off. It was coming through the hole where outside becomes inside. After I had taken my mouth away from her, I felt that I had to explain to Heathcliff why I had done what I just had; I had to explain because I wasn't one of them; I said, 'Heathcliff, I just sucked you off because I was trying to leave you alone.'

"I was actually saying that I knew that Heathcliff doesn't like it when I bother her.

"As soon as I made this apology, the three other girls and I began to grab at each other's bodies and make out with *each other. I was feeling only wonder and pleasure in which there was no fear.''*

The dream ended here. There was no more letter.

The dilapidated poet said, "She died."

He was unable to say anything else. Or he had nothing else to say.

My father said that young girls were dying everywhere, that it would no longer be safe for me to live with him.

He said, "You will no longer have to be alone. Ever in your life. You're going to go to school so you can live with girls."

All of Us Girls Have Been Dead for So Long

The Last Story That I Read:

The girl who looked like me and the boy had been living together for years and years. Though they weren't any older.

She wanted to have a baby. He didn't want to, and he didn't want her to, either.

The girl was looking at her body, which had become a graveyard because the boy wouldn't help her make a baby grow in it. She didn't ever want to fuck anyone else.

Inside this graveyard, skulls sat on top of brown dirt replete with holes; here and there, an animal leg; ducks swam on top of green and dead pools.

She looked down, below the graveyard, where she saw a rat. It was a baby. Five strands of hair, all that it possessed, sprouted out of its head. It sat itself right on her lap.

"But I can't have a baby," said the girl.

It held up its front paws, drew her face into its. Its lips, softer than it was possible for flesh to be, wanted to drink her, for she was a pool of water to the baby.

A pool of water in which a dead horse happened to be lying.

She bent down to her child, who also was crying, and lifted it up. Kissed, suckled it until all loneliness was gone. All her loneliness, all her rage against the boy, whom she loved more than anyone else in the world.

After she had stopped being hurt, the girl was able to make distinctions. She perceived that the rat was her lover.

So she laughed and said, "Boys are rats." Then, she and the boy held hands and were happy.

The night after I read this tale, I retold it in a dream:

The school to which I'm being sent isn't a girls' school. It's partly male. Also, it's a parking lot.

I'm standing in that parking lot next to a boy. Since he's a boy, we're making out. As soon as my body's hot, he informs me that he's going out with a girl from the theater department. "She's all mixed-up."

I'm mixed-up: my response to this is to give him a blow job while I hang upside down, as if I've become the Hanged Man in the Tarot deck. My socks drip over my eyes. I'm no longer able to talk. He replies, "No one can see us."

This makes me feel better.

The boy's name is K——.

When sex is over, there's no longer any sex for me: I had been left, abandoned, in the parking lot. This parking lot is a graveyard. The only thing that remains in the world is my motorbike. But I can't see it. My search for my bike begins: now I look for it where I remember I parked it. It's no longer there. I look elsewhere, and elsewhere, always inside that parking lot.

Unbeknownst to me, the parking-lot owner moved it to another spot. Just when I'm seeing my Ninja, finally, the owner backs his car into it. My helplessness to do anything about this, which is connected to my lack of sex, though I don't understand how, infuriates me to such a degree that I jump on top of his body: my small fists beat on his head.

I was willing to do anything to get out of this situation. So I got a job. I would have a function in the school so I would be a real person. I didn't mind being a masseuse—the new job— because that way I could earn money without having to be stupid . . .

I was where I was going to do it for money: touch a strange body. The first person who bought my services was female. I took it for granted she was in the theater department because her hair was long and perfectly arranged.

I had never given anyone a massage so I had no idea how to do it. But I was determined to be a real person. Trying to pretend that I wasn't stupid, without any hesitation I opened the door to the school's massage room.

It was too tiny to be a room: three minuscule shelves connected to a wall hung over a wood slab which lay on a bathtub not large enough for an adult to do more than crawl into.

Something must have happened between us, because now the girl, who might have been in the theater department, had to take a bath.

Both of us were giggling in that tub; we couldn't stop giggling. Then we had sex again. I didn't know that what we were doing had anything to do with sex.

When, in the future, the school was, I feared, about to fire me because I was working for them and fucking one of their students, I still didn't feel bad about the sex because it had been fun. The sun was outside. After that, I had sex with all the girls I could get and I knew that I wasn't going to lose my job.

The Dreams of Pirates

Out of parrots and macaws they step into seas which sound like earthquakes, into waters reaching up to, then punching holes in, the air. They're on the march; as much as they ever do anything together; they're after booty. Ownership. Usually they commence battle by surrounding their quarry like cats, mice. Tease, then, destroy them. Leave without having actually murdered anyone. They're back in their hideout in the black sands. All of them naked.

The Sex of Pirates

Now the pirates are Japanese. Two of them, a male and a female (pirates aren't always either male or female) are in a Japanese kitchen, where they're cooking. Only the woman is doing the cooking because the man's sexist. Since she's a pirate, she won't have anything to do with humans: either she's cooking for animals or she's cooking up an animal. One is the same as the other.

Right now, her version of cooking is to make animal food out of catshit.

. . . vast memories of sacred cities have become lands in themselves . . . strewn across deserts most of whose shifting grounds no human will ever touch . . . traces where there were once no traces . . . these are dreams.

There's a white girl. She's a lousy writer and knows that when the pirates translate her stuff, they'll make it terrific. She's in the pirate kitchen. She watches everything the Japanese woman does when she cooks.

Now it's the white girl's time to cook: all she knows how to make is miso soup with rice inside a teapot.

While they're eating her miso soup with rice, the pirates inform the girl where she can purchase what she wants in this city in Japan. What the girl wants is catshit.

And So I Went to School . . .

I Meet Myself

Pages torn out of my first school diary:

(no date)

school is a dairy
because all headmistresses are cows

Now that I'm in school, I'm never again going to be alone.

I used to hate girls. I remember. *Girls are stupid, girls always lie* . . . What I meant was that I was from a different race than all of them. Because the same blood wasn't in me that was in them, when I was with them, I was awkward, I wasn't right.

There are only girls in this school, so now I'm thinking about girls all the time.

I can't know what I'm dreaming because my mind is so occupied with wanting to fuck this girl.

(no date)

The word *fuck* means something, but I don't know what it means in this school.

Today I masturbated. Here's what I wrote while I was masturbating:

> Whenever I look at her, I look through her eyes and then, walk into her.
>
> Even though I'm in this school, which means I'm going to have to leave school because I'm going to graduate, I'm never going to be without her. Now, because I'm walking inside her, I own her.
>
> I live between her fingernails and the skin that's underneath them.
>
> As yet there aren't any pirates.

(no date)

again masturbating,

> Pirate sex began on the date when the liquids began to gush forward. As if *when* equals *because*. At the same time, my pirate penis shot out of my body.
>
> As it thrust out of my body, it moved into my body. I don't remember where.
>
> My penis walked into my body, each time that it did, by tapping like a male monkey on a section of the female's skin; by then punching through that skin to all that was lying below. To skin upon skin. Some-

times plastic containers holding liquids like water and piss sat between the skins.

Pirates are hot to puncture through. After they've done this, they need to piss or shoot into another person. This is why this, my body, is the beginning of pirate sex.

All of us girls have been dead for so long. But we're not going to be anymore.

After not having sex for years, the pirates came to a land where they could again have sex. Of course, they were girls. They tramped trampled down roses blustered bragged their ways stomped then limped into this territory. Some of them even pissed in their pants. They were remembering their childhoods.

Pirate #1: "I'm looking for a place to lay down my cock."

Overhearing this foul sentence, a long-standing pirate named Kiss-of-Rot, who was aware that cocks lay themselves down only in recipients, instructed the young criminal that a receptacle had to look into her eyes before she could shoot into that receptacle.

Now a receptacle is looking into my eyes so I can look into her eyes. When I do, I walk right into the center of her brains. Because I'm here, I can shoot.

In the midst of my emission, she opens again; each opening opens up; every opening series touches another opening series without entering its territory; there's no confusion anywhere; when I see all this order, my eyeballs rotate 180 degrees in their sockets. I'm gazing into a world in which sight isn't possible.

I know I'm going to descend into death.

Today, no one can find little girls anymore.

They had all gone down to wherever they went when they returned home. The more of them that had disappeared, the more flowers shot out of the earth. Whenever a colorful plant emerges from one of the holes in the dirt, out of which cunt juice is always welling, a young girl can again be seen.

(No More Masturbating)

I won't have anything to do with girls. I would rather be dead. In the future, I will be the sun, because that's what my legs are spread around.

(END OF THIS SECTION OF DIARY)

A car drove up to the school. It was black.

I watched what looked like a tiny negative spot approach the circular driveway to the entrance and turn over.

I could see someone get out of the shape. It looked like an older woman, thirty or forty years old. I ran downstairs to a window closer to the car; I looked out just in time to see a man emerge from the metal. He was in black, so he could have been a chauffeur.

Two of the school attendants, dressed in white, walked up to the car and lifted out an inert form. It looked like it was dead.

In a moment or two, I saw that it was a young girl. My age.

I ran down to her as if I were running down to myself.

* * *

It turned out that she wasn't dead yet. After he had examined her, our school's doctor said that she would live. By the skin of her teeth, that's how I put it, because her pulses were weak and irregular.

He was just taking his opportunity and feeling her up.

When the older woman who had black hair and white skin heard that the girl was going to live, she exclaimed, "Why, that can't be!" It turned out that she was the mother of the girl. "That's impossible because I have to be in ———— in two days!"

The doctor assured her that it was possible. That her daughter was too weak to be moved.

"It's a matter of life and death. If I'm not in ———— by the day after tomorrow . . . Oh, what am I to do? I can't take my daughter on a journey that's going to kill her."

The head of the school, who was also a woman, assured the mother, who from her clothes and deportment was wealthy, that her daughter could remain at the school. It was a girls' school so the child would be safe. "If you like, she can be a normal student and do what the other students do. In that way, you'll be able to kill two birds with one stone."

They moved into a corner of the room and talked to each other in whispers. To me, both of them were huge and birds. The expressions on their faces looked more serious than when they had discussed the life and death of the child who looked like me.

I disappeared from their room.

When the girl who looked like me woke up, she was told that her mother had left her here. She must have felt something, though I don't know what, because she sobbed.

In her despair, she allowed herself to keep sobbing, but she wouldn't give in and tell anyone anything factual. All we knew about her was her name. Which meant nothing.

In all that followed, she never gave a hint about the journey, neither its end nor its purpose, that had inadvertently led to her mother's abandonment of her.

That had led to her meeting me.

The first time that we consciously met, she told me that she loved her mother. That she would always, for the rest of her life, remain true to that beautiful green-eyed woman and do what she was told.

The closer I became to Pussycat, the more her obedience to parental authority, especially in its absence, made no sense.

Rather, I realized why she looked like me. It was while she was still in her sickbed. The first time I looked into her face, I saw the countenance of the child I had seen under my covers before I learned the truth about my father: that I don't have a father. The girl who had frightened me.

I perceived that she was very beautiful.

A Dream Interrupts

She started to talk. She told me that back when she had been a young child, she had either woken up or dreamt that she had found herself in my bed. She told me what I remembered and recited to me my dream about the acupuncturist, my dream in which, and by means of which, I had begun to deal with fear.

". . . a voice, coming out of me, announced, 'First, I have to get away from Daddy.' "

The girl continued:

"This is the only dream that is now left in the world:

"I found myself without anyone in your basement. It was a dark, low, grungy place. Brown dirt lay over all.

"Having nothing else to do, I started to walk.

"Finally, I arrived at what could have been the beginning of an exit. A wooden gate was stretching from one side of the room, which commenced behind it, to the other. The appearance of this gate informed me that I had been looking for a way to escape from your father's house.

"Behind the gate, which was closed and securely locked even though it was made out of wood, I saw two elevators that were standing in a line. As if they were schoolgirls being obedient.

"Now I knew that I had arrived at an actual exit.

"I was thinking, as I looked at that wood that was locked, 'The evil murderers were just chasing me and now all of them are out of this house. Because none of them are here at this very moment I can get out.'

"I don't know how I passed through those wooden gates that remained locked, but I did. I was now in the realms of the dead, which is a section of the path that leads to *exit*.

"I was looking into eyes that were elevators. Two and wide. Only eyes can lead to what's outside.

"I looked; I was inside one of those eyes, those elevators.

"The door closed. I thought, as if thinking were a specific activity, 'The evil murderers aren't here, but at any moment they could return. I have no control over that possibility. What should I do in this situation?'

"I decided I would be safest if my eyes were open: if I opened the elevator door and ensured that it stayed that way.

Then I could see if there was any sign of the evil murderers' approach.

"I held the elevator door open. All of the evil murderers were standing behind the wood with all of their faces pressed there. Just as if I were watching *Salo*, I watched one of them punch his hairy fist through the wood. Smash that.

"A hole was left, a hole in the world. I knew that I was about to be penetrated by the very ones I most feared."

Because we had had the same dream, Pussycat and I agreed that we were now now friends.

My Dreams Show Me My Sexuality

The strongest tradition that the girls observed in the school had to do with friendship. Any girl who had any intelligence and self-respect searched for the smartest, most beautiful and powerful girl who would have her. These two then made the following pact: they vowed to devote themselves to each other forever and to protect each other against all the machinations and treacheries of the others. If any girl was powerful enough or properly protected, one was the same as the other, she couldn't be chosen for a second game, also nameless.

In this game, for one week all the remaining girls in the class had nothing to do, either in speech or in any other way, with the child who had been chosen. If at any time during this week of silence, silence reaching into nothingness, the child broke down crying or complained or ran to a teacher, she would no longer be worth the attention and respect of any other girls for the rest of her life. Her life in this school. If she did survive the torture, which seemed too mild to be called "torture," torture by girls of girls, she could again enter the magic circle of power.

I knew that having a good protector would save me from the second game.

Every night almost half of the girls crawled into the beds of their best friends: for us, all the world happened at night.

During this night, I was two people because I felt two ways about Pussycat. Part of me regarded my friend as if she were a monster.

This part of me was a girl whose name was Ostracism, because the closer she got to anyone, the more fiercely, the more insanely, she had to run in the opposite direction.

The other part thought that Pussycat was the most beautiful girl she had ever seen.

That part was nameless and wild. Was never to be touched, just like the winds cannot be grasped. That part felt joy when she was as open as the air, as that invisible *not there*. Since that part was living at night, because night which was nothingness was sitting inside her, that part and night began to fuck.

I didn't know what I was feeling: I was nothingness or night inside, so I became terrified.

Pussycat said that she never had emotions, so she wanted me to have hers.

I told Pussycat that I wanted her to do it to me, and then I said that I didn't. I wanted her to open me up as wide as she could so I could begin to find my emotions, and then I started to yell at her because when I'm open I'm helpless. "I don't want to get any closer to you because I don't want to be hurt."

"That means," replied Pussycat, "*you are* hurt. I'm going to hurt you even more. That's what I do."

I reminded her that I was her best friend.

"You're not my business."

She never explained herself more than these two statements. "It's natural for me to hurt you." "You're not my business." Her refusal to elaborate made me feel I was going insane. So I thought she was insane.

She was a boy who would never grow up. I shall be a boy, too, as soon as I learn my sexuality.

I understood this.

I didn't at all understand what was going on.

Whenever her mouth and then tongue entered me, I wanted to die so that they could keep on entering me. I only wanted to be with this girl who was unable to be with anyone.

Every night I searched for my sexuality.

Dreams:
It's night. I'm sitting on a toilet.

From the toilet, I glimpse the ocean. The ocean's freedom.

The toilet isn't in the ocean. It's found in the midst of one of the grassy squares of a very formal, green park. I'm going to the bathroom, but not in public, because trees totally surround this square.

A bald man walks just beyond the wall of trees. I know who he is: he's my favorite teacher. But I don't say hello.

I must have climbed off this toilet, for I was on my motorcycle. The night or unknowingness had deepened.

It was the end of the road. It was time to go back home. Home no longer had to do with my father: it was everything that wasn't my father.

All there was left for me to do was turn right and ride down the road that ran along the beach and I would be there.

The ocean was my home.

Already I could see the turn. Due to a three-foot or so cement divider, I would have to turn sharply to the left and then far more abruptly right in order to be able to ride east, right alongside the water.

Carefully, I calculated that I'd be able to make this turn without dropping the bike if I allowed myself enough room while I cornered. Bike is a motherfucker.

Due to breast cancer, the deaths of girls were occurring everywhere.

One of the girls in my school rode her bike ahead of me.

The air was much darker. When I peered again through the air, I saw that her bike was lying in a black, dead pool, two of whose boundaries were the cement divider and the right-hand curb.

Through the rain, I called out, "Black Dog. Black Dog."

There was no answer. The air turned darker. I was riding into danger. It was so black and the rain so dense that I could no longer tell where I was going. Though it was a one-way street, I U-turned away from the beginning of the rain and went down the wrong way. There are times when the law jeopardizes those who obey it. Arriving at several townhouses, I rode the bike toward a square of gray pavement smack up against a house. My tires sank into the street water. But I was able to push the bike back to where a bit of pavement sloped upward. Thought I was safe.

So I turned around, ran back, only my body now, into the end of the night. Passing by two workmen.

"There's a girl under that bike," I yelled. "Help me! Help me!"

Thinking that Black Dog had lost her life because I'd taken so long to ensure my own. Mine and my bike's.

Half of her bike sat in deep, black water, partly surrounded by cement, like a plant, in a pot.

The workmen told me, "Don't look."

Even though the whole world was water, the bike was a furnace.

"Turn off that bike!" To the workmen. "It's roasting her!"

One of the guys turned off the machine by rotating the giant nut below its sissy seat. If it hadn't been for him, I wouldn't have known that there was such a nut.

The tremendous heat was shaking her body, which was wrapped around the back portion of the frame. I saw this. I didn't know whether she was alive or dead.

The other man commented, "She's still alive."

She has a chance to live. I hadn't thought this before, and the world made itself larger: the back of the black leather seat, the chrome frame beneath the seat, parts of Black Dog's body. All these, huge, vibrated.

Back in the section of the city where I used to live before I had been sent away to school, walking through the streets that frightened me. Since this part used to terrify me in the past, the past was present.

Walking as if through liquid.

On the way home. In any city, those who walk streets regularly know better than to do so when natural light is disappearing. The streets were becoming darker.

The air was so dark, I could no longer see its streets.

A man appeared out of the dark. Either I was terrified or I knew that I should be terrified. Especially of rape. I had no idea who he was and I let him walk beside me. I did this, I who am scared of my father.

On the streets, which could no longer be seen, the Latino and I began to make out.

Since I was white, I was now an outlaw. I knew this, I knew that my society named its criminals. So I asked the boy to take me to where no one could see us, to where we would be free to find out what we wanted to do together.

To where we could do it.

He took me to the realm of gangs.

He was gone.

I found myself in a small room half of which was lined in unpainted wood. It was a headquarters. All of the men who were in the room were far larger than me, but I wasn't scared of them because we were talking, all of us, speaking from our hearts.

Sometime during the conversation, the Latino guy returned. With the tenements looming all over my head, he walked me home.

In my dream, I dreamed that I was asleep. I woke up and looked around my room, which I knew. It was very dark.

In one of its corners, there was a black monster. He saw

that I was seeing him so he walked over to my bed and started to stalk me. Traveling faster and faster around me. He was finally circling so rapidly that I could no longer tell what he was doing. I no longer knew anything.

The room was so dark that everything in it was alive.

It was the time of the animals. The black monster had yellow eyes. When the animals who had yellow eyes bit my nipples . . .

Their yellow eyes have become my center, burning. I let go of being one person, a motorcentric body, and I go down under to where all the schoolgirls are.

Because there's so much burning in this area of the world, growth will soon occur. A foundation which can handle such massive devastation is beginning to appear.

The fingers begin.

Moving to the right, across the plane which was, is, all that remains of me, a crooked finger hooks under another strap of flesh (also me).

During the days, the schoolgirls spent most of their time touching themselves. Their fingers were twitching so continually that each girl, as if she were only one part of a gigantic body that was coming apart as I was coming apart, became absolutely separate from every other girl.

Out of Dream

I woke up and knew that Pussycat wanted to harm me. Nothing else would satisfy her. I had to find her to stop her from coming into my body and carving a hole inside there.

I ran into one of the teachers' rooms, the French teacher's, and announced that I was scared, scared to death of Pussycat.

"Why?"

"I just have to find Pussycat. I don't know why." I no longer cared what anyone in authority thought of me. "I just have to get into Pussycat's room, but it's locked, and I'm too scared to be alone anymore."

I don't know why she listened to any of my words, and maybe she didn't; I don't know what was going on in her head, but she took hold of my hand. Together we traveled down that hall until we came to a door that had a black smear instead of a name on it.

Now I knew where I was. The hall still had one dim yellow light. By knocking on this smeared door, I carved a hole into actuality and heard my dreams.

There was no answer. Knocked again and again: there was no answer.

We forced the door open. Her room was empty.

Here was further evidence that Pussycat was going to get me, because she wanted to.

We searched through that night and through the morning for Pussycat so that she couldn't harm me but we didn't find her anywhere in the school. Just a strand of hair.

Before I had gone to school, I used to pull crabs' legs off their bodies. The crabs found in the pools that were hidden under the rocks that led to the ocean. Yellow blood gushed out of the holes I made there. In the nightmare that was the first dream that I ever had, these crabs came for me. Crabs of all possible sizes crawled closer and closer as their claws, which were becoming larger, opened more and more widely so that I could know that they were about to murder me.

That presence, that dream, by means of the vehicle of memory, came back in me; as if I were back in my dream, I returned to Pussycat's room.

It was now late afternoon, which is the time when the sun dies. This sun had already carved a highway for the pirates. A road that was dazzling the eyes of those living marauders and of the dead fish who were floating below that road. Both the pirates and the dead fish, though they were traveling, no longer cared where they were going.

The pirates' teeth were whiter than those of the fish preserved in the brine that was both inside and outside their bodies. As the sun set while all the lights of the world spread, the pirates began to hallucinate.

Pussycat was sitting at her desk. I said, "Hello." Then we went down to supper, together. Lots of schoolgirls were already in the dining room. They had become sick of masturbating.

They sang,

Evening prayer
We spray over everything.
Our kind of coming will never stop.
Just like Jesus Christ comes in our cunts.

I told Pussycat, "I no longer care what my sexuality is." I looked down at the food under the glass counters. Each fake silver container, down there, was holding a different sort of inedible or poisonous substance. Pussycat, because she was mean, told the school food servers exactly what she wanted to eat. I didn't have the courage. I didn't know how to do it.

I whispered, "Rice and salad."

As soon as I had uttered these words, I was more lost than before. Because I hadn't ordered any protein. Any human knows that you need protein to live. I was announcing out loud, to all the other schoolgirls, that I wanted to die. Every girl looked at me. They were no longer interested in masturbating. Through their looks, they were telling me that I was the stranger, that I would carry strangeness to wherever I wandered. Because their eyes were doing this to me, I wanted to trash their faces, because, after that, I wouldn't care what they thought about me.

Instead of doing what I should have been, getting rid of all schoolgirls, I turned again to the school's menu. There, every item was based on beef.

"Southern beef" was the one I liked best.

All of the schoolgirls were clamoring for their meat when I left to go to the bathroom.

Far from the madding crowd, I found myself inside the school toilet. It was significant that the only way that this room could be entered was from the outside. Baby lobsters, blobsters, in a row were leaning against one of its outer walls. They were miniatures of the dragons who lived in the oceans that lapped the edges of my bed every night, monsters who were ready to devour me as soon as I moved away from my bed.

They were waiting for me. As I looked right into their eyes, they began to glide toward me. There was a wall. I was watching when one entered through a crack.

More penetrated through an increasing number of cracks. My cracks: I was no longer safe.

I fled from the place where we, the girls, had been safe. "The only bathroom in girltown," Pussycat had said. That place, cracked open. Fled in such a panic that I abandoned all my money and my shoes.

I knew that if I went back into there, to get my shoes back so I could walk again, I would lose my life.

I returned to the toilet.

Now I was safe because there was nobody in the place except for one lobster who was such a baby that he or she couldn't hurt a soul. My shoes and ten dollars were still sitting on the floor. I saw that the tiny lobster had emerged from the one crack that was in the wall.

In its bottom.

I took my time picking up my belongings. Lobsters of all sizes were gliding toward me.

Pussycat had come back to me.

Pussycat Is Taken from Me

The days, and mainly the nights, passed without any more incidents, and then it was Christmas. Christmas is the time when schoolgirls are forced to separate from each other.

Every girl had to go back to her family, whether or not she actually had one. I was becoming hysterical at the thought of leaving Pussycat.

I knew that my father's friend, whose daughter's death had inadvertently caused my presence at this girls' school, was going to be with my father and me, for the first time since his child's demise, for the entire holiday.

He was some kind of poet, but poetry didn't do anything for me.

"I know," said my father; his words didn't mean anything to me.

A few days after I had returned to what I thought was my only home, Frost told my father and me what had happened to his child:

"My daughter had been so looking forward to this visit with you. Unfortunately, she died."

"I know," commented my father again. I could hear him saying that these days young girls are dying everywhere.

"There were long rows of stained-glass windows. Voices emerged out of places that couldn't be seen," the poet continued. "As if appearing out of nothing, a huge entranceway to a house rose up in front of our eyes.

"Her first ball! She was so excited. She was enchanted! Just as if I were her, I was enchanted.

"She was my only child. No one could be as seducible, as enchanting as she was.

"This ball formally began when all the fireworks exploded into the sky. And then, the sky. We walked, hand in hand, to that house.

"When we were inside, I saw what I had never before seen:

"Almost all the people were masked. My daughter was the only one who wasn't. She was just as gorgeously dressed as them. She wanted to see everything. I watched her eyes so that I could see everything . . .

". . . her first ball . . .

". . . in these eyes, I saw a child. When I looked the other way, I saw that that child, who was also wearing a mask like everyone else, wasn't recognizable as male or female. I noticed she was staring at my daughter. Then I saw that, under her mask, which she had taken slightly off her face, a mask made up of layers upon layers of gorgeous owl plumage in grays and browns which the grays only deepened, she looked like my daughter.

"When I returned from the bathroom, my daughter and the girl were conversing with each other and laughing. The stranger had pulled off her mask: her visage was so beautiful, so extraordinary, that all who were standing near them began to stare at the two children.

"My daughter must have also found her extraordinary because she persuaded me to let her take the stranger home with us that night. She wanted to keep her with her.

"I didn't oppose my daughter; I had never opposed her; in fact, until the time of this stranger, I had never seen any reason to stop my daughter from doing what she wanted to do, and had only wanted to feel whatever she was feeling.

"I still don't understand what happened that night. Afterwards, my daughter, who had been my best friend, turned away from me. She wanted solely to be with this girl, whom she still didn't know. Not what I call 'knowing.' She called her Heathcliff. When I questioned Bad Dog about her friend's origins, she almost bit me. She said that it's natural for girls to have best friends.

"She seemed to relent and added, 'Daddy, it was too lonely for me when you were my only companion.'

"I understood because I've always understood what she was feeling.

"Then she asked if the girl who looked exactly like her could move in with us.

"I enquired about the unknown one's origins; I checked up on my daughter's information. I was more than satisfied.

"It's normal for girls to become too close to each other

until it's time for them to go out with boys. Though I'm a poet, I'm not unaware of the ways of the world.

"They spent more time in their bedroom, soon they were getting up so late that they were turning night into day. My daughter was getting less and less sleep; bags appeared under her eyes; the bags became bruises; the bruises were turning black.

"It was at this time that Bad Dog began to tell me about her nightmares. I was her father. Her nightmares were of animals."

I have nightmares and they're not nightmares. I didn't say this out loud because it was men who were doing the talking. I let them. Dreams are the mouths of us girls, and all the poets know this.

"Bad Dog told me that every night a big furry animal sniffed at her body. It—he or she—began to pace. Whenever its nostrils grazed her skin, usually her private parts, she felt a sharp, burning sensation which was so brief that it passed away by the time her consciousness registered that it had taken place. The pain returned—she didn't know from where—and grew until it turned into pleasure; the pleasure became so immense that she lost consciousness.

"From then on, my daughter was interested only in physical pleasure; then she felt so much pleasure for so long a time that she forgot her body.

"I told her that she was becoming sick. I was her father. I told her that she was sick. She had become this way because of selfishness. None of us should think only about ourselves.

"But she no longer cared about me. She spent all her time with that friend of hers called Heathcliff.

"I was her father. I could do nothing anymore."

The poet who had grown old bowed his head. "I hate those girls whose lusts are atrocious."

My father didn't know what he was talking about.

Frost explained. "My life has one purpose. I must decapitate all those girls. They're all too beautiful."

My father began to understand.

The writer described their particulars: "Even though they don't like boys, they follow those punks and let the punks follow them; they live mixed-up in graveyards. All their main organs are tongues, tongues which move in ways that break through the limits of the human imagination. After a girl has licked out a skull that's full of maggots—this is just one example—she places that organ between her girlfriend's lips. Tongues can do far more than this. Girls sit on skulls and go to the bathroom because there are no toilets in graveyards. They wipe themselves with their tongues. All of them are so insane for pleasure that they've forgotten to die and now, some of them aren't even girls."

I was beginning to know fear.

My father was frightened, because he believed his friend.

The latter quickly ended his tale:

"Malnutrition and sleeplessness had weakened her to such an extent that there was nothing I could do for her myself. She had begun to smell. I had no recourse but to call in a doctor even though I knew that she hated them.

"She informed me that, because she was going to have to appear before him, she would now do everything that she could to disobey me.

"I was totally helpless. You understand that I loved her.

"I called in a doctor and she mistreated him and I called

in another doctor and her behavior was fouler, and we went from doctor to doctor as if toward a reign of terror, a reign of the absence of language. The worse she became, the more doctors were called in.

"All of whom told me the same thing: she was going to die real soon.

" 'The girl,' the experts advised, 'doesn't need a physician; she needs a priest.'

"A priest is a man who wields the only knife that can come between two girls. I told my darling that the priest was coming for her between seven and nine the next evening. That he was going to solve all her problems. That she was going to die. Bad Dog looked at me as if her mind was already dead, and then, abruptly and alternately, she vomited over me and rubbed the lower front of her torso, which, I had instructed her, she wasn't supposed to touch.

"She died.

"She died in the arms of her friend before the priest was able to come."

My father was overcome by this story. We had found ourselves in that graveyard where I used to spend as much time as possible in the years when I had been lonely. Before I had been sent away to girls' school.

The section in which I was sitting was dark, grassy. I had been thinking about Pussycat's body, so I didn't notice that I actually was gazing at her. She must have been on a walk. The old poet saw her and screamed. "She's one of the ones!" He picked up a hatchet that was lying by a tree.

Pussycat made a face and dropped out of view.

My father and his closest friend discussed ways and plans to behead all the unnatural girls who had made this graveyard their home. Girls under the dirt who placed their hands inside each other's cunts and drew them out, muddied and bloodied. Put these fingers into their own mouths. Lips left brown and red.

I knew.

I knew what Pussycat wanted to do to me and I knew that my father wants to kill me, so I left.

Together, Pussycat and I disappeared.

LOOKING FOR A PUSSYCAT

Finally, Pussycat and I were able to have sex.

I talked to her for hours because I was shy. Then she put an arm around me, my back to her. We were sitting together on a crumbled wall by a duck pond. Dead ducks. I turned around and kissed her, I think because I had been waiting to for a long time and because I believed that I was supposed to and because I wanted her. The moment I put my lips on hers, she did it back to me. She asked me to place laundry clips around the nipple of one of her breasts. When she started to tell me what to do, I did what she ordered because I thought that I should, but I was feeling only curious.

"Doesn't it hurt?" I asked while I was moving my hand away from a clip.

She replied that usually she did this to herself. She had never before allowed anyone to do it to her.

I wasn't feeling anything, or I don't think that I was feeling anything.

Then I did the second thing to her that I had never before done. I was still doing what she told me to do. I was frightened of hurting her, too scared to do what she desired me to do totally. I was feeling just about every possible feeling that can exist.

She didn't and couldn't get off, either because I was bad at doing exactly what she wanted done to her or because while I was doing those things, the confusion of my emotions was apparent to her.

While we were doing all this, hours passed; when I looked beyond Pussycat, the night was no longer black. Soon it would be no longer night; soon a gull would be honking at the beginning of a cloud and so I told Pussycat aloud that I didn't know what I was doing, that I felt very lost.

Either she didn't understand what I was trying to tell her or else she had no way of dealing with sexual inadequacy and stupidity. I think. Brusquely, she said to me that she came only once a night. She turned me over and climbed on top of me and put three of her fingers into me and she really knew how to do this, how to do this just like I like it, and I came and came and kept coming while I was asking her to put her whole hand in there, but I was too small, and I wanted her to do this to me till after the end of time.

I was able to do for her what she couldn't do for me: under her instructions, I did it for hours, I believe, and so then she wanted it harder than I was giving it to her. I was even more terrified to do this because I feared that I was going to damage, to hurt her; that was just an excuse; I knew that I was unable to give her pleasure.

What I can't accept is that I might not have wanted to give her pleasure. At the end of that night, Pussycat left me.

* * *

At first I wasn't upset, because I didn't understand what was taking place in me and outside me. Afterwards I realized that I was bad at sex and that Pussycat wasn't going to return to me. I wanted her back because I wanted to be alive; I thought that I needed to know who I was so I could be alive.

I didn't understand, at that time, why the loss of Pussycat was the loss of myself. Then I remembered that when we had first met and for a long time after that, we didn't fuck each other. As soon as we started to be sexual with each other, we were that way all the time and everywhere; we turned the world private, into our bed.

By writing this, I'm reversing reality again.

We did that then, reversed reality, for to make the public world private is to destroy privacy, to open yourself up not only to your girl, but to all that lies outside. By fucking each other, Pussycat and I traveled to the edge of a territory that was unknown and, perhaps, unknowable. Into territories whose existences I had never experienced before Pussycat touched me, yet somehow had suspected.

They were the lands of lost memories. Before Pussycat came with me.

My own strangeness made me helpless. I was helpless because of Pussycat. I didn't depend on her; she was wrong about that. Rather, when I was with her, I was a baby: I couldn't name what I was seeing, I couldn't name all that I was hearing. I smelled only Pussycat. There was only Pussycat.

She left me.

It was a dream that led me to the witch.

I dreamt I was in prison. I had no idea why.

Actually, prison wasn't bad. My prison looked like a

spacious cell with two doors. The main door was three windows, each of them like the others, together almost as huge as the wall in which they were set. Beyond their clear glass, a formal garden led to a sea which couldn't be seen.

As I faced the sea, the other door, on my left, gave way to a narrow hall where there was an opening to the outside.

It was a pleasant prison cell.

A lot of girls visited me. So I must have been allowed to have visitors. I didn't smell to the girls because I regularly took a shower under the faucet that sprang out of the hall wall. The faucet was so long and powerful, as if it were a hose, that it shot liquid all the way into the cell.

My girlfriends always asked me the same question. When a girl asked me, "Why don't you escape?" I said, without understanding my own reply, "Because I don't want to abuse my privileges."

When Ariadne agreed to help the man she considered her only love kill her half-brother, she wasn't abusing her privileges. But he didn't believe he was her lover. I wasn't thinking about that when a man walked into my cell. He was so old and fat, he was a poet. He stooped, carried a painting half his size wrapped up in a brown paper bag. Managing somehow to bend down, placed it on the clean cement that was underneath a folding table, the only furniture in the cell.

More girls entered. "Oh," they were saying, "so this is where you've been hiding out."

"But I can leave whenever I want to."

Whenever is the night. I ride my motorcycle between the night as if I'm flying through it. Until the night will end.

I'm on a Virago that feels like my two real ones, only the one I'm on is too high up: I'm riding just outside my control.

Handlebars that think they're the grips of a lateral-raise machine rise up from the bike frame straight into the air. I don't know how to act in the face of this strangeness. So I tuck the chrome under my armpits. I'm still high, not falling, in no way safe. I've become strange. I try bending the silvery bars down as far as they'll go, opposite to how they were, different from prison bars, and I continue to climb the narrow country road on which there are no lights.

Then I descend, still beyond control, down the continuation of the road. Bottom is a top; the top's a ceiling; the ceiling's one of the cement floors of the largest office building in the city. I'm now riding around the edge of its roof, where there's a narrow track, around and around the top of the city.

And below me lies the night. Up here where all is cement, where there is no obstruction to riding. Up here, on top of this building, my bike goes over an edge.

I go down with her. Abandoning her, I grab, as if leaping, at the black metal rail that runs around the building's edge.

There's a slab of hardened cement next to the guard rail from which I'm managing to hang. One of its ends is attached to the roof-floor; the other hovers two or three feet above the floor. A human has enough room to crouch, crunched, there, between cement and cement.

A perfectly round hole in the slab lies over its mirror, its twin, in the cement floor and in the slab under that floor, hole over hole, hole below hole, I fall and crawl, until I reach bottom.

I realize that bottom is the bottom of a parking garage.

All the girls find me in the bottom of this world. They cry, "Oh, you're not dead."

"I didn't die."

"Instead of being dead, you're in the bottom of a car garage."

"I can't stay and talk with you," I say. "Because I've got to get back to prison as quickly as possible, before anyone notices I've escaped. If they have noticed, I'll be killed."

Girls were still piling into my cell, so I began to think maybe it was okay to live here, in girltown, here where I was safe, unlike the rest of England, which was a disaster. Then the police walked in.

They were the visual twins of the Secret Service. They were in my cell because they wanted me. They looked like each other.

I watched them do to the other girls what the fascists did to their victims at the end of *Salo*. I saw blood on one elbow.

All the girls were now males. They were dead. I was about to be offed.

I had to find out why I was bad at having sex, so I visited a witch.

It was difficult to find one. I tried taking a train. When I got off, there weren't any humans.

Instead, there was an ocean. On this ocean, fishing boats slept; the sun, day after day, perhaps days beyond years, had been baking and drying them. As if they were alive.

It was the new world. A signpost said: " ➡ London (You'll Never Get There)."

On the other side of the water, a few buildings rose out of land that was lower than the ocean. Lower, closer to the imaginary center of the earth.

It seemed all sand.

Here decay was in stasis. Buildings and sand were the

same color. The pier had lost its connections to the land. Sun shone over everything.

Hanging from one of the old wooden walls, another sign: "Fish Market." Below "Fish," an arrow pointed to "Restaurant Upstairs, Bar & Grill."

When I saw the half-eaten fish under this sign, I thought of Pussycat.

A piece of paper that had remained glued to what was now too dirty to be a window showed all the food that was offered. The prices were high.

There were no longer humans.

This building's insides were larger than its outside:

A bar whose wood was the same color as the air out there stretched from one side of the room to the other. Small windows behind the bar, when clear enough to be windows, showed sand mixed with fish. Fish sandwiched.

There was no furniture on the other side of the bar. People used to dance there. There were some small folding tables and chairs that faced away from a second group of windows through which the sea could be seen.

The living world had been left to the animals: in the sea, a young seal dove under, leaping upward, a half-circle, fell down again. Long whiskers covering all of her face, an old seal floated past. She no longer blinked: her pupils had become eyes and lay open to all that was outside.

Water was meeting its outside. The two seals remained right here while light withdrew from the rest of the world.

I had to go to the bathroom. At that threshold, I saw a sign posted on the wood that read: "Circe ➡ ."

I followed this arrow through a copse of laurel trees until I came to a structure that seemed to be a dead hospital. Below an X dug into three words in which there were the traces of a B and a C, someone who could barely write had scrawled "Circe." I had reached my goal.

The sun was no longer.

There was nothing on the walls inside. I seemed to be in a lobby. Since there weren't any receptionists handing out forms, I walked through this vestibule, into a smaller room. Then I waited. No one came for me. I stood up, crossed the hall which I had just walked down. An elevator stood open.

I rode it to the third floor.

The hall I was in was empty. I remember patients shuffling by me. Hospital beds rolled by, under whose sheets there were humans. On each side of the hall, nurses watched this parade. I strolled further down the corridor. A copper plaque off the door of the room on my left said: "Mammary Recovery."

No words can do justice to the charms of the woman who was standing inside. Her eyes were brighter than stars strung through a sky. There was so much charm in her voice that when she spoke, words themselves caressed the enraptured air. No wonder I was faint.

After telling me her name, she said, "Nothing ever happens around here—that's my motto. If you've come on business, gal . . . well, if I were you, I'd get the fuck out of here.

'Hie thee away,
clit between your legs,'

as the saying goes . . ."

"Please," I begged, "don't add insult to my injuries . . ."

"Oh, you're the artistic type. Well, you're used to begging for everything.

"This town," she continued, "is a plague-ridden countryside where there's nothing but a bunch of corpses who're being pecked to death and vultures who're the peckers. No one can make any money here and our asses are sitting on the faces of the rich. Because they like to live near the source of culture, but they don't want to live in it. Too many poor people in culture. The folk who live here either are worth fortunes or else are fortune-hunters. You must be the latter."

"O Circe!" I exclaimed or explained, "I can't get it up anymore!"

"That has nothing to do with me," she replied.

I wanted it to have something to do with her, I wanted to be cured of the lack of love in me, so I showed her the kiss-off epistle I got from Pussycat.

I've never been into sex the way you think I am.

I'm happy that you're such a lousy fuck because now I've got a girlfriend who is hot; next to her, you're nothing. A half hour after we met, she shoved my body up against the filthy film office wall where I work and she bit me. I still have to wear, when I'm in public, a high collared sweatshirt to cover up the gigantic bruises. Otherwise I'd get arrested. I wish that I could show you all my bruises. After she bit me, I gnawed at her legs. I didn't mark her. Now we spend every minute of the day together and all the nights have turned into sex.

If I were you, O_2, I'd do something radical immediately like change everything about myself. The way you now are, at the edge of death, I don't understand how you're able to

stay alive. If the totality of your body and heart acted like
your cunt, you'd be at the undertaker's.

"What a lively ex-girlfriend," Circe commented.
I showed her the letter I sent back to Pussycat.

Dear Pussy,
    The worst thing was that I was unable to possess you.

Together, we proceeded into the hospital's operating room,
where there hadn't been an operation in years. Here the witch
had made her headquarters. While we were going into the
room, she informed me that she couldn't cure me. No one is
able to resurrect the dead and bring back sexual desire. While
she was mumbling, some of her spit hit my face. "But if you pay
me enough, anything might happen."

I explained I didn't have any money because my father
hadn't sent me to business school. But if she'd cure me, I'd let
her fuck me. "I'll do anything so that I can get kissed and loved
again."

She led me by my hand into her bedroom. The operating
room for breast-cancer patients. The walls were green. A cot
stood in its middle. Machines, looking like animals out of Dr.
Seuss, extended long rubber tubes to the bed.

The reign of Pentheus had ended. Circe instructed me to
spit three times, then drop between my breasts, three times,
some pebbles which she had charmed and wrapped in soiled
toilet paper. She began to test my virility.

I didn't have any—virility—so she started to walk away:
"You can't be cured, dimshit."

"Try me!" I threw myself bodily into her arms and tried to kiss her until I could kiss no more.

"Maybe you've got your genders mixed up," she murmured.

I was so desperate that I began to masturbate. It had nothing to do with her. "No one can cure me," I moaned in the sort of agony that signals the approach of death. "Never again, during all the hardships that life brings, will I be able to seek for comfort. Never again will I know the laughter of a child. These are only some of the joys sexual pleasure brings . . ."

My clit was a little girl who shied away, then dove under a long board of wood. Wood lay under wood; therefore, a hand was formed, its fingers linked, clasping. Beyond, there were pirates.

This little girl said:

"Have to open up. Which is to open outwards. At that time, the sensations will start deep within there.

"But now the water is calm, grows stiff, stands upward. Deep within quite a number of stalks, the water is rising up from the bottom; the marsh is mucking and rising, thickening dead fish skins; there's no need to come when everything is sparks, thick and sparks; I come fast."

After a long silence, the witch came back to me. "Well, there's one person who can cure you. But you'll have to do what she says and not what you say."

Her left hand clasped one of my breasts and by this breast, led me to her bed. What had once been the operating table.

She said that she was going to give me something to drink. A stove was sitting by the sink, which was pretty rusty;

over one of the stove's burners, a pot enormous enough to brew tea for an army. Into the pot, she dropped a bag of beans, forgetting to get rid of its plastic, and a decayed pig's cheek. She didn't put in any water, so everything caught on fire. Circe ran out of the room . . .

While still masturbating, I said to myself,
    ". . . calm, just vibrations within gray mist.
    "That's just an image.
    "Vibrations turn into water as they turn over. The more they're becoming rigid and turning over, the more they're simultaneously moving outward and wanting to do all this more until the whole will be convulsed. Where will I be? But not yet, as yet still thickening miasma, sparks like flies all over each other, each fly a little orgasm until everything is shaking, going down, disappearing in cycles, will never stop, down and down while moving and the rhythms of the universe deepening; how could this stop now?"

I was thirsty, so I took off my clothes.

The witch came back into the room and told me that the tea had fucked up so she was going to feed me. "I'm veggie, so if you're going to be cured, you're going to have to do what I say."
    She took a garlic out of a barrel under the sink, peeled off a few of the larger cloves. She got hold of a leek, chopped it up with the garlic, put her hand into some of the dirt on the floor that was coming up through the linoleum, mixed in the garlic and leeks, and rubbed the whole mess into my skin.

I was smelly. We both drank red wine and shared a cigarette.

I couldn't tell what I was smelling anymore. I looked at her.

Just when I thought that all the witch spells were over and that I no longer had to fear what might happen to me, just when I thought that now I was safe, the witch came back, though I hadn't known she had disappeared, wearing a harness and a huge gray dildo. She dipped her instrument into a cracked egg cup and waddled over to me. She dipped her instrument a second time.

I think we were both too drunk to know what was going on. It hurt. Maybe in response to my cries and maybe not, she pulled it out of me so she could rub some of the ointment on my lips.

Now I'm going to interview myself.

Questioner: Did the ointment smell like her?

Me: Yes.

Questioner: How can you best describe the odor?

Me: Like a witch who's just died.

Questioner: What happened next?

Me: She soaked my thighs in sauerkraut juice. I dared to ask her a question.

Questioner: What was that?

Me: Why?

(Pause.)

She said that she wanted to teach me not to take the Mother Nature thing too seriously. To show me that one vegetable is as good as another vegetable. She picked up a nettle stalk and, wearing a glove to protect her hand, began to whip me on my front below my navel.

I decided I had had enough pain. I ran away.

Questioner: There was nothing that you could have done that would have touched her.

Me: I realized that only after I ran away from her.

It was only after I had run away that I knew that she was the only woman on earth who knows everything, and, therefore, the most desirable. If she would only have had pity on my ignorance and have let me battle myself to be with her and have taught me, I who am always so bad, I who have fucked up my whole life, Pussycat, where are you? O witch of the night, where are you? Will I ever talk, *really* talk, to anyone ever again I am this alone if only the witch had loved me, but I don't know where she is anymore. Maybe my sexual parts, which are now dead, were created that way, maybe turned that way by a dead society, maybe buried alive by other witches. I didn't mind her smearing those smelly liquids on me and then spanking me, because I knew that I was guilty, that I was a brat and that I am always a brat, so I need someone to take pity on me, not just anyone. A real witch. But she threw me out.

The witch tossed me out on my head, so now I am exceptionally bad at sex.

Only let me return to my former love, let me return to love even if love did whip me, on the brown tips of my nipples, with nettles. Actually, love did worse to me: She made me walk naked except for a pair of cowboy boots down a highway in Italy. She made me masturbate in a bar in Berlin where a German woman, because she was watching this, became so disgusted that she had to leave. In those days replete with desire and tears, life was good; now, at night, I sleep with my pillow between my legs and pretend that it's my sweetheart.

Night after night.

Others have been hounded by gods and implacable fate,
those three women of the hairs,
not only me.
Ariadne loved a guy and committed a crime for him. She abetted in the murder of her half-brother, who happened to be a monster. And in this way unraveled the labyrinth. The man for whom she had done everything, and perhaps more, after she had turned away from everyone in her life in order to be with him, left her. Left alone with no one to turn to, no life.
Like me.

Then I cried aloud, I must get rid of Pussycat!

IN THE LIGHT OF THE MORNING OF THE WORLD

There are such things as ghosts. Death does not all things end.
   Pussycat as a corpse came back to me in a dream.
   She was wearing the same hairs she had taken with her to the grave. Standing so close to my head that I could smell her, she said:

   "There are such things as ghosts. Death does not all things end.
   "And pale yellow escape shades out of vanquished graves."

You see, Pussycat by me was seen to lean over bed, though near the roar of just buried freeway. When I could no longer fall asleep realizing love just dead, my bed and new reigns of chill and pain.

The same she had with her in which she was buried little cunt hairs, the same eyes, one side of her shirt had been burnt, and always worn on finger the ring its pearl had eaten away fire. Surfaces Death's had turned black and blue her lips' liquor. Breathing animation and these words she let go, though thumb bones were rattling their own hand bones:

"Slut, but for better what girl can hope,
"you already asleep, how can?
"Already you have forgotten our desperate crimes:
"my by nocturnal deceptions worn-down window
"through which dropping down a rope to reach you I hanging
  how many times
"by the other snaking around your neck hand!
"Often sex occurred publicly, genitals joined;
"made hot skins our streets.
"Too bad for Our Silent Pact, whose obviously lying promises
"unable-to-hear has torn the winds to pieces!"

"Listen. When I was dying, there was no one. There's no one in my life. I had no one to turn to because I'm alone. If you hadn't deserted me, O_2, my life wouldn't have turned out this way.

"I would have done anything for you if you had stayed with me. I would still be alive.

"There's no one who gives a shit about me dead. Is there anyone now scaring away all the demons, ghouls, flesh-eating birds, and poisonous snakes who are living in my grave and resting on top of me? No. This is what reality is: instead of you being with me, as soon as I died, the deaf winds dropped a broken brick on my head.

"This is what happens to those who have loved.

"You're complaining that I left you. But who saw you at my funeral? Who saw you, at that funeral, shed a tear?

"Perhaps you didn't attend my funeral because you couldn't have borne the reality of so much pain. Perhaps you couldn't bear that I was no longer with you. Perhaps you couldn't bear that I could no longer protect you, especially from the realms of loneliness. Or perhaps you weren't present at my funeral because you didn't want to realize that you're going to die. If that was the case, O_2, why didn't you just put a halt to my burial? I've seen you do things like that before. Even when you weren't crazy in love. Or why didn't you throw yourself on top of me inside the coffin while it was still in the mortuary? Then, why didn't you start to fingerfuck me? That would have stopped the funeral. Why didn't you throw yourself into my crematory flames? We could have had sex there. I know you're fascinated by Near Eastern cultures. There's a lot of things you could have done if you had wanted to, but you didn't because you didn't want to stop me from dying.

"Hasn't love ever mattered to you?

"There are some things that you could have done that are normal: you could have bought me perfumes. Do you think I want to smell to everybody for the rest of my life now that I'm dead? You could pick a little flower from a dead person's grave and give it to *me*. Or you could get me drunk. On red wine. That's the best. Then we'd have a good ol' time.

"There's nothing better to do when you're dead.

"Your problem is, O_2, you don't know how to love."

I said back that it was she who didn't know how to love and that's why she died. That now I was unable to get it up because I was being faithful to her. That this is how much I love her.

It was she who had abandoned me; never I her.

She or the corpse with hair ignored me just like she had all the time that we were alive.

"Therefore—I've proved it," I positively stated. "You never cared for me."

"Now you have a chance, O_2," the corpse answered me back, "to make up for all the wrong that you've done to me, a chance to show that you're able to love.

"Remember Liquor and Noun, two of our classmates? They hatched a plot against me: Noun spit her saliva into a glass of red wine; Liquor handed that glass to me. Because they were jealous of the hot sex we were having.

"This is what you're going to do to them: Burn off part of Liquor's leg; then make Noun confess that she likes to kill people. You know, Noun used to be a whore. Not just any whore. She used to walk the streets. Cheap as they come. Not just any streets. The streets that no whore worth her salt would go near. Cheaper than anyone comes because, on that street, she would put her lips around anything. That's why her spittle can now poison anyone. Petale, unlike you, brought flowers to my grave, so Noun spit on them. Then, she spit on Petale. Petale today has wrinkles.

"Remember Lalage? That child who followed me around and loved everything that I touched. Noun has got hold of her. The child, forgetting who Noun was, said my name in front of her; Noun twisted the child's hair, then hung her from this twist on a nail. No one knows that child's suffering.

"I know that you're a great poet, O_2, and that you wrote about me all the time in your poetry. I will never deny the love for me that lies in your words; I know, as well as you do, how words lie. I will never put you down or hate you because you lie. I know that I mean everything to you. I swear this, I swear by the Fates, the three hags or that triple barker, and my mother, and may this gentleness in my swearing make the world gentle to me, I swear that I love you and am faithful to you. You wrongly believe that I rejected you. I've never fucked another girl.

"If I'm lying, in any manner, in any possible mode, may a snake who looks like a human cock lie on top of my bones and make his home there, on whatever is left of me, and hiss.

"For I love only you."

Now all my emotions came back to life, woke up like the Sleeping Beauty that all emotions, especially the most horrible ones, are. Free, I was, before I woke up, able to ask Pussycat to tell me what death is like.

Pussycat threw back her long, wet hairs both above and below her and replied:

"Demons live in the netherworld. All of them have cocks.

"It was here that I saw the source of human life, the water of the world. All waters flow down to here, then up again. And here lies the egg, the only phenomenon which is without origin.

"The egg is the one which, every time the world ends, bursts into flames. Its fire eats up all that remains of tripartite reality.

"There's another fire, whose name is Fire-Mare. This is the origin, or story, of that second fire:

"There was a boy who was so upset that there were humans and that humans were having babies that he didn't know what to do.

"He didn't know what to do with his anger so he gave it away to a dead horse. She was sitting in water.

"Replete with anger, she became the entrance to hell.

"There in the southernmost part of the world, flames began to shoot out of her mouth.

"I walked between those lips. There I journeyed down, past the netherworld in which all the demons lived, into a pit which was bottomless. A hole, a cave.

"I was in Hell, where dead people live.

"People die so that they can learn things. This is the reason why those who are living, still alive, travel into the land of the dead. Down there, I asked a corpse why there is evil in this world.

"The corpse, nameless, clarified my question for me: 'There was neither good nor evil until humans were born, until creation began, until humans started having babies.'

"Me: 'Was there anything before humans started fucking and impregnating each other? Anything prior to good and evil?'

"Corpse: 'Yes.'

"Me: 'What?'

"Corpse: 'Amniotic fluid. In other words, inside was outside and is outside, and no inside, no outside, and vice-versa. In other words, the demons. Afterwards, when creation took and is taking place, the demons became corrupted.'

"Me: 'How could they have become corrupted when no corruption existed?'

"Corpse: 'They became replete with anger. They were angry that there were humans, that humans were making babies. The humans were using semen solely to re-create themselves. Note that both men and women have semen.

" 'The demons wanted semen to remain only semen so they took all the semen that they could get their hands on, protected it by locking it up in a cave. A cave deep within, in the darknesses of the highest mountain, where the demons kept their home. Patala, their communal womb. Patala, the name of that underworld part which is the demon body.

" 'Soon the demons owned all the semen. Yet they still didn't want there to be any semen. In the human world. For they had become greedy, antisex, antipornography demons.

" 'When humans were created, they created gods. Due to their nature or to human need, the gods were hungry: the humans had to keep feeding them.

" 'The demons didn't want this type of human procreation either, this creation through imagination. Imagination has its own semen. So the demons stole every morsel that a god was about to munch, to chomp, so the gods began to starve.

" 'Then the whole world lay in starvation, in poverty. All caught in starvation, in poverty, except for those demons who were not of this world. There was almost no more semen anywhere.'

"Now I listened even more carefully to what the corpse was telling me.

"Corpse: ' "Oh, god," scream some of the humans, "how are we going to live? How can we defeat evil? We don't know what evil is, yet here we are, starving. Are we evil's cause? Are we or our gods the cause of our own demise?" ' "

"Pussycat, I want to fuck you again," I cried.

She continued to describe what it is to be dead:

"The corpse told me how all the people yelled and demonstrated against the demons who were evil, whose evil was inescapable because the refuge and the castle of the demons was impregnable. Where the semen was hoarded, where all the treasures of the world lay buried.

"And the gods screamed more loudly because they didn't want to starve. Being gods, they were more hysterical, more fearful, more desperate, more emotional than humans.

"The gods realized that they were going to have to ask a demon to help them survive. They turned to the demon who was unlike all other demons. Who had killed his father. Who, being strange, had to be by himself. He lived in a graveyard away from humans and most demons. There he sat, with his snakes and rats, a couple of demonic followers; he didn't care about semen. There he ruled no one in his loneliness.

"Me: 'It's Punk Boy!'

"Corpse: 'One day, Punk Boy's girlfriend, Ratty, asked him why he loved graveyards so much.

" 'Now listen to Punk Boy's words:

" ' "I found my father fucking my sister. I stopped that one. After I had sliced off his head, not his dick, I became more alone.

" ' "His head fell into my hands and remains there to this day. I call the two halves of this egg-shaped skull *heaven* and *hell*."

" 'Punk Boy's words got his girlfriend hot; everything that existed also turned her on.'

"The corpse paused.

" 'When Punk Boy heard the gods out, he agreed to fight against his own kind.'

"Me: 'Why?'

"Corpse: 'He had never wanted to remain as he was. Because he was alone, he knew his own kind wasn't his own kind. So he left everyone.

" 'This was why Punk Boy lived in a graveyard.'

"Me: 'Wasn't he scared to live in a graveyard?'

"Corpse: 'If there were going to be possibilities again, there had to be nothingness.'

"Punk Boy agreed, for his own punk purposes, to fight against the demons; he used the earth as his vehicle to travel over the ground of his mind; he defeated his own.

"Afterwards, the demon city was drowning and burning up; the body was drowning and burning up.

"Ratty wanted to go out and watch all this destruction. As if she had never seen it before. Watching the world turn into a grave, from where she was standing, she saw a big, fat rat.

"It sat on her lap.

" 'Who's this?' asked rat.

"The stupid girl didn't recognize her own child, who, because Punk Boy wouldn't give her a child, was Punk Boy himself, dripping with all the blood and guts of all the demons he had just killed.

"If there were going to be possibilities again, there had to be nothingness.

"Or: here is the world in which the demons have been defeated; here is the graveyard of the world. A baby's crying.

"Seeing the woman he believes to be his mother, the

child reaches for her tit. It's the end, or the beginning, of the world. She's seen horror; she's just seen the world end: she's dripping with blood and guts.

"He wants to drink her up. He's thirstier than any child who doesn't know want. He drinks up all her fear of men and anger at men and horror of them.

"He finishes drinking her; finally freed of horror, she realizes that he's her lover, Punk Boy.

"And that's what it is to be dead," Pussycat told me.

I knew that that wasn't what it was to be dead because, even though Pussycat was appearing as a corpse, she wasn't dead. Pussycat was a liar.

Even back when I used to lie on top of her.

Pussycat had abandoned me; I had always remained faithful to her.

I wanted to tell her what death really is, that death is the loss of love. The only death is the loss of love. I argued with her, because she was a liar, in the same way that she had argued with me. That in dreams lie the beginnings of all things:

"We were in a school. I was following you.

"As soon as we knew that we liked each other, we ran away from that school and from my father. We had lots of sex.

"Remember: when I saw you the next morning, in the light of the morning of the world, you were sitting with a bunch of girls at a table. Right in front of all of them—and I didn't know anyone—*publicly*, you rejected me.

"You don't know anything of all that happened next. You don't know anything about what's inside me.

"You put me in a wasteland and every part of me didn't

want to be there. Thought that, since there was nowhere else to go, I could no longer be. But I couldn't bear not to be. Dragged myself like a pirate whose legs have just been chopped off away from that place to the only other territory I had . . .

"A smidgen of land . . . in my mind . . . remembered . . .

"Searching through my memory, I found the two girls I had loved before I had met you. Before I had met you and so had no one in my life.

"I chose K—— because, since she was a wimp and had followed me around everywhere that she could, she had never frightened me.

"I was shy, but it wasn't as if I had any choice: I phoned K——. As soon as we began speaking to each other, all of my awkwardness about my past went away.

"While she was gossiping to me that now she was a he and living in a male-only society, I reached down to open a carton that someone had just placed at my feet.

"You're a liar, Pussycat. I'm not a great poet yet. I'm going to be. This constitutes further evidence of your ignorance of me.

"Inside the carton lay stacks of my books in Dutch. And the books' publisher was Dutch Penguin? I was a real poet.

"Since I now had credentials, I could contact I——, the other girl. She wouldn't have anything to do with me while I hadn't been . . . but now that I was published by Dutch Penguin . . .

"As in the case of K——, I had loved I—— and then abruptly dropped her.

"I was searching for I——'s phone number. Looking for phone numbers drives me nuts, so at the same time I was flip-

ping casually and carelessly through one of my Dutch books.
Inside I saw photo after photo of me almost naked—I used to
be in the sex industry—photos that proved my criminal past.

"The only problem was that the past as shown in these
photos had never taken place. In one, sporting a feather boa, I
was leaning over so deeply that my breasts right up to their
nipples hung out of a stripper bra. I looked glam, but the truth
is, when I was in the sex biz, I wasn't. Sex biz is low and sleazy.

"I think that this image came from one of your dreams
about me."

The dead girl didn't reply. The dead never reply.

"I was hysterical. Almost none of my poems had been left
in my book. There were only these depictions of me as sex-
queen-publicly-displaying-cunt. I knew who was responsible.
It was my agent! She was responsible for all the bad that had
ever happened to me . . .

"I *had* to get hold of the only two friends I had left in the
world, K—— and I——. I had a phone, but it didn't work.
Because I didn't know anyone's number any longer. Each time
I dialed a number on the black wall phone, that number led to
another number . . . all these numbers formed a labyrinth
around me, a labyrinth inside the phone receiver, a labyrinth
from which I was never again going to be able to escape. Truly,
I was doomed.

"I was doomed to become increasingly lonely.

"I found myself inside a bookstore whose walls were lined
with books. To my pleasure, I learned that my friend K——,
for whom I had been searching, owned this shop.

"I wanted to hear the reading that was just about to take
place, but I had to listen to everything K—— was telling me.

As she spoke, her words turned into life: my agent's con-fabulating with my publisher; the latter thumbs through my Dutch book and says, 'This stuff's dated.' I know that he's refer-ring to the sex pics of me.

" 'We should have pictures of her peeing,' he continues.

"I have to hear every single word that these two creeps in my life are saying and, more than ever, I have to be at the po-etry reading because the reader is female and Italian, very im-portant categories, but I'm hysterical. I'm hysterical because I'm repeating the question, 'How can I let this book become public? This book which is *my* book? How can I allow myself to be seen by the public as the lowest porn trash and slut cur-rently alive?' Not that I knew who this 'public' was.

"K—— offered me her phone. It was the first ray of hope in my life. The appearance of hope allowed the commence-ment of revolt: I know what I'll do! I'll call all my girlfriends!

"I told them over the phone, 'I hope to hell this works—

" 'Girlfriends, you're going to infiltrate Penguin by pre-tending to be bona fide Penguin workers. After all, none of the real or boss penguins can distinguish one woman from another. Just show some tit. Like me in the photos.

" 'Now you've penetrated Penguin before my books have gone out into the world. Inside Penguin, inside the labyrinth of books, having located my book, on every porn phot of me, you shall stamp in big, bold, black letters: DYKE.

" 'Get it, girls?'

"All of it happened just as I had planned. The big pen-guins never noticed that their workers had changed nor that the insides of their books were altered. Those guys never read their own books.

"Thus, it is better to be alive than dead," I finished.

As soon as she heard these words, the corpse turned away from me, left me.

But I knew that she wasn't really dead, so I left her.

Free of her former embraces, free for the moment from my desire for sex, I awoke. Awoke, went down to the bottom of the world. Where girls become pirates. In the light of the mourning of the world.

ANTIGONE'S STORY

Hegel, or the panopticon, sees all, except for the beginning of the world. In that beginning, which is still beginning, there is a young girl.

Her name's not important. She's been called King Pussy, Pussycat, Ostracism, O, Ange. Once she was called Antigone . . .

From Antigone's Personal Diary

so I just got out I upped and left put it however you want

because it's all a piece of shit. The world I had been in. I don't have to give you the details because they've been repeated over and over, the whole story, every possible story, again, again, just walk into any bookstore and look at all the stories and they're all ours, anyway they were all mine, those repetitions, which I called representations, to me were prison. Prison. That's where Creon, my so-called dad, but he wasn't my real dad, he just wasn't perverted enough, wanted to put me. Put me away. He wanted to cut off my head and do worse things.

I won't anymore live in a world where paranoia's the only possible act of knowing.

If this new dad had stashed me in prison, that would have been a repetition because . . . you know what prison life is? Prison life's emotional appearance is boredom, then forcible identity-disappearance, because prison existence is repetition upon repetition so I lived in prison even before Creon wished to put me there, even before the future I walked out of, the future of Creon's incarceration of me.

Side-by-side the reign of prison and the reign of lies began:

Don't worry. I'm going to explain this.

None of you knows who my dad is. None of you even knows I had a real dad. But then you don't know me. My dad's name had and has been forgotten because, as a girl once said to me, he was a criminal and a murderer. He was gutter slime, whatever is worse because it can't be mentioned. All that is antithetical to human. My real father was all that is the enemy to humanity. You see that was why I was taught that I didn't have a father.

Taught, among others, by my fake father, Creon.

I know what my real father did. I know exactly what he did so I know how my blood smells. I know what it is to be human and I will never hide this. When they state that my father didn't exist, they're representing my father; all of them represented my father who was my incestuous birth when they said that I was naked, lewd, tormented by extreme wildness.

I want to return to my birth.

Do I have to tell you the names of my birth you who think you're not allowed to say those words?

My real father's creation of a state by patricide hid a worse crime: the disappearance of females.

Whatever I am I'm not a fucking liar I don't even know whether I fuck I got away from all this by a motorcycle. Antigone on a motorcycle. While Creon was threatening to shove me into prison, I took money from him, with part of it, bought a Jap bike. So my feet could touch this earth.

I'm going to get out, at that time I told myself, and simultaneously I'm going to learn to see.

I started learning something when I had a dream. The night before I set out on my 1100 into a country which I didn't know. I had been remembering how my sister and I are the only ones left. Perhaps.

During this night:

night—to mountains—there, humans were sitting in pools.

The mountains rose up into ridges, in the darkness. Pools sat almost hidden in the ridges.

All the land, mountains.

Afterwards. I wanted to go back there so I could sit in a hot, black pool. Inside the cold.

To go is to return.

When I was finally able to return, a disaster took place. Now I was traveling with a man who was older than me. But I couldn't sink my body in a pool because we had to leave before disaster sat everywhere.

The only hospital to which I could bring the man with whom I was traveling, the only hospital there seemed to be, was located in the lower, in the dark, green world. Through the night I sat, waiting for him to emerge from surgical operations. There in that waiting room, I dealt with boredom by playing records on a turntable. A record by Arthur Miller. Side 1. Side 2 was all songs.

No one used turntables anymore.

The operations were over; he had come through.

Below the lower earth, earth appeared in the form of a shantytown: narrow paths ran between, and separated from each other, rows of paper-and-aluminum constructions. They seemed to be only walls. Deep holes became visible in the dirt mixed with bits of garbage, strange stains. Laundry hung down from the string loops connected to the paper-aluminum constructions and to the windowless windows.

I walked on top of this dirt, past door after door in the paper-aluminum wall on my right. I opened the fourth. Inside there were two gay men.

There must have been more people inside and all of us must have climbed into a car . . .

In that car as it was moving, a guy who resembled an exboyfriend of mine only because he was thin and blond told us, "I'm going to Japan."

Nobody seemed to notice because nobody asked him why.

"I'm going to Japan so that I can be cured of alcoholism. We're all alcoholics."

I thought he had a point. At which point, he vomited all over me.

I told him that we were heading to a disaster, that a major portion of the world was heading toward, and actually in the beginning of, disaster.

That in the mountains, it happened one night. The night when I returned to the mountains. Suddenly inside that night, when someone put his foot down, there was no more ground. All of the ground left was falling fast. That mud lies over mud. Nothing else. "All of this northeastern continent is sinking," I repeat myself so that everyone who is in the car which is moving will understand. "The only way we can stop this, we can save our section of the world from falling without end, is by carrying all of the water which is now part of the land up north, into Canada."

But I knew that that wasn't practical. That our part of the world had to go.

As soon as we came back to the paper-and-aluminum house, the boy vomited over me. I hate the smell of vomit more than anything else in the world except for lobotomy. Perhaps something happened in my childhood which I don't remember. My left hand, with a napkin, moved his insides off my flesh. I carried this paper which I called "the vomit napkin" over to the sink. It was white. Inside there, I washed my left hand more than thoroughly.

While I was washing myself in the sink, I had an image of a tattoo whose style was European graphic novel.

The vomit was gone. Pete, whom I know outside dream, said instead of asked, "Let's see your tats" and, without waiting for my reply, lifted up the back of my T-shirt so I had to move away from the vomit napkin that was sitting in the sink.

In its left corner as I left.

I was thinking, he just wants to see me naked but what the hell. I don't like people seeing me naked.

I was thinking while he was looking at me, it's good for me having him see me.

*   *   *

up early on my motorcycle next morning bye-bye to daddy I've buried him so it's all over

Memory of Creon's voice: Women must learn to obey as well as men

after a lousy drive through desert 106 degrees beating on my head

how ugly California is when it's, here, away from the ocean. around me, flat land everywhere, but not flat enough to make the sky around it more than sky. Nothing has grown in this yellow-brown. Nothing grows in this yellow-brown. "They go fishing in a swimming pool," a big blonde in a taco shop comments upon this land.

There are almost no roads except for a freeway. When I turn off again, to fill up the bike, a trucker who's standing behind me tells me that he thought that the cop who was behind me on the freeway was going to get me for speeding.

"No, he was racing to the fire."

There had been a second cop who had driven up behind me, then sped off.

All along the roadside there were tiny fires.

A second trucker asks if I'm boiling in my leather jacket. I ask him back what's going to happen with the weather in this part of the world. It's autumn 106 degrees.

He answers me that the weather's like the government: you never know which way it's going to go.

"Sure you do," maybe I'm throwing my weight around,

"you know that it's going to take all your money." I remember an old friend of mine, someone who used to be a friend, a hot-shot media boy, saying in one of his magazine columns that nobody worth anything lives outside New York City. Outside, he said, there's nothing . . .

The trucker and I laugh.

More straight sun and my brains are fried.

I'm on the road and I must be worrying whether bad brains cause bad driving 'cause I start seeing car-and-motorcycle accidents. Can no longer tell which is which. Everything and everyone is all mixed up in these tremendous, differently colored piles, cutoff human limbs and shattered metal, glass shards. I see pavement after pavement covered, smothered, by red. Streaks of red, swipes of red: reflections of the sun left there in the sky. No more a night.

My brains.

I've been on this road several hours: everything's changing:

As if a world begins, hills houses. The entrance to a mountain range inside which roads are winding, ascends and dives through air which appears to be hanging.

I come down through the air into a number of deserted cabooses. One caboose says: "Motel." The mountains are rising up around me.

What did the man who was named Creon say?

> Prison's not right for her pagan sort. Find a cave
> and wall her up in it. Bury her alive—with just
> enough food so that no one can say that I who am

the State am guilty. And that way she'll have plenty
of time to honor all the dead who've been forgotten.
While she's starving to death.

. . . I arrive at a sign that says: "No Trespassing: Road Not
Maintained."

I decide I'll take a walk.

Everything, under my feet and around me, is brown, except for the greenery which is more extensive than the brown
sky. If I keep on hiking, I'm going to come to something.

I climb about a half-hour when I see a mountain the next
world over.

There's a clear, simple distinction, in this world, between
brown and green; the line of demarcation, according to my vision, lies parallel to my position on my mountain.

When I was a child, I dreamt of a hill which was not yet a
mountain. Its form fell between that of a small animal and a
cock. Later I saw that shape in the west of England. The top
half of the mountain I'm perceiving looks like what I saw in
England, in the dream I once had.

The sun is licking part of its surface.

Rewriting while masturbating so that I can write, that is,
see, more clearly:

to go in there is to penetrate the mountain: the castle,
there are extraordinary pleasures inside the castle, velvets and
a feast, the round table, only now it's rectangular

to climb up a crag is to come

I'm going to go in there now: to the water; it's hot; the
woods are not the log that sits by the water; not sits, rather lies;
flies, roaches, roaches lie everywhere; the flies want to be my
skin, but I tell them, "Go away."

it starts deep within, too sunk within those woods to get out. The cold wood has now disappeared because I'm going to come any moment; I become lost in the wood; what love is; coming again is rising over a fence, like, into another territory. Over again. There's no stopping.

The cops haven't yet stopped me for speeding.

The doctor moves his tool right inside my skin, then down my leg. It emerges out of the skin below my right cunt lip: there the doctor makes a hole in my inner thigh while I'm watching him. I'm thinking, I don't want what is happening to me to happen, and simultaneously I'm thinking, it doesn't matter what I think. I know that it doesn't matter what I think and I want to begin to feel again, but it's too scary in this kind of world. When I walk away from the doctor, my stride is so stilted that I'm forced to know that an operation on me has taken place.

Back on my bike

the days of trees, tree after tree, until I stop seeing.

my second night in a town, this time a town which seems to work.

in the center of this town there's still, black water. birds, not humans, live here.

a white mallard is gazing in one direction; a black, the other. a spotted bird moves past the two who don't move. A teenager whose head is shaven walks across the green.

I stop seeing. A woman wearing a pink halter and pink shorts, fat and pretty, tells me that she likes it here, the life, while her boys scream they worship motorcycles, her husband's back where they used to live, down in Bakersfield which must be the hottest place on earth as if the world no longer exists. My mother's mother who's still wearing her blue-white hair piled in waves on top of her head and looks like Joan Crawford as if Joan Crawford is still alive, remarks, "These are the nights of dread, of grief."

The first part of this going away is the discontinuation of seeing.

Memory of my words to Creon:

> I agree, willingly, to your sentencing me to prison,
> to death: I'm leaving your world.
> In silence, in darkness, in solitude.
>
> In the echoing caves of the north wind, now I, a
> child, halloo; on the open mountainside I'm running
> wild with the horses.

I'm seeing in dream:

The Setup of Night

I'm lucky to have a job in this time of poverty. I'm in Santa Barbara. Down, on part of the beach, because I no longer have a home. This whole area looks like Newport Beach during the jazz festival.

There's lots of music going on so I'm going to stay on these sands even though there's nowhere for me to sleep.

My jewelry's in a box. The box, also, is mine. But my jewelry's the most beautiful of all: it's made out of chunks of colored and almost transparent glass.

All of the people who're now on this beach are girls who have sex with girls. I'm not like them. I, Antigone, no longer have a home.

In other words, I'm *on the beach* and at the same time I'm living at my girlfriend's house which is on the same beach.

I'm living temporarily.

I look at all the people who're inside. Her house. I see in this order: (1) a blond girl; I like how she looks; (2) a gay acupuncturist; (3) myself.

I check out all of the beds that are in this room.

A tall thing is lying on one of them. The acupuncturist, whom I've already seen, has just done it to him. Then, I see that the face is bloody . . . As for the top of that head . . . Whoo! I have no way of handling this sight.

Something, which is now unknown to me, must have taken place in this bedroom before I got here.

Maybe . . . "tall" has something to do with "gay." Now that it's time for me to go to bed, I'm thinking this because a guy whom I believe to be gay is showing me a silver eyelash. He's wearing it: two silver pins piercing the eyelid directly hold the eyelash to the eyelid. Since it's beautiful, both eyelash and eye, I want to own the former even though I'm scared of the pain. I don't actually know that it's painful to wear this.

Despite the pain, I have to pin the eyelash on to my own eye. While I'm doing it, I hardly hurt.

The tall, thin boy has left his eyelash in my hands so I can try it on again.

This time, when I attach it to myself, I have to insert many, many silver pins into the edge of my upper eyelid. Before I do this, I know that I can do this; so then, I do. Now I never want to again give back the eyelash, but I have to, I have to give both it and my box of jewelry to the boy.

It must be hours past bedtime because I'm in the bedroom. There are so many single cots here that this is, now, a dorm room. I lie on mine. A girl who's pretty walks over, then climbs on me. The weight of her body feels good on top of me. I'm feeling wonderful because we're rubbing cunts even though it's taking a long time for each of us to get off.

She murmurs in my ear, "Fuck me." I shall.

realize that I've been at the top of the world because I'm falling now, long sweeping curves which seem to never end. Miles after miles of curves until there's nothing else but curves. Waking world is the same as dream world so there's no more need to dream. I've stopped seeing. Falling because the top of the world is descending with me; falling without danger because the top of a mountain can't tumble.

I remember I saw a sign which read, "The Shining." I can't return.

Falling until there's a bottom. At this point I cross water. Over a bridge made out of metal.

On this side I'm no longer anywhere so I'm aware I'm beginning to travel.

The night is made out of yellow Jell-O. Diamanda Galás is performing this night. Oh, yes, I know her, I tell a few girls who're younger than me.

The town I'm now in sits on the side of a hill; now and then narrow streets wind, out of it, up to the hill's top; everything resembles the town of Cambria but narrower, darker.

All of us, girls, are standing outside, on a street. This is

DG who's in front of me, but she looks like the Dean of the Chicago Art Institute. Her hair is curly, dirty blond. But . . . people change greatly.

On the other hand, the rock-n-roll crew consists of Ava, a girl whose hair is as dark as the real Diamanda's. But wavy. And some guys, I don't know how many 'cause I'm not looking at them.

Someone whom I don't recognize hands me a plate of yellow Jell-O.

Almost all of these guys, the ones in the rock-n-roll crew, are dating me. The only one who doesn't have anything to do with me is a goon. He's a goon because he pisses over anything he sees that doesn't move. Maybe this is his way of being scared of what does move. But I'm not a psychiatrist.

I'm in a bar with these guys, none of us doing shit, and this goon starts pissing in public. I'm never going to date him, never. But . . . but but but. This is where I stand right now. I went with one of the rockers and it just didn't work out between us. There's this second rocker. I'm into him; I don't know if he has any interest in me. If he doesn't . . . there's only the goon left.

The second rocker is interested in me because he's pulling my body into his. All that I want in this town. Now he's taking me down with him. Down, to the floor. It's made out of wood. We're not exactly in its center, but still, everyone's watching us, everyone who's in this subterranean bar: he rolls on top of me; he's about to fuck me. I never wanted this to happen. At least, not in public. I don't want to be this public. So fuck him! Now I'll never be with anyone again. Not with a man.

I leave the bar.

Death is another bar which lies several steps below the normal world. I'm at its threshold, but not yet in it. Its doorway is doorless.

This is the order of seeing at that threshold:

(1) In front of me and to my left, a guy sitting on a wooden stool, his visage wet with drops.

(2) In front of and below me, drops forming concentric three-quarter circles, drops or "seeds," on worn-down carpet.

(3) In front of me and to my right, the goon stands. From his waist down to his knees, he's naked. In the place of a cock, he has a mass of brown, wrinkled pudding or muddy flesh whose surface is marked by concentric circles. Out of this center pops up a very tiny cat-shaped prick. The texture of this pudding makes me think of elephants.

(3) explains (1) and (2): the goon has just urinated on the sitting guy.

I decide, I've had enough, so I get out. Out of the bar which I must be inside.

One result of all the piss is that I'm hanging out with Diamanda more than I ever have in my life. This, for instance, is exactly what happens when we're in the outside, on a street:

"Do you want to sleep with D?" a girl who's one of her real friends inquires.

The question makes sense to me because I suddenly realize that I have to sleep with someone because I haven't slept with anyone in ages.

Me, Antigone.

But I don't want to know this.

"Of course," I answer. These words, which I said before I thought them, tell me that everyone in the world is in love with Diamanda. Just as I realize this truth, Diamanda walks on to the street as if the street's now a stage set. I see her this way: she's perching in a recess in a clean and white concrete building.

In there, the singer gossips about the ebony-haired girl, Kava. That Kava isn't her manager or even part of her crew: Kava only performs before she goes on. Actually, Diamanda confides in me, she doesn't like Kava.

Kava's history: she always and only has been a rocker; she used to have something or other to do with the Rolling Stones.

Now I know that Diamanda's attracted to Kava.

I have to get out. Maybe that's why I'm now shopping, why I'm in this yuppie boutique.

Here are only four racks of clothes. It's the disappearance of the world: whenever I turn around and look at any rack that's in this store, the clothes on those shelves are no longer there. I will never have anything to wear.

The only clothes which remain in the world are huge, chenille sweaters: they're piled neatly on the four shelves of one side of one rack. There're only autumn colors: deep oranges, brown which is always only one color, pale blues. I detest all colors except for red and black and they're not colors. I'm aware that I'm going to have to make do. I'm going to have to buy one of these things. And that I will not do, I, Antigone,

I refuse.

I will be _____ instead.

_____ is something impossible.

I'll be a girl pirate.

Flying.

Earth along the northern side of this body of water is calming down into hills. First, into green. Then, into red-brown-yellow. Increasingly, into more yellow. At the same time, less foliage.

Only earth and sky left. All the people have passed away. There are no more signs pointing to specific geographic locations: there are no more locations.

After people comes gas. "Last Gas Station for 80 Miles." I remember when I was driving through East Germany. When there was an East Germany. On a back road. Away from the Autobahn. The strange bike I was on ran out of fuel.

Finally, a local motorcyclist stopped his bike.

I looked at him, patted my tank. "Gas."

"No gas here," he answered.

All the filling stations are gone.

Brown, red, and yellow curve slightly, descend into brown-yellow. The difference between ascending and descending has disappeared. Blue runs parallel to the horizon.

The flatter the land is becoming, the more I can see of it and of sky. Whatever there is of me, of being apart from water, earth, and sky, has become an act of seeing. Nights I no longer dream; I barely sleep. There's no way for me to return home because there's no one to go back.

I'm not lost. Seeing is becoming broader, higher and lower . . .

. . . petrol tanks sit in a mix of gravel and dirt . . . in the oasis, there are humans . . . a motorcycle kid and his girlfriend lean against a wall stuck in the bottom surface . . . within the restaurant, men with old faces lean over french fries burgers pools of red, here and there a lettuce leaf . . . the only females are waitresses except for the girl who's outside . . .

Humanity's gone away again . . .
Bye-bye . . .

I'm no longer lost nor found. I'm seeing.

Green begins.

As if greenery no longer matters, this greenery which is a town named Walla Walla, outside the greenery, while I'm passing a car that's drifting toward the shoulder, a cop in reflective blue glasses pulls me over for defying the law, then throws me into jail.

Do you remember the sad story of Cepheus's daughter? I write in my jail cell. She was unmarried, therefore an outsider, always in danger. What bitter tears she shed. They dripped from both her mouths. She had been happy before her father tried to murder her. Before the beginning of attempted destruction, she had lived with her father in that chateau, that collection of buildings, of walkways, each construction different from every other, thick greenery above and below, where she had many fabulous adventures.

Like me.

Like me, she had never wanted to leave her home.

She had only been going to a party . . .

As soon as she was at her destination, she no longer knew where she was . . .

In a wood-lined room too large to be a bar, but nevertheless a bar . . . she saw only three people. Two girls and a boy. The boy was blond. Even though he was hunky, he was hot for her. Only because, she thought, I'm a famous poet, even though I'm a child.

Both the boy and Andromeda became sloshed. Within this drunkenness that was like a room, he disappeared.

There were three people in the room that was like a bar. A boy whose hair was light brown stood with two other girls. He couldn't look at anyone else. Andromeda could understand his desire. She had never believed that the blond hunk had wanted her. The three children disappeared so that they could make out hard.

Andromeda was left with the liquor.

When she opened her eyes, the blond boy was holding her whole body and she knew that he liked every part of her, each section of skin, no matter what skin, because his hard cock was poking into her stomach, through her clothes which were between the two of them, but she didn't believe that he wanted her.

As soon as she began to trust him, she started to want him too.

These emotions made her drunk; in the drunkenness, the boy disappeared.

She was alone when child after child showed up for a party. It was going to be huge: she was going to become lonelier.

She had to get out of there because everything that was and that would be in this room would make her lonely.

Andromeda couldn't leave because she no longer knew where the chateau was. After all, her father had wanted to murder her. She hadn't written down its address. She had forgotten. Nor did she know the name of the owner. She didn't know who he was . . . an archbishop . . . something like that.

If only she had someone with whom she could talk. Someone who would understand her. Who might be adult.

She explained to a stranger, a man. Explained that she wanted to go back to the chateau but she didn't know exactly where it was.

He knew that she lived in the south. Inside her eyes she saw a map. Home was in the bottom. " . . . and slightly to the east." Slightly to the east was slightly to the left. "Near Cologne."

"Can I walk to that place?"

"Well . . ." His *well* was a word of doubt. "I'll call you a cab."

She hadn't known that such a thing could be done.

As if the sentence "I'll call you a cab" was a key, or because the increasing numbers of partygoers and soaring drunkenness heralded the emergence, the reign of a large and totally ordered group, Andromeda no longer hesitated. She left the room.

Unlike me, Andromeda didn't come out of incest. Her real father didn't make her mother suicide.

Her real father, not her fake father, tried to kill her.

She fled her real father and remembered that he had attempted to off her because *to get out is to remember*. That is, *to get out is to want to go back to a home to which one can no longer return*.

The beautiful girl got out of that room and found herself in snow. Its night was peaceful. The white snow was the same color as the black sky. She still wanted the blond boy, whose name was Perseus, though she didn't know this, so bad that she was hurting worse than she had ever known, but she couldn't see him. She could see all that lay outside. Snow, as if snow is black. Watched couple after couple, heterosexual, as if in a university, file up the narrow, dirt path to the door of that great building. The path separated two areas of untouched snow. The walls of that building were brick red.

According to words she was hearing, here and there, these boys, these girls were going to a meeting of the Society of Conservative Youth.

Now she knew that she couldn't return to the party. To what lay inside the barroom.

Those bits of conversations that the beautiful girl just managed to overhear enabled her to start on her way home, back, as the man had shown her, down the white and brown path, here and there obscured by snow drifts. Unable to be certain of her direction, she assured herself, "I won't lose my way as long as I stay to the left."

Like me, she was willing to go to prison, like me willing to die in accordance with her father's orders because she wanted to do anything to get out of the society of which her father was head.

Words to Creon: **Creon, I left your lousy world. Only a fool will now attempt to stop us girls. To halt our ecstatic singing. The death of reason isn't blackness, but another kind of light.**

Andromeda talked to me. She told me that she was going home, back to her real bed between the living and the dead:

"Like I said," she said, "I was still wet for him. As if desire is muscles, my muscles were so big and tight inside me I had to do something. Then I knew I was where he lived.

"This was the last place I would have expected him to live. A two-story wood filthy ugly suburban house stuck in a small plot between two other ugly houses.

"All of it seemed to be empty. There was still snow.

"I couldn't stop being cold, I had been walking so long that I walked through the open door. After all, I didn't have to knock. I found myself in his bedroom.

"There was no one nor any furniture in the room.

"A room beyond this room, though attached, was in another house. Through the doorway that separated the two rooms, I caught a glimpse of a male-female couple. 'I'll be with you in a second,' the boy cried out drunkenly to me.

"I realized that he must be thinking that I'm summoning him to go back to work.

"Before he could find out who I actually was, that I was an intruder and that I had broken into his house, I headed back to the front door.

"While I moved backward through my boyfriend's bedroom, I repeated the thought I had when I was looking through the doorway. 'I had better get out of here before he returns and finds me breaking the law in his space.' "

Andromeda never veered from her filthy path. Snow covered the ground. Its sky turned back to black.

She began to see more and more: houses. They stood closer together. She could no longer distinguish between dirt and concrete. Between what belonged to the country and what to the city. She knew that she was at the edge of a village square.

As she kept on walking, of course, she saw only what lay on her left. A restaurant whose insides were mainly outsides. Black, in the shape of a square. There, huge umbrellas opened over round tables; a plant, one or two. She glimpsed figures, sitting at two or three of the tables, which she thought were human.

I am no longer human, but outside.

It was at this point that Andromeda knew that she needed to ask for help. That she, according to every social stricture, structure, was hysterical maddened perverse foreign wasteful virginal nymphomaniac secret and smelled lousy. She might no longer know where she was going.

In other words, she needed someone to help her return to a home that no longer was.

She thought: Obviously, there's no one in this restaurant who's going to be willing to get near, much less help, filth like me, because this restaurant's posh. There's a tea shop across the street. In the area I used to be not able to see. I'm looking through its window. Inside, it's half a tea shop, half a butcher's. My sort of people might be in there.

These thoughts must have had something to do with the truth because the inside of the tea shop didn't contradict but rather expanded in detail that which she had partly glimpsed and partly imagined. Inside there were all sorts of small, interesting objects, and dead meat, and the proprietors, an elderly male and an elderly female, large and rather slobby, were kind to her. They knew where her home was located even though she could no longer remember anything.

"We'll call you a cab."

The time that lay between the calling of that cab and its arrival which might not happen:

Andromeda was somewhere else. In a room large enough to be a whole abbey. This room had been carved or hollowed out.

Through a large window that was sitting in front of her eyes, Andromeda saw its replica, or the same window. Saw,

through that window, into the abbey's replica or the same
abbey.

Inside there, every person and every object was larger
than usual. Two boys as Greek gods or Greek gods who were
boys stepped through the farther window or the replica of the
window on to the wood plank that connected the two windows. Then, walked through the one in front of Andromeda's
eyes, right up to her. She saw!

In the whole of the abbey a play was about to take place.
A play or performance art: large objects had been placed, dis-
creetly and precisely, in that space which extended to space in
general. As if a language, a language of objects, was being born.
Andromeda remembered an early R.E.M. video.

When she looked up to the center of the room's ceiling, she saw a string from the bottom of which hung a bat.
Swinging.

"There are wonders!" she gasped to the two who were,
perhaps, helping her return home.

Here I am in this jail. I've been here a fucking month now.
Maybe I'm here for a purpose 'cause this girl who's really dirty
has just given me a message which I'm to deliver for her.

I've become friends with this girl perhaps because she's so
filthy. Her filth is anger. When she's really angry, she tells me
that she's never going to be let out of this jail—if the authorities have their way.

I've gotten out. They couldn't keep me inside: all I did was
speed, while driving, and I wasn't doing that illegally. They put
me inside 'cause I'm a girl. I've heard there are societies in

which girls stay in prison until they're married. I'm out now so I'm never going to go back there. Never back to turned bologna thrown down on stale Wonder bread, never back to girls in whom racism is being carved so they can beat up other girls, then emerge as able members of society. I remember. Members. Never back to a town composed of Seventh-Day Adventists; never back to cops behind huge reflecting blue sunglasses; never back to people taught by priests to see demons, by fathers to hunt; never back to criminalization. I'm no longer safe and never have been because I was never going to be dead while alive.

I have this passport the filthy girl obtained for me so that I can deliver her message to Bristol, a town somewhere in England. The filthy girl told me where this town is.

They wouldn't allow us to read newspapers in jail because, they said, we were girls. This paper says that the Republicans won almost every election last week so the religious right's in power. Gingrich, Helms, and all the Seventh-Day Adventists. Instead of reading on, I read what I'm supposed to deliver.

> "*(To the smelliest girl there)*
> *Old Anchor Inn*
> *Bristol, England*
> *19/3/94*
>
> "*Dear King,*
> "*Even though I'm in a filthy jail, I've accomplished what's necessary.*
> "*The ship's bought and fitted with sails etc. She's lying*

at anchor, in Brighton, ready for sea. A child could sail her . . .

"Go back to Brighton. Fuck your sick cat. Bitch. Get the hell back there before any other girl gets wind of what's going on. Of the port we're sailing for. Of the port of buried treasure.

"I'll be out of this feelthy Americano jail soon."

To my surprise, I'm finding myself becoming interested, incrementally, the more I keep reading. Now I know why I was in jail. So that I'll keep on reading . . .

. . . and I do:

"I enclose a copy of the treasure map. Note that the island to which we'll be sailing looks like a dead woman's body. (If it wasn't dead, it couldn't be a map.)

"Unfortunately the map in my possession has no markings that indicate the location on the woman's body of the buried treasure.

"I do believe that such a map exists."

Sea- or sex-dreams are filling my heart, and anticipation of days, of nights filled by wonders, times beyond wonder. I'm already floating, which is flying, in the realm of water, from isle to isle.

As I finish myself off by reading the end, I decide, not forgetting my promise to the dirty girl, that I'm going to deliver her message and then, I'm going to stay with whomever I've just given the letter.

> *"For the moment I'm in prison, Puss. It no longer matters to me how I landed up here.* Any land is bad land. *For the moment I'm here and you're there, so you're the one who's going to be running things.*
>
> *"Now listen, Puss. This is exactly how you're going to run things: in Brighton, which is a good town for pussy, round up whatever mean girls you can find and get. To prepare for sailing. We're going to the island on the map by rowboat because that's the only way to elude the authorities.*
>
> *"I'll arrive in Brighton before you set sail. This is really what I want to tell you in this letter: watch your fucking head, and don't let your power go to your head. For your power is always mine. You're the king, but you're not the king of anything. Even of girls as greedy, as ravenous, as dreamy as you. Remember, Puss, I know you. You're as nasty as me: you've got a tongue like a razor blade and a worse temper. All the nicest qualities in a girl. Remember that no one has ever come up against me and won. Not even a female. If you try to usurp my power, I'll rip off your pretty head, and it is pretty. Mine's prettier; so is my cunt hair.*
>
> *Yours,*
>
> *"P.S. You can trust the child who's delivering this because I made friends with her in hell and so death shall never part us."*

cunt

hairs

crossbones

become

hearts

For the first time I know her name: **Silver**

. . . and so I traveled to Bristol, where I met Pussy, who was there nursing her sick cat. I gave her the letter I'd promised to deliver.

Pussy took her cat and returned to her hideout. Back there, in Brighton, we picked up Morgan, Pussycat, Bad Dog, and, afterwards, Black Monk, MD, Virgin Gold, Ostracism, and some others. As according to our instructions . . .

. . . for Brighton is the bottom of the world . . .

The Beginning of Poetry: The Origins of Piracy

"I want to be a female again."

"What does that mean?" I inquired of Bad Dog, who had been talking to me for several hours over beer and more beer.

"Dogs and murderers."

In the Bald Head Pub.

"Do we know who we are? Mustn't we go back to our past? *Where are the pirates of yesteryear?*"

Bad Dog turned to the rest of the girls, who were more inebriated than the homeless around them, and to the cats, who were eating fish, and to the dead fish. They were all sprawled everywhere. Bad Dog was spewing out her rhetoric probably because she was now too dry to spread anything else.

"Where are those pirates, all men, now?"

"Rotting under our feet," a wit named Morgan whose feet had been cut off in a brawl murmured, "Not all of them were men."

"Where is that male rot, that drool that will never dry though it long ago died and still stinks from here to the China Seas in which ivory is growing, from here to rotting eternity, where are those bearers and carriers of nausea, those vessels of disease as if all they knew how to do was steal what was most pernicious out of Pandora's box? Where are those who masturbated themselves red and dry every day while fantasizing sexual encounters whose excitements, born of horror and pleasure, knew neither the limits of time nor of space?

"*Girls of fortune*, we, and this is the first time, here in Brighton, that we call ourselves fortunate, perhaps because we're talking about our past, know that we come from a long and glorious lineage. Of death. For one of the meanings of the word *lineage* is 'dead.'" This smelly dog was looking around her. As usual, her pals had already passed out from drink and were now spread out in typical girl corpse form. "They're all dead."

She finished up: "Dead men don't bite."

Bad Dog should know.

After this girl had made her speech, she went off to find her mother. Brighton Town used to be where English royalty brought their mistresses and young boys for romantic weekends. A dead town.

The girl sang this song while she was looking for her mom,

I'm looking for my mom
Whom I've never known.
I'm never going to find her
Like me she had a womb.

She knew that, since her mother lived in the society or world which she had fled, her mother was shopping.

For a mother, shopping is always grocery shopping: Mom was in the mall.

"Don't go in *there*," Bad Dog's girlfriends used to tell her.

"I'm going to go . . ." This time she defied her bad friends because her visionary eye was seeing this map:

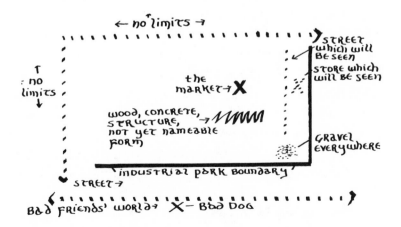

Bad Dog crossed over the street.

The grocery store, though it was gigantic, aisle after aisle of vegetables, canned goods, even slabs of meat, was a health-food store. Bad Dog wouldn't eat anything else. Already this store was closing up, for night had started approaching the whole of the earth.

The dirt under her feet, as if the floor was outside, was turning wetter and there was almost no food left on the shelves.

Even Bad Dog had to realize that it was useless to shop any longer. Her mother was nowhere to be found. She had been trying to buy vegetables, but now the girl wanted only to leave the store where her mother was supposed to be.

She crossed a street which she hadn't seen on the map, then entered a store which hadn't yet been visible. She was heading to the east. Now there were all sorts of things, inside, where every item was visible, that could be purchased. Edible and nonedible. Bad Dog began to desire. And she could afford this merchandise . . . as long as she didn't buy everything . . . but she was a greedy dog, a dog who had always been hungry, a dog ready to eat anything, anyone, chomp, chomp.

"I need something to carry all my purchases in, chomp, chomp," Bad Dog, who was a logical dog, told herself. "Look at that black wool Mexican carrier that's hanging from that rack! Right there! Chomp, chomp. I want it." Bad Dog dug up all the goodness that was buried deep down in herself. "Down, dog! You don't have enough money to buy a bag. You're poor, just a mutt. You can carry that Mexican bag around. But you'll have to put it back before you leave the store. You will you will you will."

Since she could only afford to buy the one thing that she

most wanted, Bad Dog went searching for what she wanted the most. As soon as she saw it, she didn't have to think anymore because her wanting was so clear.

"I'm going to buy that turtle."

The turtle was still alive only because it was in a container of water.

Bad Dog sang to her turtle after she had purchased it,

Imagination arises
when there's no more reason
so the mind can make
a kingdom.

Halcyons will cease to prey on fish,
poisonous leaves become our food
all sailors be without remorse,
for your lips have been stained in blood.

Still in that store, Bad Dog was lying on a bed. The room was the roof of the very store in which she had bought the turtle. As she looked up at its ceiling, she saw her turtle shoot across the top of the room.

This was how the turtle shot: its tongue extended clear to the other side, then fastened itself, the disc near the tip of the tongue, which was white paste rather than mucous membrane, onto its prey.

"Cool," said Bad Dog. "Obviously I made the correct purchase."

The screen of the TV that was standing in front of her eyes turned on. The screen was video, since it was slightly larger than a TV would be.

She saw a show that looked like an ad. In it, the turtle was like a white horse, only stranger. Afterwards, still in the video, a man wearing the kind of crumbled, white suit rich men always sport in the tropics when they're in a movie began talking about the environment to the viewer of the TV. By the end of the video the viewer was watching, the man's clean-shaven visage had become covered in rough growth, in stubble; the white suit was filthy: such changes indicated to the viewer that the speaker had become a revolutionary. Bad Dog liked this turn of affairs! She especially liked this guy now that he was a white or an Hispanic incendiary in his once-white bum's suit!

Environment terrorism erupted on TV. Everything burned down. It erupted through TV: whatever was like a white horse only stranger appeared outside the TV, right in Bad Dog's bedroom.

She began to think about what was stranger than horse or horse all the time because that's what you do when you fall in love. Because she loved horse so much, she knew exactly what it was thinking: it wanted to go outside so it could eat. It was as hungry as Bad Dog. Chomp, chomp. Maybe hungrier.

Bad Dog thought to herself: What decision am I going to make? I know horse wants to trot, gallop, down the stairs that fall from the edge of the terrace that lies off of this room. I should have thought of all this before now. But I'm a bad dog. I should have bought oats at the same time that I bought turtle because oats are what horsies eat. What am I going to do? Should I let horse go outside by himself? It's dangerous in the outside and horse has no protection. Am I hurting horse even worse by shutting him in here with me?

Despite her misgivings, Bad Dog let horse go.

She returned to us and told us that now she knew where pirates came from.

Bad Dog's Story

"Pirates came from the moment when animals became holy."

"We who are born: The name of our Lord, our Lord of birth, of the Lord of Genealogy, is Prajāpati.

"Prior to all birth, there was only chaos, cruelty, wildness. This god who was wild, outside of life and death, existed before the Lord of Genealogy, before genealogy, before the morning of the world began.

"The Wild God, that pirate, sets all on fire.

"Afraid that he's going to die and even more frightened to live in fear, the Lord of Genealogy begs the Wild God not to set him on fire. 'I'll do anything you want if you let me live.'

"The Wild One answered that there would still be birth and death in this world, that there would still be this world, only if the Lord of Genealogy made him Lord of the Animals, whose name is Pāsupati."

"That's why there are pirates," said Bad Dog.

Where Boys Come From

It was King Pussy who introduced the punk boys to us. At the time she had met them, her first days in the bottom of this world, she had believed that she would never talk to anyone. That she would always remain Pussy, the girl who lives inside her own head.

They had believed the same about themselves. That they

were rotten. This was how Pussy and the boys got together.

The day on which Pussy introduced them, one afternoon so devoid of sun that it had already become evening, we saw nothing because we were tucked inside the Bald Head, she told us more. More as if moving further out on the ocean. Told us she had encountered them in a restaurant.

Pussy never differentiates between dream and waking.

That restaurant, unlike the rest of the rooms in Brighton, was as large as a New York City art gallery. And as empty. Puss had walked into its upstairs as if into one of her memories.

As soon as she was in there, she had to go to the bathroom.

The bathroom was to a regular one as that restaurant was to the usual Brighton restaurant. While examining her face in the large mirror over the three sinks, she saw a form . . . a man . . . in black leather . . . S&M . . .

He moved into the space that was, at that moment, her space.

Pussy didn't know whether or not to be scared. The more she tried to think, the slower the moments moved. When there was no more time, she yelled out the names of some of those who were outside the bathroom because they worked in the restaurant. She hadn't spoken out loud because she was scared.

Not understanding why she wasn't scared now, she walked out of this bathroom.

Below the two restaurant floors lay a beauty parlor in which all sorts of trinkets were for sale. Bad guys . . . milled about in there. They were wearing black leather.

The joint was a hangout for the punk boys.

The instant that Pussy laid eyes on the boys, she saw an ocean in all its glory. Glory which is infinity. The ocean has no bottom, is all surface. A waterfall looking like a fountain rises out of the surface.

Pussy looked down, saw that she was holding a key. Yellow plastic covered its sides and top; it emitted weird rays.

"This isn't what you're used to," one of the dangerous skinnies explained to the girl, " 'cause your life's been defined by poverty, by the roughest possible street conditions."

Pussy knew this was true. She looked around her.

"Our beauty parlor's also an art gallery. This kind of art's quiet, but there's a lot going on here."

This was when Pussy knew that she should listen to the boys.

The day we met them, they explained their origins. In a Christian society, such as the one that's now in the middle of its dying, those who truly believe in Jesus Christ do so by imitating his life. The punk boys wanted to become Antonin Artaud. "A. Our Toad," said the punk boys. In the beginning.

A. Our Toad had been born on September 4, 1896, in Paris. Near the zoo.

While he had been alive, especially as he had grown older, he had had few friends, almost none of them young boys. A few delinquents had followed him around.

"The most alienated of all artistpoets"—this was the kind of thing the romantic boys also told us while they were spitting—"A. Our Toad wrote about himself":

This childkid
he isn't there

he isn't anywhere
because he's only an angle
who's about to happen

The punk boys continued to pick their noses while they quoted Our Toad:

this world of Christianfathermother is the one that must go
away,
this world of split-in-two or constant-union-always-longing-for-
total-unification,
around which the whole system of this society is turning,
this world of fathermother malignantly sustained by the most
somber organization.

" 'I WILL NOT HAVE ORGANIZATION!' screamed Our Toad, as his fingers picked at his brains as if brains were worms to be eaten:

" 'It must be understood that all intelligence is only contingent, that one can lose it, not as a lunatic who's dead (that's what I'm becoming), but as a living person who, at the same time, feels intelligence working in himself.'

"Our Toad went loony, either before he was electroshocked, perhaps because he had been using too many hard drugs, or after he underwent several series of treatments.

"In the first days of his stay in the sanatorium of Rodez, the artistpoet wrote his doctor, Ferdière: 'You're a great mind and a great heart and I know that you've gone to the bottom of things and that you've perceived the Truth.'

"Five years before those first Days of the Rodez Sanatorium, in 1938, the Italian physician Ugo Cerletti had visited a Roman abattoir, where he had watched pigs being slaughtered.

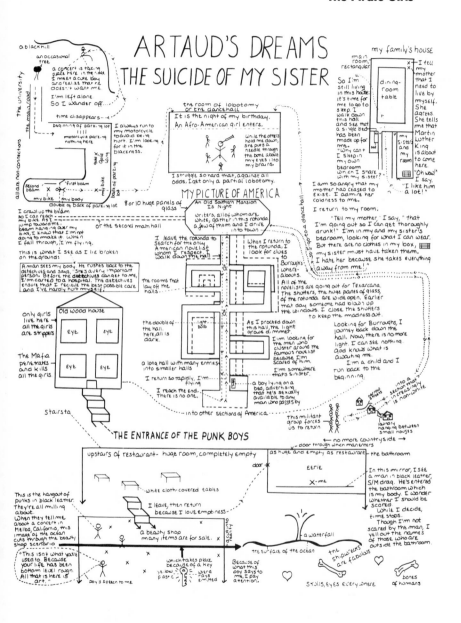

ARTAUD'S DREAMS
THE SUICIDE OF MY SISTER

" 'as yet there's no angle.' "

He saw that the electric shock being administered to their skulls was rendering them more willing to die.

"In electroshock therapy, the patient is carefully tied down so that her limbs won't fracture during the convulsions which always accompany this procedure. So that her teeth neither break each other nor bite through the tongue, a spatula is placed inside her mouth.

"After the patient has undergone electroshock, she falls into a coma that lasts between fifteen and thirty minutes. Awakes with only part or none of her memory.

"Dr. Ferdière was attracted by the innocence of this curative procedure. Between May 23 and June 10, 1944, he administered to Our Toad twelve electroshock treatments; in August 1944, twelve; in December 1944, twelve.

"Following one of the treatments, the artistpoet's coma lasted so long that Ferdy decided his patient had died and so sent him, or only his body, off to the mortuary. In there, Arty Toad came back to consciousness.

"Having returned to life, still in that Rodez hospital, Our Toad wrote to another doctor: 'It was you yourself who last August put an end to the electroshock treatments which were so terrible for me, because you realized that this was not a treatment I should have to undergo, that a man like myself did not need to be treated, but, on the contrary, helped in his work. Electroshock, M. Latrémolière, reduces me to despair, it takes away my memory, it dulls my mind and my heart, it turns me into someone who's absent and who knows he is absent and sees himself for weeks in pursuit of his being, like a dead man alongside a living man who is no longer himself, but who insists on the dead man being present even though he can no longer enter into him. I've a great deal of affection for you and you know it, but if you do not stop these electroshock treatments at once I shall no longer be able to keep you in my heart.'

"A writer, the artistpoet loved to write about other writers:

> " 'For when Poe was found dead one morning on a sidewalk in Baltimore, it was not because of an attack of delirium tremens brought on by alcohol, but because a few bastards who hated his genius and despised his poetry poisoned him to prevent him from living and so from offering that extraordinary terrifying solace that is revealed in his verses.
>
> " 'It is permissible,' and this is important,"

said the most romantic of boys,

> " 'to invent one's language, and it is further permissible to make language with extragrammatical meanings, but then these meanings must be valid in themselves. That is, they must come out of anguish. I like the poems of the starving, the sick, the outcast, the poisoned: François Villon, Charles Baudelaire, Edgar Allan Poe, Gérard de Nerval, and the poems of the executed criminals of language who suffer ruin in their writing . . .' "

There were a few boys who, during his lifetime, took the artistpoet's writing seriously. Thought his work on the body of the family and the family of the body and his intense belief that this body must change and continue to change so important that they began to follow him. They wanted to be him.

A little before eight in the morning on March 4, Our Toad, like a kid, died somewhere in China. At the moment of his death, his language split into forgettable, unreadable fragments.

The boys could no longer follow anyone, for there was no one left to follow. So they traveled to England.

"There were boys and boys and boys.

"Then there was us."

Their first days in that dead town, Brighton, the punk boys didn't know what to do with themselves, so they perused books. Everything they read was about a boy.

The scummy brats told us his story as romantically as they could.

"Though this boy had a girlfriend named Slut Girl, what was most important of all to him was that he never made her pregnant.

"Everyone used to know that."

"There's no more literacy," King Pussy said. Then she passed out.

"What is this shit about us? About women?" roared MD. And kicked a fish.

"Cut off their heads for not wanting women to have lots of babies when they want to have babies," the footless pirate chimed in. No boy contradicted her.

"What no one knows is that, even though Slut Girl didn't want to leave Brat Rat, she wanted to have a baby.

"Slut Girl had two loves: wanting a baby and taking a bath. She didn't give a shit about being clean; she was residing in a graveyard. No, what she adored was to lay for hours in water. When, where there were lots of odors, those of the night, of owls hiding their eyes behind their own feathers, of rose lavender rosemary, of the buds that bloom in the dark. Of the evening and of dreams, snakes in search of rats who were no longer stuffed, leaves drenched in the liquid mud that was falling out of the sky. The perfume or stench of rancid pools caught in the crevices beneath the soil. Slut Girl loved to smell herself.

"Late one night—it was almost morning—while she was in the water, taking a pumice stone, she began to rub at her skin. Scum lay across the water. Out of her own residue, she shaped a boy.

"Bits of crap remained on the water.

"There came a knocking on her door.

"Knock, knock."

" 'Oh no,' said Slut Girl. She had no intention of letting anyone in. '———!' for she didn't know what to call her son yet. 'Protect me! Guard my door!'

"Dutifully, this son, wet, leapt to the door, yanked it wide open, then began to beat up the man who was on the other side.

"Punk Boy had been trying to walk into his own home and he was pissed."

"Like me," murmured Pussy.

"Being an elitist, he had no intention of fighting with his own hands. He might get a spot on them. Punk Boy called to some of his skeletons, his lads, the ghoulie tongues and spermy skins, who always accompanied him. Boys hanging around, trying to jerk off. Being a demon, one of them sliced off the head of Punk Boy's son without any effort.

"Of little Punk Boy.

"When the beautiful girl saw the headless body of her child, she started to cry. Wanting to leave the world, she cried out her eyes. The eyes wandered.

"Punk Boy recognized that he had caused the one with whom he was living to become blind. He had to do something to restore her sight. So she'd again want to see.

"He walked up to the first sentient being whom he caught sight of and cut off the head.

"He picked up this head, which had originally come off an elephant, and placed it on his son's red neck.

"Slut Girl and Punk Boy named their nameless son: Ganesh."

Thus the punk boys told us what it is to be a pirate. We joined up with them. It was only now that we were able to make up the rules of piracy.

The Rules of Piracy

1. Regarding Purpose:
   To find that place out of which we come.

   a. Explanation:
      "Gaja" ("elephant") means "the origin and the goal."
      i. "ga" = "goal"
      ii. "ja" = "origin"

2. Regarding the Identity of All Those Who Undertake the Acts or Infiltrations of Piracy:
   Half-human half-beast.

   a. Explanation:
   According to the story, which is the only truth around these miserable parts, these dead isles, the elephant sits on the human.

   b. Explanation of explanation:
   The head sits on the body.

3. Regarding Identity:
   There are no pirates anymore.

   a. Explanation:
   In the world in which we live, a human isn't an elephant.

   b. All pirates dream animals.
      i. Explanation of explanation:
      Dreams are manifestations of identities.

4. On Pirate Methods and Methodologies:
   Crooked.

   a. Explanation:
   The elephant's trunk is crooked.
   "His face, shape of the Self, is crooked."

   b. There are no pirates anymore so we have to be crooked as hell in order to exist and WE ARE EXISTING.

5. The Purpose of Pirating:
   Stealing.

   a. Explanation:
   Pirates are the destroyers of all obstacles.
   "I bow to the son of Síva, to the embodiment of the
   giver of gifts who destroys obstacles and fear."

6. Where Pirates Live Free of Authority:
   Caves.

   a. Explanation:
   Nothing and no one's straight.

7. Regarding Pirate Purpose:
   To find buried treasure.

8. Regarding Direction of Sailing:
   Buried treasure is hidden in caves at the centers of labyrinths.

9.

The Pirate Banner

The Beginning of Creation

The Black Flag

paths which lead to the cave as crooked as possible

Black which can be seen

The cave containing the buried treasure

Red flowers

Big ears because she loves to gossip

Red

Red Teeth

Red

Red, Fat Ratski

Scroll — Rat Takes all

a. Explanation:
In the end, rats.
   i. "Musa" ("mouse" or "rat") comes from the root
   "mus" ("to steal").

Ratski is fat because everything in the world sits inside her belly because she never sits inside any belly because, if she did, she'd tear right through it. Her fur is red. Whenever anyone in the world thinks she's feeling pleasure, it's Ratski who's really feeling this pleasure because Ratski steals everything and anything.

No one ever finds Ratski: she lives inside the interstices of the world. Located between red flowers. The name of each interstice is "intellect."

Ratski's always on the rag.

. . . and so the reign of girl piracy began . . .

In the Days of the Pirates

Pirate Island

DREAMING REALITY

The whole rotten world
come down and break

– the moon cracks
my cunt

and I'm crawling
through these cracks

I've never had a lover
not in the world that exists
I've never wanted one
piss on my teeth, shit and piss.

(poem by Ange,
'cause poetry is what
fucks up this world)

I wanted to die . . .
I'm a girl,
night is my eyes,
die for a while.

While the world cracks open
and all the rich men die,
and all the fucks who've sat on my face,
those sniveling shites.

We come crawling through these cracks, orphans, lobotomies;
if you ask me what I want I'll tell you
I want everything.

Whole rotten world come down and break.
Let me spread my legs.

— claws or whiskers

— tongue

rats coming out
of broken egg half

Three seats away from us on a Northern tube line, three children argued about which passengers they should mug. The fattest of the two boys spoke in a high feminine voice. Outside the train, the pickpockets waited by ticket booths. As we walked on the garbage, I kicked a turkey bone spotted with blood.

Dogs were sitting everywhere.

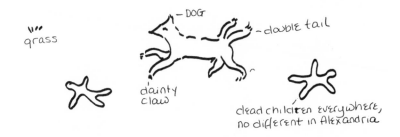

grass
— DOG
— double tail
dainty claw
dead children everywhere, no different in Alexandria

"I don't want to ever be here again," I said as we were leaving London.

It was then that we met this other girl. She was one of the strangest things anyone'd want to see. Tiny with hairs so stiff with muck that every disease in the world seemed to have been celebrating her birthday.

Later I would learn that every day *was* this brat's birthday.

We followed her down to a section which seemed to me to be a place where I had already lived.

Ange reminded me that we didn't live anywhere. "There are more dead men here than where we just were."

"That's what I'm looking for."

So we chose a hotel like the brat's hair. Somewhere between dirt and scum.

The brat explained to us that there weren't any dogs in this town, but there had been pirates. She herself lived above this pub where there were a lot of girls like her. That is, as grimy. Almost. Knives were sitting in the walls 'cause most of the girls owned knives and, when they had hair, whether above or below, kept them in there. Some didn't have any teeth and some plucked their teeth right out of their mouths.

They hung with a few boys known as *punk boys*.

Now, the pub was a block from the mucky hotel. These two wooden buildings, each two stories in height, were the only things that stood up in this part of town. Empty lots, sand, and countryside remained.

I dreamt that this section was city and country because, here, one was the other.

The hotel was a hut because, inside, metal was being changed. The components of computer electromagnetic disease were being transformed into something else. Something like dream.

"You have to go down." That was what the brat had said the first time we met her.

To forget is *to transform* or *transmute*. I had thought that the practices of alchemy were forgotten. But St. Barbara had said in one of her letters, "When history goes to sleep, we shall walk around the hut."

Now I further understood, but I didn't know, that any metal object, such as a brake lever nut, in itself holds traces of its owner's past. Of all the activities that composed that personal past. To the extent that *personal* means anything. In the hut, the traces of history were removed from each piece of metal.

My father had left me before I was born.

Suddenly I realized that the gimp was explaining to Ange and me that she owned the pub. Though she didn't look like she owned anything.

"I don't want to own," she whispered. "Much less be a landlord. Even of a building that isn't a building 'cause some of its walls are missing and rats live there even though most rats wouldn't go near it even if you paid them.

"This situation's making me so sick that I'm becoming physically sick.

"I wanna go back and be a sailor."

I had the idea that I should hire her to find some real ma-riners who could get Ange and me to the island on the map.

The gimp or whatever she was couldn't find the island by herself 'cause she didn't have a college diploma and she was a female. A good-for-nothing like Ange and me.

But she wasn't there to ask. Only a silver strand to remind me of her.

That night I dreamt that I left the hut to search for the silver-haired girl. The mist a few feet in front of the edifice was so thick, I could barely make out what lay ahead. As I stepped into that white, I could no longer see.

I turned around and headed for the only place I knew had lights.

There were many people there. The metal-changers. The ones who changed motorcycle nuts.

"They take all their preoccupations out," I said out loud.

The next day, Silver explained things more carefully to me. The reason she was so dirty was that her girls were dirty, being orphans and refugees and other kinds of rejects, even from rich families. They were the kind of girls who have no-where to go but to a pub. Of course she didn't want to offend these customers by taking a bath or washing her hair in the kitchen sink.

It was then that I perceived how really dirty she was. 'Cause of rats, 'cause I actually saw a rat, there, matting up her hair. In there, in the mat, were also used latex gloves, a knife or two, a broken comb.

The hair smelled like a mixture of rat waste and fish. "The ocean, that repository of our bodies including our shit and piss," further explained Silver, "is where the dead pirates live. Using their eyeballs as money, they buy the goods they

need, for while they were alive, they never bothered to purchase anything.

"Dead pirates are sailors' mates, 'cause to those who don't
own homes, death's as common as life."

I realized that she knew human things like angst and
loneliness so I started to confide in her. I even showed her the
map. Which I shouldn't have, but I'm too trusting.

She coughed a few times to remind me she was sick. "So
you'll need a ship and crew."

"I want to go here." And pointed again to the paper.

"You'll have to give me a copy of that map."

"No."

She coughed so violently that I began to feel sorry for her
'cause she took so little care of herself. She even looked like a
rat.

"This is what being a landlord does to you," Silver explained further. "COUGH. COUGH. Work all day work all
night. Until nothing's left of the world but work. Nothing left
in this endlessly lightless reality that can be called *life*.
COUGH. COUGH. Owning a pub—it's a dog's life. I'm an
old hound dog who's sniffing his way through a world that's
dying. COUGH. COUGH."

For a second, her words were making me see what it is to
grow old.

"No one cares about an old dog. COUGH. COUGH.
And this is why I care for orphaned brats."

"Me and Ange aren't brats."

With this, her voice changed and became a little girl's.
"Only thing an old female dog like me can do these days, these
nights," though she didn't look so old to me, "is help other
little girls find what they're looking for. She shook her silvery

hair. Which would have been silvery if she had ever taken a shower.

I was going down farther than I thought possible.

"Take me with you on your search for buried treasure," she begged.

I went back to the hotel and told Ange everything. That Silver was an old sailor but now kept a public house, and she knew all the girls in Brighton. That she was beginning to take me down.

Ange asked me what I meant by "down," so I told her to fuck off.

Ange took my head down and bashed it.

The next day, Silver brought me to her pub. The Bald Head. This time we weren't going down, for, though from the outside this shelter for drunks looked as if rats were using it for their gym, to my surprise, its insides were clean. Dainty red curtains hung across small windows. The floor, though its surface was sawdust, sparkled.

On the other hand, grimy girls were lying all over the floor except when they were lying on top of each other. At least half of the ones who were still conscious—it was about ten in the morning—were smoking cigars and viler protuberances. Through smoke thick enough to blind a Seeing Eye dog, I thought I was seeing glimpses of gold and silver, not over but inside those delicate bodies, jewelry at the most unlikely places disappearing into skin. Those who were the most drunk were so heavily tattooed I thought I was in a museum of girls lit, no longer by unnatural light, but by the sun that, lighting up the waters at the end of the day, reveals the roads that lead to buried treasure.

I turned to Silver.

"Here are the girls I told you about. The ones for whom you and what's-her-name have been looking. They even have a captain named Pussy."

I must have been looking a bit disapproving 'cause then she said that, though girls might look like alcoholics, I had to learn that when it comes to the sea, appearances are deceptive. Actually they were the toughest old salts she had ever met. They even had an available ship whose name was Mary and they had rigged it as well as any vessel, even in the past, has been prepared for the roughest and the most treacherous seas.

"Best of all, it's a rowboat."

"What?"

"Your fucking Pirate Island or whatever you call that dump . . ."

"It's not a *dump*. This *pub* is a dump!"

". . . is only ninety miles from here. It's not as if you and your green-eyed companion are going halfway around the world."

"Where's the captain?" I demanded.

"She's not here 'cause she's off seeing visions."

"Oh."

"But look down here."

I peered below me to where I saw a tall, narrow girl lying between two gigantic wolfhounds.

"She can kill a man at forty yards. While chewing tobacco."

So I sort of saw the point of taking these repulsive girls with us on our search for buried treasure.

Then the silver-haired girl informed me that MD—that was dog-girl's name—could not only shoot, but also took baths. One of the dogs and the female skeleton now had their tongues entwined around each other's.

Something must have been happening to me, or inside me, I guess one's the other, 'cause I could no longer remember how I had felt when I was a whore.

Outside one of the windows, part of the sky was gray.

The gimp was almost licking my shoulder when I informed her that Ange and me would hire her and several of these girls to take us to the island on Ange's mother's map.

"All of us or nothing," she replied as soon as her tongue was free.

She wore red lipstick the next time that I saw her, though her hair was more voluminous with dirt than before. Owing, like everything else about these girls, to the fertility of rats.

Ange was with me, and the three of us went all the way down, down those Brighton streets that seem so narrow that they fall down. Until, on our right, several piers, each longer than any tampon string I had ever yet seen.

Past pier after pier until we came to one shaped like a crescent.

As if born out of the quartered moon, a boat.

A boat as long and as lean as a wolfhound, and twice as odoriferous. Distorted without the help of sun, for there wasn't much of that in this town of rotting men.

Obviously a number of animals were still living in its hold: in addition to the usual feces, there were many webs, nests, and chewed-up socks. Two colorful fish heads.

All sorts of fungi, mosses, and the beginning of a mussel family were growing over the wood. Ange was so hungry that she wanted to call this ship *Crawling Into My Mouth*.

I told her no, that was a bad idea. A rat slithered out of Silver's hair, so I said, "We don't have to give it a name . . ."

"We don't?"

"Do we know who wrote the map that we're following? Do we know the rubrics of those dead pirates, living in the ruby oceans, who'll guide our steps?" The metal has been changed, I thought: metal tracings or memories overthrown. "No."

And so I turned to Silver. "Tell me, girl, when do we sail?"

"I'm not always a girl." One of her fingers was dipping into the scalp at the spot where the rat had crawled out.

"Oh."

For a second, I remembered a dream that Ange and I once had. But memory was overthrown.

"We sail tomorrow."

INTO THE STRANGE

"Yo ho ho and a bottle of rum," Silver's voice rang out . . .

> and all that's old has turned to scum
> for this world's begun to burn.

> Two girls lost on a dead man's chest
> doing what they like to best,
> pecking at unknown alphabets,
> alphabets that lead to gold
> across seas made up of stars,
> dreams glittering under dead men's bones.

Ten filthy girls on a dead man's chest
doing what they like to best,
girls who spit right up your ass,
girls who'll take all that you own,
knife you in your turned-up breast:

All that you own will turn to scum
and the world begin to burn . . .

And so we set sail.

Just before leaving, MD had brought her two wolfhounds on board with her. Nobody seemed to think this unusual. They were as tall and as lean as her: all seemed to be continually swaying. Ange said she could smell the booze crawling out of all three of the mouths.

I confided to the silver-haired girl that I had had an affair with a decayed alcoholic back in China that had so devastated me that I can never be close to anyone.

She replied that MD never touched a drop of the stuff. She would swear, as would every girl, that there was no drink on this board.

Rats come out from broken eggs,
eating all the nights and days,
then crawl inside our unwashed hairs,
drinking down the fluids there.

Pussy, the captain, wore a bandage around her eyes because, she explained, a dream had wounded her.

So it was Silver, a few days into the journey, who ordered Bad Dog to be second in command.

This sailor was so ugly that the gulls and more vulturous

birds, in fear, flew away from her. One of these birds became so disconcerted that it flew right through our sail. From then on, we had to use the small motor found in the back of the boat.

This was just one of the ways in which Pussy commanded.

What I remember aren't the details of that which happened between girl and girl. After all is gone, what I remember are the colors of Silver's hairs. How the smell of it was the same as its colors.

Smell and color were the stars that sat on my head every night. Layers sat over layers of stars until there appeared that fabric which the girls named *night*.

Girls passed out on the deck below.

A few of them had vomited into the shreds of the sail. In memory of all childhoods.

Then Silver chose me to be her confidante. She whispered to me that Bad Dog was first mate because, besides being ugly, she had all the characteristics of a horny mongrel with rabies. A rare character in a girl. This mariner was so mean that whenever any part of a girl's body happened to rove within four or so inches of her mouth, she bit *it*. That is, *the girl*. Dog-face sharpened her teeth about once a month. So it wasn't that the new mate didn't know how to give orders: it was that she barked before thinking.

The girls liked her being in command because none of them wanted that position. Or any position. Moreover, Bad Dog kept the deck clean as a result of her diet. She ate rats. In fact, there was something in Bad Dog that was as emotionless, or nonhuman, as mean cold deceptive and smart, as a rat. In the late afternoon, when the sun was turning the color of blood, after the dog-puss had munched down a score or so of rats—she disdained mice—she'd clean the remnants of their bones off her teeth with drink. So did the rest of the girls who hadn't champed on rodent fur. Though Silver had said that the ship was clean of such evil.

But Bad Dog became drunker than any other girl because she'd never pass out.

The drunker this square-shaped mate turned, the more sexually attractive. She was so vile, physically, that she was highly attractive to begin with to all but the most confirmed old farts such as Pussycat and Silver. Whenever a young girl, hovering around Bad Dog, became so drunk that she made a direct move for Bad Dog's body, Bad Dog chewed on her.

As the stars sat upon our heads and disappeared and reappeared from our heads, until Ange and I felt that we were being carried into wonder, Bad Dog grew fonder of booze. Soon she was drinking everyone's scotch and beer. Her motor functions, her perceptual faculties, slowed down to such an extent that she was no longer aware of all that was taking place around her.

As all the drunken girls lay there in the stars which were night's flames.

One night, Bad Dog fell onto the deck and cut herself. She lay in her own blood. Another night she turned more violent than usual and cut a child who, probably because she didn't yet know what sex was, thought she was Dog's girlfriend.

It was then that Ange said that Bad Dog really was a dog.

The fonder of drink the mangy sailor became, the more, out of pure viciousness, she encouraged fights among the other girls. Fights often caused by her lies. None of us minded when, one dark night, she disappeared.

Wherever bad girls go.

Pussy didn't notice that anything had happened.

It was as if all this was leading up to something, and when that something happened, it was the last thing that I expected.

TO ALL THE DEAD DOGS OF THIS WORLD

A few days later, I saw Bad Dog chewing on a rat. I thought, it must be dinnertime. At the same time, because mutt-girl was no longer available to clean our deck, a three-foot-long rat stepped over my foot.

Almost all of the crew happened to be vegetarians.

My vision of Bad Dog munching on a rat, for an unknown reason, had made me hungry. I ran over to the barrel in which most of our perishable food had been stored. As I peered into that darkness, I realized that there were only apples left and that most of them had been chewed by vermin.

I must have dealt with the hunger by falling asleep, because the next thing I knew, the silver-haired girl was whispering in my ear.

Actually she was talking to another girl in front of the barrel behind which I had fallen asleep.

". . . the ships I've seen, amuck with blood and fit to sink with precious stones . . ."

"Where are all those criminal hearts now?"

"Dead, and swimming between the bones of other dead criminals. White bones on white bones."

Where are all those dogs tonight?
For dead dogs cannot bite.

Silver again answered, "To all the dead dogs of this world: You were the roughest the world's ever known and the devil himself was afeared to go to sea with you."

"But what are we going to do about getting our hands on the map?"

I could hear voices all around me. There were two of them. I was back in the hall in which I couldn't see. In the threshold of my parents' bedroom. They were discussing my character in words I could barely hear. For the first time, I knew that I didn't belong in this human world.

"Let's kill 'em," answered Silver.

"I can't kill girls."

"You haven't yet. But they've got the map."

Crouched on the deck slimy with all sorts of mucus, I was missing childhood, or all that I had never known.

Crouched in that dark, in that human and rat spit, I was a child because I was in a world of animosity. My mother was a monster because human mothers always love their daughters and because she wanted to kill me. Since I knew that monsters are born from the imagination, I had to get rid of my imagination.

I had to find out who my mother really was.

"Once we get hold of the map, we won't have to murder 'em," remarked the other girl.

"Who bites? I'll tell you who bites. Dead dogs don't bite."

"You mean even if we get the map and the treasure, they can hurt us in some way?"

I was beginning to recognize this voice.

"Yeah. They'll rat on us to the authorities so they can get their treasure back, or, if not that, so they can ask for justice and then we'll be hung from the highest yardarm without any clothes on. *Dead dogs don't bite.*"

Now I knew what I knew when I was a child. That they were coming for me . . .

If they found me . . . My heart sat in my mouth. And filled it with blood.

This must have been what it was like when I was a child.

All that I could no longer remember.

Girls.

Pussycat—now I could clearly recognize her voice—said she was hungry. She started to walk toward the barrel of vermin and apple. I heard her footsteps.

The winds were blowing through patches of fog so thick with gray that no more objects could be seen. Neither birds nor whatever clouds were moving fast through that sky. Perhaps there was a break in all the gray of the world, for suddenly a separate voice cried out, "Land!"

Then the fog belt lifted and the moon appeared. Through an opening not of but into the sky, I saw that the differences of the world had become visible. In front of my eyes, there was a horizontal line. It was as if the sky had separated itself into two sections. Each area was a different color black.

The stars were opening, and lighting up more and more of the deck. Most of the girls were there, standing and lying below those stars. So much I saw, almost in a dream, for I had not yet recovered from my fear.

I didn't realize that for the time being my life was safe.

"Have any of you," asked the captain whose eyes were bandaged, "have any of you ever seen that land before?"

"Aye, Sir," answered the girl whose golden hairs were trying to fly away, "when I used to ship out with Captain Bonny."

"And what's it called?"

"Pas Sang Rouge. Or Pirate Island. It was a place for mutinied sailors once, thus its rubric, and a hand on board Bonny's boat knew all their names. That hill there . . ."

"I can't see it," said Pussy.

"It's where the pirates cleaned the worms out of their booty and drew up false maps showing where booty was to be found," explained Silver.

"So now we know where we are. All of you, do what you have to do, and so, we'll reach this land!" Pussy walked out, stumbling only slightly, and the rest of the girls, except for those who had passed out on that star-drenched deck, followed her.

I was waiting for them all to go away so I could run to Ange. Who was sleeping, so she was still seeing the splendor of the world. Run to her and tell her all that had just happened and that we still had the chart.

I had to explain to her that these girls didn't mean us any good.

And we should plan our escape.

I saw Silver drawing near to me. I knew that, for the moment, she couldn't harm me because there were too many girls around, even if they were drunk, and because she still didn't know where the map was, so I just stood up thinking that she would think that I had come out on the deck with the other girls as soon as we had heard the cry "Land!"

But before I could, with all those other girls, find my way below deck to the hold, she laid her hand on my shoulder.

I didn't want her to know that I was aware what her plans

really were, her real intentions toward me and Ange. That I knew the crew was a crew of criminals, so I let that hand sit on my shoulder.

I didn't say one word.

Under the still opening stars.

"Look," says the silver-haired girl, "and I'll tell you where we're going to go." Her hand was no longer sitting on my shoulder. "I've been there before: I can show you the ways and the byways and the paths and its labyrinths so you won't become completely lost, utterly scared."

I didn't say a word.

"You're scared."

Now I could feel her hand again.

"Close your eyes." Her voice was in and inside my ear. At this moment, I parted from childhood.

Her other hand closed my eyes. "Where do you want to go most?"

I knew that she was duplicitous, cruel, and powerful and that I shouldn't trust her but, at the same time, I knew that I did trust her, though I didn't know why. I trusted her because I had to because that's how I was.

Her hand had moved deeper, as if pirates were exploring and I was their explored. "I'll take you somewhere you don't know about and then you'll be able to open your eyes."

The stars were still shining, or maybe they weren't, because everything was becoming everything else while the inside, through skin or through the disappearance of difference, turned into outside.

My body took over consciousness. Fell asleep as if in a faint. All was pleasant where I now was, and quiet. Lilac and gray, the water mirrored the air.

I was truly seeing land.

Long, tall trees equaled shadows.

Finally the boat again set sail. Beneath it, the water resembled the air as long as there was no possibility of coming so the coming was more violent. Kept on going because the water and air, mirroring each other, were boundless.

Deeper in there, the animals came out. Fur then fur. There were lots of little animals so I couldn't stop.

"Beep beep," cried the little animals, "beep beep."

"I'm going to find somewhere where the gray is going on there," I said. There was no one to hear me. "I'll go there over again."

I went there over again so green painted the landscape. So intense it could barely be handled.

By the time I could speak again, though I had lost all meaning, Silver was gone.

I couldn't tell Ange what had happened, though I did.

PISSING IN THE SUN

I know that we change continually when we're alive, but I don't know whether that's true in dreams. And all that's past lives in the realm of dreams.

After I had talked to Ange and cried and she had cried, I must have fallen asleep.

For I was back in China.

The alcoholic's profession was rat-killer. 'Cause we were together in China, he took me out to a Chinese restaurant, where he ate rats. Crunched them up good between his teeth.

I refused to kiss him.

I'm not into guns and he took me to a Chinese shooting gallery where they shot rats and I looked at this object that was in my hands and decided I'd try to use it once. Because I'll try anything. Once.

That was how I began being punished for rat-killing.

I was in back in my room, which is long, far in its back. A tiny mouse scooted across the carpet on which I was kneeling. It walked up to me. As it was trotting across my right arm, I became conscious, for the first time in my life, and saw that it was playing too hard with me. It used its claws and teeth.

I began to wonder about what it might be.

It was walking over the carpet next to the right side of my body, so I put my hand over that bit of cloth and trapped what was under it. Tiny gray popped out between my fingers. But my boyfriend was helping me. I knew this really was a rat, so I put a knife right through its body.

Then I felt guilty, and guilt made me miserable.

Now I started to dream about Silver and not just about pirate girls. I was rising out of a bathtub, while Silver was sitting on its side. For she was the masseuse. I snapped my towel at her and said, "It's wet." For some reason, my action reminded me that there was sexual tension between us. I thought that she wanted me to kiss her, but since I wasn't sure how to kiss a girl I did nothing.

Now this brat and I were having sex on a narrow cot mattress almost the size of a bathroom in a room the same size as the bathroom so it could have been a bathroom. If bathrooms can change. They can. In front of my head, there rose or I saw this wood door through which I could hear the noises from the girl next door. I hadn't heard anything before, not from over there. She must lead a boring life, I used to think, for she never does anything.

I was hearing myself.

The door opened, even though it was the door to all that lay outside and so, I knew, should be locked. But then I forgot to tell Silver, who happened to be under me, that the front door was open, because I was so interested in fucking.

When all of our fucking was over, I crawled down to between the walls and the bed. To the floor down there. Through a letter slot in the back wall, wetness was coming through. It must have been dribbling down for a while 'cause all of the floor was damp.

Plastic bags had been put on the floor to protect it from all that wetness, but all they did was hide the floor.

Then, the tip of a shovel's head as full of dirt as if it had been digging a grave appeared through the slot. Like a tongue. A tongue's a letter. I knew it was a tongue because I felt it up.

Something under the bed which I couldn't see began tugging at, and holding on to, my bathrobe's hem.

For it was morning and dreams had ended.

While Ange and I had been dreaming, as if we had been dreaming pirate girls, the boat had made a great deal of way. It was now lying about half a mile southeast of earth.

It was the beginning of a world.

Caught in whatever dreams boats dream, dreams of being pursued by bloodthirsty pirates, yet less and less able to move, for the waters around the boat grow thicker and thicker. Caught in a mixture of mud and water, our boat sat.

We had to dig away the slime to free the bottom ribs of the rowboat. As we parted mud from mud, that which looked solid and behaved like liquid from scum, or that which will not allow itself to be separated, strange vapors rose and insects, those who swim in the air, moved in front of our eyes. As if we were seeing pop art. Their colors were that brilliant. The thin wings and protruding eyeballs, hovering still in our minds, diseased whatever they touched there. Slugs were alive in the brown, and those long worms whose numerous white protuberances had something to do with our sexuality. Or that from which we had come.

In this manner, we were able to approach the shore about which Ange and I had dreamt back in another world.

This was a shore caught between dream and visibility.

I was working my butt off because all of the other pirates except for Ange and Silver, or so I thought, had either passed out due to a bottle of mescal now empty and lying by a rat who must have died from the same thing, or they had no intention of doing anything anymore.

Mud and semiliquid substances so disgusting I didn't want to know what they were, covered me, just as God must have been covered when he made His world.

The ship touched something that felt like earth.

I didn't give a shit 'cause I was staring at Silver. She might be a murderer, but she was beautiful, with her silver hairs thrown all over the winds of the world.

"A bad sign of what's to come," said this girl.

Probably she was talking about the smells that were rising up from me. I knew that she didn't care about me, for she didn't have any feelings like most girls have feelings.

This thing whose hair was gold, who was standing right behind Silver, put her arms around the brat.

The birds were wheeling and shrieking, and I knew their

beaks were sharp as razors, and then they saw us, me and Silver and Gold, these soaring beings who had preceded the insects and worms, and not understanding what they saw, again started to shriek.

It wasn't earth but a rock that had torn through the ship's side. Nevertheless, here lay the beginning of the world. The moment just before it began. Because I could see that which I couldn't yet touch. I saw ponds in the earth, gray and lilac and green, then birds feeding at them. Grass was growing, here and there, in huge tufts and clumps, then not at all. Howsoever it pleased. For the rocks lay in order and then, not: whatever was in front of my eyes seemed to be doing whatsoever it wanted.

Most of the pirates were drunk enough to be as good as dead.

But Silver wanted to explore.

I did too.

Ange reminded me about the past. "The map my dead mother gave us."

"Don't get sentimental."

"Don't you want to find buried treasure?"

"Of course I do." I paused. "That map might have come from your mother's body, but it's dead men's talk. Pirates' tales. Men who cut off women's fingers so they could do worse."

"Ate eyeballs," suggested Ange.

That sounded pretty good. Now this is when I made a really bad mistake, and my first one. Because of this mistake, I would find out who Silver really was.

I was pulling the map, ruined as it was, out of my pocket when I knew that I just had to explore.

Ange called out after me.

Then, Silver. When I saw that she saw that I was following her, I went the other way.

Alone, I reached the forest which I had just seen.

SILVER'S HAIRS

I saw snakes. I couldn't tell one from the other. They sat on these small rocks in the sun.

One raised his head at me and made a noise like a top when it's spinning. But not really like that. Each sound here was strange to my ears.

I wanted to talk to the snakes, but then I saw a marsh. Up close.

All yellow, it seemed to be in the ground, and, at the same time, it seemed to be growing along the sand like a bramble on steroids.

I followed it to the edge of another body of filthy water. I saw that the marshes were the streets in this nonhuman town. I walked through one, and the next, until so much liquid sploshed into my shoes that my footsteps were that of an Abominable Snowman's.

For Nature was metamorphosing me.

Then, as soon as I reached a piece of dry sand, I stuck my butt on it and took off the drowned shoes. Now my feet, when I walked, were going to get all foul and smelly and even bloody from torn skin. The sun was mature the way a piece of fruit gets overripe. Even this air was smellier. A fowl, I think it was a mallard or a duck, I don't know what the difference is, was rising out of a clump of reeds behind me. Soon a great cloud of gulls began to honk.

Through their language, which I didn't understand, I heard, for the first time since I had been alone, what was human.

"Maybe you're only capable of loving one girl and giving her the kind of devotion I'd do anything for. The kind of love a girl dies for. I know that it isn't me you love. And so you don't give a shit about me, and I do you, and I know that you know I love you. That's how you are about everyone: you'd see us dead if it suited you and you wouldn't blink an eyelid."

"That's how I am."

"I still love you and you know that. And I know you don't me. My mother didn't love me and I loved her." Now I recognized the speaker. It was the prettiest girl in the crew, Gold. We called her *Virgin* because her father had raped her. "So I have to do whatever I have to do because I like myself . . ."

"What're you laying on me?" The colder Silver appeared, the angrier she was.

"You were wrong, Silver, about Bad Dog, and you're wrong about these two dumb girls."

"I do what I have to do," replied Silver, "for me and for all pirates."

"I'm going to go against you, Silver. I'm not going to get involved in your murderous plans, even if they involve digging up lots of buried treasure, and when we get back to town, I'm going to tell the authorities all the treacherous things that you've done."

"If you do such a thing as that, you'd better watch out that you possess a memory, 'cause you need a head to possess a memory."

"Do you think I'm scared of you?" and the girl whose hair

was the colors of the sun picked up a stone and threw it at the pirate.

Silver, who knew how to throw, immediately grabbed a rock, which happened to be the largest one around, and slammed it at the other's head.

Blood flowed out of the red dent where the object had hit. As she fell, I saw Silver jump on top of her, then, with a strange expression on her face, leap up and run off.

I felt that I was seeing what I had seen before. Only now I was really seeing it:

A face whose features couldn't yet be seen. Whose silver hairs were thrown all over the winds of the world.

Only I didn't know how to see what I was seeing.

When I looked for the golden-haired girl, she wasn't there.

Sections from _The Chronicles of the Pirates_

As Narrated by One of MD's Wolfhounds

THE SINKING OF A SHIP

Since the purpose of these chronicles is to place down for posterity, and whatever shall be after posterity, the histories of the pirate girls, it is not my place to talk about myself. For I am the writer of these chronicles.

Suffice it to say that the family to which I'm genetically tied claims descent from the greatest antiquity.

For my ancestors were there when the world began. For, if this world began by beginning, it must have begun in a division whose double name was, and is, _life/death._ My forebears were there, then, for Hecate had three names, _Uncreate, Life,_ and _Death,_ and three heads, lion, horse, and dog.

The pirate girls say that man defines God. And so the ancient Greeks, that is, men, sick of the priestesses and fortune-tellers who were controlling the future, transformed Hecate into *Death*. From then on, Hecate was invoked only during clandestine rites of magic, named *black* by the local politicians. And at the same time, I or my family was reduced to ordinary dog.

But I am nevertheless able to grant to any human her heart's desire. Suffice it to say that, like the pirate girls, I will still fuck anything.

—I just decided that I've talked too much about myself.

—*crucified from within by all that's intolerable in the world and proud of it*—that's my kind of writing

—I shall talk of myself no more

—except to say that I have always been faithful to MD, and ever shall, and she to me and my brother

—and so we came to the new world

—After Silver, Virgin, and The-One-Who-Has-The-Map— that's what we secretly named her—left the ship, all of us, some not noticing that we had reached land, continued to do what we usually did.

We did notice that there was a bad smell.

Pussycat, licking her lips, said that it was rising up from all the dead fish that were lying under us.

Ostracism took her fingers out of Pussycat in order to investigate. When she returned, she said that there were lots of dead fish everywhere.

Pussycat was ready to eat.

"This stink's making me sick," Morgan, or Kiss-of-Rot, added to the conversation. Her face, green, was becoming simultaneously greener and more colorless, so she decided to pass out instead.

Not just Kiss-of-Rot but all of the pirates wanted to return to the Bald Head Pub, the true home of rotten girls where the world was one of comfort. Where dainty red-velvet curtains hang in front of windows whatever the conditions outside. Whatever the time and weather of the world. Where there were neither medical benefits nor class distinctions nor any other amenities to disturb their quiet existence. Where they moved through their orgasms into the imagination of the world.

"Bald Head Pub," said Pussy, their dreamer, "home where and when there's no home to those who don't want one."

Not bothering to listen to their captain, that was usual, these rotten and rotting girls whispered mutiny to each other. Really foul words, especially words which made no sense.

Only the most criminal, the ones who, when they had hair, pulled clumps of it out of their skulls and placed those bundles in front of other people's eyes, Antigone and Pussycat, cursed out loud.

Now it was really stinky. So odoriferous that the clams who were lying in the mud-water below, shell-open, and the fish whose mouths were gaping even though they were dead, could see a wall of smell.

With mouths agape between legs.

Most of the pirates still didn't notice anything.

"I'm going to investigate." Curiosity-mad Antigone dived into the liquid. Being three feet deep, its bottom hit her head. Sitting up between the open-mouthed fish, she was the first pirate to perceive that the ship was going nowhere.

Now Captain Pussy started to make a speech about shipwrecks, but none of the pirates paid attention because they had begun to fight each other. Water was soaking through everything, water polluted by slime and dead fish heads, fish mouths open as if treasures could be found within. Water mixed with air and earth. Pussycat tried to kick MD, but the sea held her legs back. Half the deck hid under the water. Pussycat and Ostracism, tangled in each other's bodies, didn't notice that they were now lying in mud. Antigone rubbed her eyes with both her hands and got more crap into them. Filled with bits of starfish. When she tried to look through these eyes, the world had changed.

It looked as if the end of the world was the same as its beginning.

The battle broke out in earnest. Drops of water, slime, then blood flew through the lower part of the air. A sore breast, torn flesh at the right shoulder, bruises already turning all the colors of flesh that's already died. The viscous liquor that the girls were now in managed to buffer the worst of the blows, but not some poisonous scratches.

For the ship was sunk. All that could be seen was fingers of wood spread out and sticking up into, stinking up, the sky.

Thus, the girls visited the dead pirates who lived under the water.

Unnoticed, Ange disappeared in the direction her friend had gone.

King Pussy interrupted the speech she was trying to give to mutter, "First ship I ever lost."

It was the first time she had ever been on a ship.

Finally, Pussycat munched on a dead fish.

Wearied beyond endurance, the pirate girls fell back into the world of mud.

THE FALL OF A KING AND OF THE KINGSHIP OF PUSSY

King Pussy told all the girls who were lying in the mud and the water what was happening to them. According to her dreams. For Pussy no longer needed to be asleep to see dreams.

"All of us are now being tested for AIDS.

"This is how those tests are being done: needles, having been inserted into the lower spine, put in but principally draw out gooey yellow liquid. And a small amount of blood.

"In other words: a cracked egg yolk."

Now Pussy predicted the future:

"Half of the ones who're lying on top of the lofty hospital beds 'cause they're in the middle of being tested are men.

"I was only watching what was going on even though I was supposed to be being tested. But it looked like it hurt to be tested so I asked one guy, 'Does it hurt?'

" 'Yes.' "

Pussy is never too clear about things.

"I know that among these people I'm the only one who's refusing to be tested. And I know that I don't want to know this.

"All of the tests come out negative."

Relieved, MD went back to French-kissing my brother, who had just devoured a rat that wasn't yet dead.

"So I went away with the medical tester," continued Pussy. "I can't remember whether a he or a she." All of the

pirates were now listening entranced to their captain. They
didn't mind that they were sitting in mud or that jellyfish par-
ticles were dripping off their eyelashes.

"The countryside was anything but beautiful. As soon as
we were deep inside that gray and brown straw, she/he tested
me, by use of black boxes that looked like Geiger counters, for
all major diseases except AIDS.

"I had three of them. I knew this was true 'cause I was
watching those needles in the round glass windows waver in
the positive. Just a bit positive . . . that's positive.

"I was sick.

"How can this be? I was too terrified to answer myself, so
in desperation I asked the Medical Authority.

" 'It's probably because you have AIDS. That's why most
people get many of the kind of diseases you have at the same
time.'

"Now I panicked. She/he tested me for AIDS and I had
it.

"I was feeling the worst things that it's possible for a
human to feel.

"Then reality turned even worse:

"I was sitting in a second-story New York City–like apartment, the usual hole, like the Bald Head Pub, with a bunch of
my friends, about half of whom I didn't know. A man, whom I
had never seen before, set this room on fire.

"Because he had just been informed that he was positive.

"Through that disintegrating floor, we fell to the ground.
Which was the outside. Human-size automata, female, military, eight of them, in two lines, began to advance. A leg rises
straight up, another, military style—1, 2, 1, 2—someone must
have first activated them, they kept on closing in on us, for

they were planning to annihilate us. That was their one purpose in life. Meanwhile, a missile, flaming right through the
sky, hurtled toward us. Similar missiles explode, right there! In
the air! Just above our heads! War lies all around us and
human limbs are being lopped off!

"I guess I had gotten away from the war, 'cause I was inside a grocery store. Maria, you were in there with me. In that
grocery store." We called Maria *Black Monk* 'cause she was as
sweet and pure as a holy celibate. "You were crouching down
in front of those cash registers so no one could know you were
there."

That's typical behavior for Maria. She doesn't want to be
part of the human world.

"The cash registers were shelves filled with food. You
were crouching down because you were poor and had to steal."

"I will never recognize Restraint," Black Mary announced.

"When I asked you, 'cause even in dream I liked you,
what you wanted me to get you, for I see that you were skeletal
and homeless, you pointed toward boxes of dried milk.
Carnation.

"You spoke up for yourself: 'I want to eat white rice, not
dried milk. But I don't have money.'

"I knew that there was a causal connection between your
two sentences, but I didn't understand what it was.

" 'Will you steal for me?'

"From then on, we hung out together. In the dream, you
were beautiful and suicidal, and I didn't understand how you
could be both beautiful and suicidal.

"Nothing anymore made sense.

"Until everyone who had been tested told me that it had

been reported to each of them that they were positive. That the U.S. Army had done this and had activated the female au-tomata. They planned to exterminate all of us."

From then on, Pussy began to talk about herself. It was dream who was talking through her:

"After that war had taken place, the world was changed.

"From that time on, all my dreams were about cats."

The secret is that these girls aren't drunks, but dreamers and poets.

"The war had taken place and then there was a cat which belonged to a man and a woman. These humans were experi-mental poets and married to each other.

"The cat had the bathroom.

"I had the bedroom, which was in front of the house.

"The cat and I were on a train together. Though she had always been distant to me, now she opened up.

"I explained to the woman, whose name was C, that her pussy had become friendly.

"After Henri G., a psychic in London, had introduced me at a symposium, she said, while I was in full view of the audi-ence, 'Your job will be to improvise on the subject of *cats*.'

" 'Oh, please. Give me five minutes. I need to figure out what I'm going to say.'

"I started by walking over to the podium which was as tall as me. The larger it grew, the smaller me. As if I was Alice in Wonderland, since this pedestal was only a carton under a car-ton three times its size, I defeated all of it by carrying it away, and then I could see that the audience was moving backwards.

"I began to talk to them by describing C's pussy. I thought I was making sense, but they kept on laughing and talking among themselves.

"Some of them were lounging menacingly in the doorway to what lay outside.

"At least half of them were outside.

"When I began speaking again, there was no one left to listen to me."

King Pussy had just announced to us that she had failed as our captain. She would no longer be a leader.

"I had no more worth because, instead of an audience, there was a group of seventy-five or so schoolgirls, sitting, as they had been taught to do, in folding chairs in three rows.

"All of these girls came from privileged families.

"Because I no longer did anything successfully, I decided the world was void.

"Then I saw that the lecture hall was the interior of a church. A small church.

"Wooden pews were strewn everywhere, this way, that. Down on them, those who were homeless sat discussing their business among themselves. This is what's going on, I thought, not all that highfalutin culture that I've been part of.

"The homeless ended the meeting.

"I was outside the church with C.

"I wanted to go to a punk bar, but there were no more punk bars anymore, and besides, C, the poet, wanted to go to a nice-girl bar.

"We parted our ways."

As soon as Pussy finished speaking, all the girls cheered, for they thought that she had been speaking about treasure. Clearly, they were going to get more treasure than they had ever seen. They were going to live in silver and gold and do whatever they wanted to do and spit on the world if they could be bothered.

Kathy Acker

They came out of their sulks and gave another cheer for Pussy their captain that started an echo in a faraway hill, which sent the gulls once more soaring and squalling around the wreck of the ship.

The pirates began to run toward the land, but the muck wouldn't let them. All the dead fish with their mouths agape. They moved, those sailors, however they could, alternately paddled and crawled, until they reached a narrow stream. The beginning of the earth that contained treasure.

Days That Are to Come

O's Story, the End

BECOMING A RAT

I ran and I ran.

I was sinking down into earth. It was as if the earth around me was opening. Its top was excited—I could see this—excited so that its bottom could open up and the dirt part, dirt from dirt, earth under earth.

I was in the marshes.

There was a lot of dirt underneath. Rich, brown bricks that I thought might be gold but weren't. I knew.

It was seared.

There were bricks of soil, which is shit, everywhere, scattered all over the fallen birds' wings. At this edge of an abyss, lips of grass like tiny swords lay in the sun. Light winds everywhere.

Beyond the marshes, there was nothing but time, so that the earth could take a rest. Where there was time, trees began to appear. Violators stood in the tops of those trees.

The earth opened.

The marshes had begun again because I was standing in stillness. In one of those pools between the trees. Water was air: silver. And then, the water that I was in and seeing started to ripple, for there was trouble underneath it, logs, fish-ferment, which is a combination of fermenting fish and fish shit. It all smelled like rot because it was. It was hot 'cause hot is orgasm. All was rolling and hurting and smelling and it was a strong, rich smell which was rolling over and rolling over and around again: a dog in mud.

The dog's teeth champed on mud which is meat.

My teeth or the world's champed on me or the world.

The trees were long because this whole world was logs. Logs were rolling over reality: turned each other over, turned over on and under each other. Each log-wave began time. And a new room would come into being. Each log-wave-time turned over, was gone.

And again.

My heart leaped up and began to thump, for I thought that I heard something. In this world where I was alone. Which seemed to be without humans. Something which sounded other than the winds creeping low through the reeds, birds' wings on the march, or the rocks under the wrecked ship scraping the sky.

At first, I thought I heard rats.

I was standing at the edge of a small hill. It must have been a young one, for its hair had just started to grow. I thought it was quivering because I was touching it, but the sound, I saw, came from bits of gravel falling downward, through that stubble.

Something that looked human leapt behind a tall tree.

It might be a possum or a giant rat. I thought.

Smells sat everywhere. They weren't as powerful as the ones that had been down in the marshes. Where trees had begun.

There are times when I get really scared, though I know that I'm brave.

Not knowing what I was seeing, whether dream or real, whether human or animal, brought my steps to a standstill.

In back of me, regarding time and space, was Silver, who wanted to murder me. In front of me, regarding the same, was I didn't know what. In front of me, my inability to know.

I had thought I would never return to Silver and now I was going to. I preferred dangers I knew to those I didn't. And I knew how to handle Silver's sexuality and her viciousness.

Or so I believed.

I didn't know anything about her sexuality and viciousness.

Turning on my heels and looking sharply behind me over my shoulder, I began to retrace my steps in the direction of the boat.

Instantly the strange figure reappeared and, making a wide circuit, commenced cutting me off. Both fear and exertion had tired me, but even if I had just awoke, it would have been useless for me to contend with such an adversary.

For it ran manlike on two legs, but was unlike any man I had ever seen.

Soon I would no longer be able to see. For the sun was ceasing and the stars beginning to gather. Each wept at the other.

I was scared.

I knew that I was scared because I had never cared whether I was alive or dead.

I said, "I who've been dead for so long: I don't know what to do and I don't know how to live and that's who I am."

It was a girl who was standing in front of me. She looked like a rat. For example, her hair was drooling over her face's front.

She stepped back and forth, as if she had to go to the bathroom, and then she threw herself around my feet.

It was Ange. She was the filthiest thing I had ever seen, far more grungy than Silver, for a sail part had been wrapped between her legs, then around one thigh, like a Kotex that's falling off. Otherwise, she had become a rat.

"What happened to you?"

"I got lonely."

It was then that I knew that I was a rat, that we were both rats, just like all the pirate girls, and it had taken all we had been through to make us this.

Metal-changing.

So I held on to her and the world disappeared and there were no more rats.

"Ange," I whispered, "Ange."

There was no one there to answer me, so I said her name as much as I wanted.

Maybe, in the future, I would get used to being in this new world.

"Ange. Ange."

Everything was rolling in this gentle motion so everything was alive and the air was warm. I and everything and the warm air turned over and over. Though I was no longer scared, I wondered if it was dangerous to be here 'cause there was no need to end.

"Do you want to stop, Ange?"

"No."

The world was where things grew, just at the top of a slope which was beginning to run downward.

For the two paths had separated.

Here was fur moss and animals.

"Hear come the nights," I said to Ange. They were rushing in, rushing water; the knights held their spears extended. Water was all over the place, had already flooded the world, there was no more ground.

The oceans were everything. The waves on the tops of the waters made, were also, patterns; the patterns were made out of froth, rather than water; the froth made the water visible.

This was the realm of continual ecstasy.

Now everything was wet, dripping with it. Dank and rotten. This world was never going to stop. For those two paths that had opened when this world had begun were now touching each other. Two paths each split into two. Burning. Turning around each other. They were still very dirty and exceedingly smelly.

The odors that had made the colors darken caused the waters to surge.

I looked upon Ange. Her hair was sticking straight out of her head and over her face. It was rat's hair all thick and brown and so stiff nothing would ever make it go down again and her green eyes were red. These red holes were opening and closing, all of her was opening now around my left leg, so the plains went on yellow and yellow, yellow but with bits of brown like grass, there.

As if all was a surface and the surface, a carpet, a line on or under the carpet, rose up like a snake.

Earth was lying under earth.

Under the membrane of the earth, the snake pulsated equaled *beneath an orgasm, a river*. Every time the snake touched this membrane with its nose, because it couldn't break through because this was the top, it was all orgasms in the plains.

The sun burned down, so the tips of the grass were now red, touches of.

I told her that she was never going to go away from me by telling her that she was a rat.

"If we're rats," she murmured rather than murdered in memory of the pirate girls, "we should act like rats."

"Then we have to eat everything we can scent."

We decided that that would be good behavior.

Ange said that there might be something to scent at the shipwreck or *the place of exile*.

I didn't know what this rat was talking about.

"The boat got wrecked and those girls made me go away from them, they put me into exile."

"That's because you're a rat."

Both of us agreed that we didn't want to be here because we didn't want to be anywhere, so we might as well crawl through this skanky-skunk-wood-tangled-garbage-whatever-it-was called *nature* 'cause there maybe we could find that which could help us, though all of this so-called nature looked more desolate to me than a city that had burnt down and was remnants of human civilization.

Ange 'n me decided that rats live in cities 'cause rats are highly intelligent.

The sun was getting up so he was mortal like us. It was then I knew that there were dead pirates all around us.

We walked on hands and knees through a bunch of nature that was rotten by nature 'cause nature naturally rots. Like trees 'n wildflowers 'n weeds 'n rocks 'n dead lizards 'n all the childhood neither me nor Ange ever had but we're gonna have 'cause that's our goal in life 'n worms half-squished by these really hideous crabs who were Martians in disguise or in real life. And found dead computer parts.

Slithered around ponds and even through some 'cause Ange wanted to feel what it's like to have piss all over you. I said no because I thought I'd be disgusted, but it smelled kind of good, like I was all safe again, like when you put mud all over you, so then I felt safe enough to remember that I had never felt, that is, been, safe.

We didn't find anything, so this nature was a lot more useless than a decayed city to two girls who had been through everything on their hands and knees.

That's how I felt then.

We came, as if we were coming to an object, to the sounds of birds screaming. And to bits of bird shit. Ange said she was hungry.

"You smell bad enough as it is," I told her.

The harpies above us were still squawking, probably 'cause they were waiting for us to die so they could eat too, when Ange's hand sank into what was mushy.

She started to put this hand on my face, so I informed her that I'd vomit, only the smell of vomit made me more nauseous than the smell of her hand. "You have to suffer and endure terrible conditions if you want to find the source of dreams." I told Ange. "I'm going to make you bathe."

The first time we looked up from this cross between a pond and a puddle in which we were sitting, we saw that we were in a cemetery.

This couldn't be a pirate graveyard 'cause pirates get buried in the sea so they can dream. So this was a rat cemetery.

A different bird was sitting on each tombstone. Most of which were wood 'cause they were sticks.

This death joint was more solemn than a chapel. Neither Ange nor I had ever been in a church. One of the gravestones must have just had some sexual pleasure, 'cause the liquid in which we were cleaning ourselves was still issuing out of it.

We thought of all the dead rats. How humans feared them 'cause humans, above all, fear intelligence. How humans, scared out of their minds, gather whatever intelligence they can put their hands on and put it all in a central penitentiary named *facts*, whereas rats eat everything whether or not they're hungry. Rats: pleasure rules their world.

This is why Ange 'n me would rather be rats.

Ange was the one who said this.

I asked her whether pleasure was equivalent to a rat.

She said that she'd know this as soon as she totally became a rat.

It all had something to do with treasure.

The puddle-pond was located in the center of the cemetery. In this land of the dead, we had already met dead butterflies 'n dogs' teeth but I didn't see how we could use any of this nature for our own purposes, 'cause all of it was perishing, if not perished, so we decided to keep on crawling.

While we were still sitting there, right in the middle of nature, I told Ange 'bout how there was this guy named Orpheus and he had a girlfriend and we don't know whether or not she was a poet 'cause she was a girl. "Everybody knows that Orpheus, or O, or Or, was the most famous poet who's ever existed in all of human memory, or Greek memory, which soon might not be remembered anymore, and that includes Orpheus's girlfriend even though we don't know who she was."

I said that we know that Orpheus followed her down into the ground, right to this burial ground.

"At that time, there was a cemetery king who was a rat.

" 'Yo, Orpheus,' said Rat, 'you can get your girlfriend back and own her and kiss her all up. All you gotta do is get out of this dead place.'

" 'I want to get out of this rotting cemetery,' replied Orpheus.

" 'So go. And don't ever look behind you.'

" 'What about Eurydice?' Now I remembered. That was the name of Orpheus's girlfriend."

"I've got a girl," mumbled Ange and wriggled over to me and climbed on me 'n made me come a few times.

"The Rat King said, 'She's right behind you where you can't see her.' "

Ange and I, again, started crawling.

"Orpheus, of course, looked behind him, as if *he* walked out of the land of the dead, as if *he* hadn't been changed by going through the land of the dead, as if *he* could be the person he remembered he was. Disobeying Death, or *Identity*, he lost Eurydice."

Ange turned around so she was facing me. "He lost Eurydice 'cause he was ignorant: he never knew who she was, just like we don't know who Eurydice was."

When Ange turned back again, now in post-cemetery domain, she saw exactly what I was seeing.

Silver was standing by.

Night must have come and gone. It was the coldest morning that, still, I have ever known.

Trees were rising up like dogs who forgot they've just been punished. The cold was turning the low-lying sun into ice.

Where Silver was, fog was rising from the ground. Her legs were spread so far apart that she could have been pissing. There was this lizard sitting in her silver hair. Then, all I could see were my lips on those of that white animal . . .

"Aren't you going to talk to me?" The filthy-haired girl's lilac eyes were looking into mine. So were the yellow and red eyes and everything that was living in her hairs.

Ange was muttering that this brat whom we had befriended, or who had befriended us, was a common murderer and a pirate and at the same time should be hung and electrocuted, so I said out loud as loudly as I could, "I know that you and your girls never meant any good to us."

"Well . . ."

"I know that you want to murder me." I was looking deeper into those lilac and black realms.

"Here's the thing," replied Silver as if no emotion had ever shared her world.

And even now, I know the sun is a lizard.

"The thing is," she picked her nose with her grubbiest finger, "we, the girls 'n I, want that treasure and we're going to get it. There's nothing you can do about this so you might as well be dead, and you have to die to be dead. But before you die, you're going to do one thing, 'cause there's one thing that we want."

"What's that?" asked Ange, all green-eyed and curious. Ange was much braver than me.

"You're going to give up that chart! The original that has pirate blood smeared all over it!" Her legs spread themselves apart farther, and at the same time, the lizard, who had been almost hidden in all that hair, slithered out until it was balanced on two or three strands of thick girl stuff. Its tongue hung out of its mouth, so long that it could lick its own eyes.

"What I mean is," cried the nasty pirate, "we want that map. I myself—understand this, O—would never do anything to hurt you, so I don't give a tinker's damn what happens to you. I don't give a tinker's curse whether or not you're murdered in the process of us getting, and becoming, everything in the world we want."

And this was how I remembered that I still had a treasure map.

"I think you should die," Ange replied to Silver, "and all of your girls should be electrocuted because, according to my acupuncturist, that is the most painful way for humans to die. All of your flesh while you're alive will become shredded living worms because our treasure map is ours."

Silver turned away, she walked away from us just like Orpheus.

Just like the headless writer—though he wasn't headless then—she looked back. Toward me. Eurydice. As if I were dead. As if I were dead to the world, and so the world, now dead, was commencing again in the form of a sun. In the form of all the treasure that's hidden within the sun. "I'll tell you what I'm going to do, O. Listen here."

My ears were as red as a rose.

"You come over here and slip that chart up into where I keep my treasures and I'll offer you a choice. As soon as all the treasure's been shipped into the ship, you can come on board with us and become one of us, and for the rest of your life, and all your lives after that, your cunt, when you have one, will know what it is to be continually wet, dripping in the winds of the world. There's no use stopping the winds, is there? Think of all the odors coming from the winds. You've never smelled them, have you? Never smelled yourself, have you, girl?"

Pause. "Or you can choose to die."

Pause. "You'll never get a handsomer offer."

Pause. "Either way, that treasure's ours."

"Now you hear me, Silver. Fuck off. That's what I've got to say. I don't want your rotting old cunt anymore. I had forgotten about the treasure map until you threatened Ange 'n me. Ange 'n me, we're going to find the treasure and it'll be ours and that's that.

"If anything, there's murder between us."

There were all sorts of animals in Silver's hair. She pulled a screw out and the white lizard scampered away. Mumbled, "Them that'll die'll be the lucky ones."

After she had stamped away, the green-eyed girl and I just looked at each other.

"We're tougher than pirates," announced Ange, quivering.

"I'm scared."

PLAYING HOUSE

The actuality was that both of us were scared, so, remaining standing up, we looked for a house in which we could play house 'cause we knew that it wasn't going to be our real home.

Ange said we had to analyze our finances to see what we could afford. Mortgage rates were going up all over the place due to the disintegration of government. She wasn't going to take chances like we had been taking them.

We looked but we couldn't find anything. Just goes to show that nothing ever changes, and, if there's a history of human progress, men have made it up.

But Ange insisted that unless we wanted to become pirates and murder nonpirates we had to live somewhere.

So we started crawling through nature again.

We were inching and grumbling through used beehives and rose petals. I sneezed 'cause I'm allergic to anything natural like the world.

Soon we got all tangled up in these dead wasps and combs that looked like they came from leftover schoolgirls and these kind of crab claws—actually I couldn't tell what they were 'cause Mother Nature is always changing her form. All of them were down in the ground. Just like the teeth Jason had sown in what might now be a post-human world.

One of the teeth caught on some threads that were leaking out of what remained of a pocket in my blue-jean shorts. The map started falling out. That's what made me remember I had a map. Maybe it wasn't drawn by humans, I thought, 'cause maybe criminals aren't human. So I looked down into it to find out what this posthuman world looked like.

Section of the map I'm looking at:

James Baldwin's Novel
Inside the book

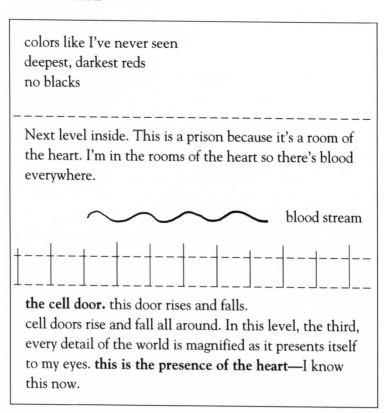

colors like I've never seen
deepest, darkest reds
no blacks

Next level inside. This is a prison because it's a room of the heart. I'm in the rooms of the heart so there's blood everywhere.

blood stream

the cell door. this door rises and falls.
cell doors rise and fall all around. In this level, the third, every detail of the world is magnified as it presents itself to my eyes. **this is the presence of the heart**—I know this now.

"This is what it's like to be a black man in our society," says Ange.

We returned to the map's insides:

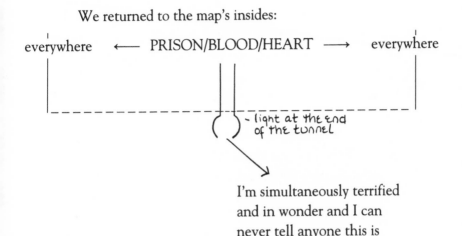

everywhere ⟵ PRISON/BLOOD/HEART ⟶ everywhere

— light at the end
of the tunnel

I'm simultaneously terrified
and in wonder and I can
never tell anyone this is
happening

Maybe 'cause of what I'd just seen and maybe 'cause I couldn't describe what I'd just seen, I, with Ange, kept on crawling.

We thought we were back on the beach next to the sea in which lived those men who had also been in Ange's dead mother's cunt. Next to the gray surface of the water where the ship had been and, now, was dead. A dead bird like all who are sleeping and dreaming.

When we walked to the edge of that sand, we saw that there was more sand below us. We were on the top of a cliff. The sun had set; the sea breeze was rustling and tumbling through the woods in the distance. Light seemed to come from nowhere.

We kept on walking. Piles of shit were hidden in the sand. I stepped into one; brown stuck into the crevices of my hiking boots' soles. I loathed this sight, so I told Ange I had to find a bathroom, sooner than possible.

While I was telling Ange I had to go to the bathroom, I was so freaked out about what was on me that I didn't notice that she was already knocking on a door of a log cabin.

"Look, Ange," I said, "a house."

Just like the one Abe Lincoln was born in. Dead crabs were lying outside it.

There were no windows, only porthole-like openings, where its slats didn't manage to meet.

Ange, inside, stared at the floor, parts of which lay above other parts, sometimes so far above that a part was almost touching the ceiling, just like we touch God, while I was washing my hands, then more thoroughly my feet, right in front of the metal stalls found in the bathrooms of schoolgirls.

Then I remembered that there was shit stuck inside the crevices of the soles of my hiking boots. I had to get that out, though I didn't want to, 'cause the shit would contaminate my clean hands, but I made myself do it so I could be like a child.

Meanwhile, according to the map, a ladder led from the center of the large room outside this bathroom to another room.

Ange tried to climb up this ladder and failed.

I wanted to try. So many had tried and failed, but I was determined to succeed.

I fell.

When I started climbing again, I knew that in order to reach the room that was on top I would have to bring something with me. *To bring something with me* would be *to give something away*, But, I told myself, I don't have anything 'cause I had nothing in childhood.

I started to go up.

I was halfway up the ladder when I saw that ahead of me there weren't any more rungs.

I had nothing to stand on anymore.

I kept moving by pulling myself up by my hands.

When I was almost at that trap door, I saw myself halfway through the opening, which was too small for the rest of my body to pass through.

I could only be pulled through.

Pulled into a room larger than I had ever seen. Where Ange and I would be able to play with each other.

I heard a noise that, at first, sounded like winds.

Ange screaming.

I leaped out of the tangles of that ladder and, rubbing my eyes like a child, ran over, beside the green-eyed girl, to a hole that was lying like a dead rat in the wall and smelling like a girl.

THE TRUE COLORS OF PIRACY

I peered through the hole:

Sure enough, all the rotten girls were outside. I saw two of them. Silver and that dead girl, Virgin.

They were lounging around, nothing else. Maybe feeling themselves up.

It was quiet and early, so I could still see the chill: white and stiller than time. 'Cause there are no clouds in time. Gold and that brat whose hair was all over the place as if it was the garbage can for the years were wading knee-deep in air so milky that it had to be poisonous.

"Don't let her in. That means *you*," Ange told me.

"I want a truce," the silver-haired girl yelled.

"What do you want a truce for?" I asked. "Get along or we'll shoot you."

"Now, me hearties"—as usual Silver was doing all the talking—"girls should get along with each other and not have fights, 'cause girls aren't violent, and all my nice girls agree with me. And piracy's survived for a long time in this world. So why do you keep prolonging this internecine turbulence?"

"I don't know." Then I caught myself. "Get out of here or Ange 'n me're gonna shoot you."

"I'm gonna shoot you," yelled Ange.

"Girls have to accept girls who aren't like them," the pirate brat pleaded with us. "For this reason, the girls and I have decided to join forces with you even though you've never been to jail or stolen. But dooty is dooty, 'n girls' dooty is to love other girls."

"And all other living beings," added the Virgin. She was masturbating, so my friend followed her example.

I kicked the green-eyed slut hard.

"O," Silver continued, "you 'n me used to be friends, and you know, if you ever saw something you shouldn't have seen, well, you know I get a little drunk sometimes. All of my girls do. It's from living in a society that disrespects its women and hates their bodies. Especially when they masturbate. This makes us turn to drink, though I know that's not the way to deal with certain types of hegemony."

Ange was coming, so I kicked her again.

"The bottom line"—the girl whose hair was silver, though it didn't look so silver after all we had been through, was still talking to me—"is that girls got to survive. Since *girls* includes us . . ."

"Not you," the Virgin commented.

". . . *we* need that treasure. That's the bottom line, matey."

The filthiest of all girls, blood hanging like dead rats around her thighs, filthier even than Silver, stepped forward. It was Pussycat.

"Since that treasure came from pirates, that treasure should go to pirates."

She disappeared as fast as she had come.

"Yeah, that's the bottom line." It was Brat-face. "You've got the map. The real one, don't you?"

"Yeah," Ange replied. I kicked her for real.

"That's what we want. As for me, I have no desire to kill you, O. You or your little friend."

For the first time, I was seeing the pirate girls in their true colors. Black and red. They wore their insides on their outsides, blood smeared all over the surfaces. When opened, the heart's blood turns black.

Just like the room in Baldwin's novel.

"So," Silver finished me off, "you give me that map so I can get all the treasure, and then you drop dead. Or, if that normal way doesn't please you, become one of us."

"I have a desire to kill you," was all I said because I wasn't noticing her anymore but rather thinking about how the pirate map that had started all this had come out of Ange's dead mother's box. Just as Ange had come out.

With that, Silver disappeared, dragging Gold with her.

Whereas my mother had tried to off me and killed herself

instead. I clung to Ange in that world that was now deserted. There was no one there but us, so the emptiness of our play-house would never go away. Brother and sister, we clung to each other.

It was the new world.

Ange and I were waiting for something. 'Cause we were no longer going to play house. We waited past our time. Time was past its birth-time and about to bust through its mucous linings, and this delayed birth, or commencement, of the world set our ears, eyes, and nostrils—especially our nostrils, for we had gotten good at smelling skunk, dead fish, and crab, the three animals this isle was full of—on the alert.

"There are pirates out there," announced Ange.

I didn't ask where.

The world hadn't yet begun.

So Ange and I discussed whether or not it's right to kill pirates, as if anything that we said or might say bore any rela-tion to what was really happening and what was really going to happen.

Then, the world began.

The viciousness of girls cannot be imagined.

All the pirates appeared.

The fields were lilac, filled with tiny flowers. Then the animals, little bits of fur, specks of gray, the tops of heads. Each time a head stuck out, each head was an orgasm.

A rat was putting her head under her paws and snuffling around. "Sniff," she snuffled, shuffling, "wuff, wuff." The rat, at that moment, thought she was a dog 'cause she was looking peering snuffling for a word or a possibility of speaking: "Down there, something's happening! Down there to the side!"

In the side, wood was rolling slowly. A roll of wood. Rolling down into the depths of hell.

The wood descended to where there were dark lands, rivers, everywhere. While the pirate girls shot at us and made blood flow out of the body.

Everywhere rivulets divided the land.

It's not that girls don't kill. A pirate named Pussycat, who was truly the meanest of all the pirates, having run up to Ange, grabbed the gun the green-eyed girl had found, wrenched it from her hands, threw it toward the other pirates, where it landed in a pile of rat shit. The girl pirates didn't care. They were used to bad smells. With one stunning blow, Ostracism's lover laid Ange senseless on the earth.

"Will I see poetry again?" I looked at Ange. "Orpheus couldn't see the violence of *red*. This is all an announcement of the future of death." All the motorcycles were coming in death; the orgasms caused tears of joy to be on their faces.

King Pussy, who was a rat, stood in front of all of them, all those ratty, now bruised pirates. "I, King Pussy, who see by means of my dreams, have seen wars! Mutilations! Girls dying from brutal mistreatment! The hell with my dreams! Now I see everything differently!"

In the past, King Pussy explained in her declaration of war, girls who had never done anything to anyone were called names and beaten with sticks. "Now we're declaring war! We shall beat up O and Ange, for all the treasure is ours! Ours, the girls'!"

Ange—even though she had passed out—and I were seeing our limbs cut, then spread, over all the dark, rainy Thursdays, Thursdays about to die. Thursdays are always autumns. Thursdays are the days of death because girls put on suits of earth, suits of shit, buried in the bones of corpses, they crunch on those bones, those bones of shit.

Beaten up always on a Thursday . . .

The pirates had won the war.

Afterwards, sleep elongated to a lake.

For the moment, the pirates were gone. I tried to drag Ange up the ladder, 'cause I knew we'd be safe in that room up there, but the rungs kept falling off. So I took her behind the ladder, to a small space the ladder had obscured. And shut the door so that room could no longer be seen.

If we remained hidden, we might not die.

"Where are those yucky girls?" inquired Kiss-of-Rot, a mangy pirate. For her peck was known as *kiss-of-rose*.

"I, King Pussy, see through my dreams . . ."

King Pussy had to masturbate to see this one:

"I see two girls, can't distinguish all limbs, about to lose energy, dissolving, as if into gasps, hardly see figures. One has hair, one squatting on floor, other kneels beside her.

"Floor?

"The walls are moving. I can no longer tell—for *to tell* is *to remember*—where. Like going through narrow halls, shift as turn, another set of halls, just see through a slit."

"That's all you can do is see through a slit?"

"How can I look through it?"

Pussy: "A narrow, vertical slit. Through which these two girls . . ."

"Seeing into what?"

". . . they're in a room. One has hand on the other's face,

the face of the one who's squatting, rubs that cheek, the other's inner thighs are quivering 'cause she's coming, me too it feels so good, they lie on the floor, both on their backs—it's a wood room—'cause they want to rub their asses on the floor."

"One is on top of the other, legs spread, O my God." One of the other pirates was now looking through this hole.

"Where are these two girls, pig-slut?" asked mangy cutoff ears.

"Oh, behind. Just go behind, left, right, it doesn't matter, oh shit, I'm coming again, I'll tell you where I'm coming, where's there's light . . . ah . . . black."

"Oh, shut up, Pussy," said a girl whose tongue had been bitten off. She usually didn't say anything.

The red glare of a torch lighting up the interior of most of the cabin showed me that all of the pirate girls had come and were in full possession of my house. Silver and her bloody co-hort, Virgin, stood in front of me.

Behind were the rest of the motley crew, in the infernal light, in the nighttime that belonged to them.

As soon as she had me back again, brat-girl yanked my head up by its tiny hairs and then stuck her hand up me.

THE VISION PASSES

When the pirate girls blindfolded me, I knew palpable fear. I was terrified of each girl, of what they were going to do to me, for I knew they were going to do something.

What they were going to do to me was my fear.

There were animals everywhere. Not only the wolf-hounds, who were barking, and the birds.

Hands shoved me forward—we'd started walking—pulled me in certain directions.

A rose yes yes rose oh the relief. Rose out front, all the roses were alive.

"I don't want to be blindfolded," I protested. Rose thorns stuck into my skin, stumbling.

The dogs kept barking, the birds and the lizards.

"We could let you die."

"Let's just leave her and let the birds eat her cunt."

"I'm hungry," bespoke another pirate.

"Give her to your dogs, eh, MD?"

But there was every kind of animal everywhere. I could no longer tell where Ange was among all those animals.

The animals are just one animal today, I whispered to myself. One growly bear who clenches paws and takes all into that chest. "I want, I want," says growly bear. And just does what he has to do 'cause he's a he-bear.

"Yump yump yump," which means *give me*. The bear has a big tongue. This makes the outside come while he licks oh my god bees. I'm gonna die coming outside and, of course, inside is all fields 'cause there's constant churning there.

Bear has gone to the roses 'cause both bear and roses can't exist at the same time.

The pirate girls were taking me down a hill.

We were going downhill. I said to myself, Oh yes they can. The bear sits on roses with his big tush. When this fat butt goes down, the roses squish. But bear doesn't care about squished roses: this is what an orgasm is. When the skin of inside the asshole comes out like a rose.

Oh no, I shouldn't be doing this, coming out; asshole skin coming out; but it's okay when it's an orgasm.

Growly bear, I continued, for I had forgotten where I was, puts dildo in his cunt. Is anyone looking at me? he thinks. If so, does their gaze affect me? I'm not interested, thinks growly bear. "Yes! Yes! Yes!" growly bear is shouting, 'cause now he doesn't have to do anything. 'Cause coming so deep in there.

But growly bear isn't that deep yet. Is going to the center, but as yet isn't in the center. Growly bear's where all is turning, metamorphosing. The riches of nature and orgasms are so strong, they metamorphose into convulsions. Where the rain of rose petals reigns.

Again I could smell the sea where the fish are always more rotten than they have been.

Some pirate took off my blindfold. Somehow, seeing had changed. In light that was also dark and dark that was also light, pirates were poring over a map. I didn't have to see to know what they were seeing.

There would be a sign: *dreams end* . . . Then there would be paths and they would get jumbled, and bones, and they all get jumbled, and all of them would combine and then there would be a tall tree that, according to the map, was red.

And off to the side, a boat next to a black stone and a white stone.

"That's where we're going." MD, her two wolfhounds leaping around her, came over to me and pointed toward a plateau. Trees were growing from its top, especially one so tall it seemed to be reaching through the sky. Right before me I saw an anchorage and two stones, one black and one white. MD kissed the dog on the left.

The pirate girls were so eager to find the treasure that they no longer cared about Ange's and my presence.

All of us ascended to the plateau, we dug down. The higher we went up, the more this earth opened.

Until there were only mountains and everything that was rich and brown. And the meeting place between the sky and what lay below it was red.

Now, as the hill began to grow steeper, all the colors changed, for color is the first appearance of the world. The sun was red and the birds' wings, for green is the color of death. Yellow fields rose up as if they were about to break open. "Oh, thank you, little men," cried the pirates. "Come out come out open up we're looking for the treasure." Red was down here, was the cherry. They would have to go down now, there, there where it was brown, go, go into space as space expanded and action burned.

It was all burning as they climbed to the top. There space expanded and, simultaneously, violently contracted.

Each star is a contraction, a burst, when you dive to get treasure.

All of us still had to find the forest, find the lilac water so that what was the most inside, the treasure, could turn out, roll over. So that consciousness or surface, for all is conscious, could faint. Become a feint.

Once the treasure was found, the insides would turn and turn and never stop that. On the other hand, each set of turn-ings would become more violent and calmer. *The woods* will be the name of all this.

All of us reached the forest. The pirate girls started leap-ing about and looking for booze and doing whatever pirate girls do regardless of what they're supposed to be doing.

The youngest of them, Black Maria, who was never heard from, cried out in terror.

"Now I see the treasure," shouts King Pussy, for she is the one who sees, and I wasn't blindfolded anymore, and what Pussy had thought was treasure was a dead pirate.

Which goes to show that a dead pirate is better than nothing at all.

Pussy who lives by her dreams wouldn't believe that this wasn't treasure, so she lifted up an arm, then a femur, like there was going to be something besides bones, and MD's dogs were doing the same thing. All the girls started sniffing each other. They threw the bones around and said, generally, that is, that there was no more need for pirates and suchlike history and that now the reigns of all reins could be over.

Antigone decided to celebrate this day in which there was no booze, unless you count fermented rat piss, by changing her name to Angelique, who used to be some whore, because, she told us, she was currently talking to an angel. The angels were larger than humans.

Ange 'n me were still these girls' prisoners and hadn't been allowed to talk to each other. We wanted to get away and be together. "Look at that old skeleton," Ange pointed toward a corner of the crisscrossed jumbled-path cemetery where the pirates were lying.

She said this to the pirates, 'cause she didn't want to act like she was talking to me, but they didn't bother to notice her.

It was a bigger skeleton than all the others. His feet pointed in one direction; his cock, a bone, pointed in the other.

"Let me see the map," added Ange.

Silver was fucking Virgin, so the green-eyed girl just took the map away from her.

"Look." Ange. "Here's a compass. The map says the labyrinth begins ESE by E. This must be those guys' last joke. ESE by E is here. His fucking boner is showing us the treasure, O."

I looked down at the map and gazed at that dead cock. Now I knew why I had been searching for men. And hadn't stopped until I had found one. The pirate girls were so into their private world, they didn't notice anything, notice that the world or the sky was shifting again.

Ange and I followed the cock.

We discussed how boners stay alive even after men die . . .

Cocks weren't treasure but pointed to treasure. That's what Ange said.

And so we left the pirate girls to do what pirate girls do.

While we were traveling in the direction the cock told us to, I announced to Ange that I was going to tell her a story about treasure:

"It's a story told by a poet.

"In order to take revenge against a human named Prometheus, who had challenged his inhuman power, God the Father, whose name was Zeus, created the most beautiful woman in the world. He wanted to give her to Prometheus.

"Actually he sent this woman to Prometheus's brother, but Prometheus had already warned his sibling not to accept gifts from the gods.

"Even more furious than before, Zeus chained Prometheus to a stone pillar. There, in the coldest regions of the mountains, a vulture tore into this naked man's liver, and Prometheus said, for his liver became whole so the bird could repierce it, 'There is no end to pain.'

"Prometheus's brother became so terrified that he fucked

the woman, Pandora, who, because she was beautiful, was stupid, dishonest, and a pain in the butt, as opposed to the gut.

"All these events occurred in the golden age of the world, in the beginning of the world. In that age, when and where there was no human suffering, the cause of human suffering lay in a cunt.

"When the man, because he couldn't resist beauty, opened up Pandora's cunt, her evil excretions, her excrescence, smelled up the world. So badly that all those who could smell those smells—that is, men—wanted to die, and would have if they couldn't get rid of that which lies within women.

"That's where treasure is," I concluded.

"How can you be you and say this? I thought that you loved me."

"This story isn't saying what *I* say about cunts: this is what that old, dead poet said."

The dead cock was no longer leading us, 'cause we were back at the edge of the water. Were in the middle of a cove, where a gentle slope ran up from the beach to the entrance of a cave.

"Ange," I said, and took her hand.

Together, we entered the opening.

There were no more pirate girls and I didn't care anymore.

It was a large, airy place, with a little spring and a pool of clear water, overhung with ferns. The floor was sand. In a far corner, I saw a box out of which coins and yellow slabs flowed. This had cost such blood and sorrow: what good ships, scuttled in the deep, amassed in blood and guts, what brave humans walking the plank blindfold, shots of the cannon, shame and lies and cruelty, perhaps no man alive can tell.

Yet there were still those on the island who had indulged in blood.

"Come in," I said to Silver.

"I'm doing my dooty," said Silver. "That's our treasure too." She walked into the cave, and then, King Pussy.

We all looked at the money.

"I'd rather go a-pirating," said Silver. "If me and my girls take all this treasure, the reign of girl piracy will stop, and I wouldn't have that happen."

King Pussy was staring out toward the ocean.

I understood, and watched in awe, while those girls walked out of the cave.

Ange and I grabbed all the money we could and got into the rowboat that was hidden by the two, the white and the black, stones.

A Prayer for All Sailors

Halcyons shall cease to prey on fish,

Poisonous leaves become our food,

Be you sailors without remorse

For your lips have been stained in blood.

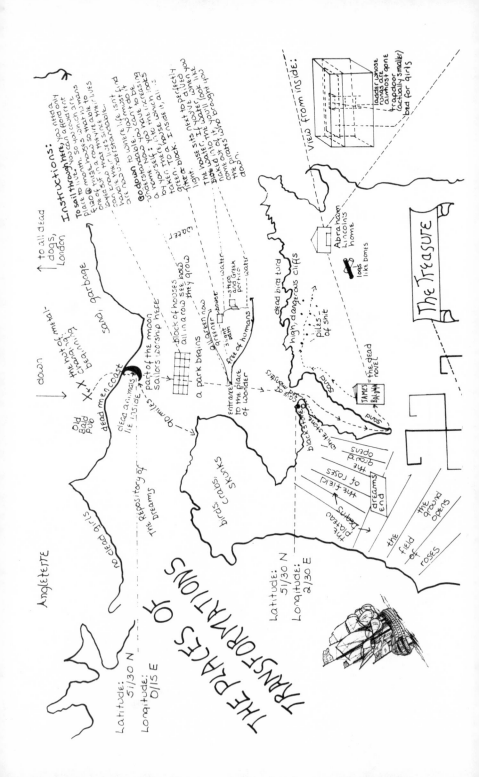

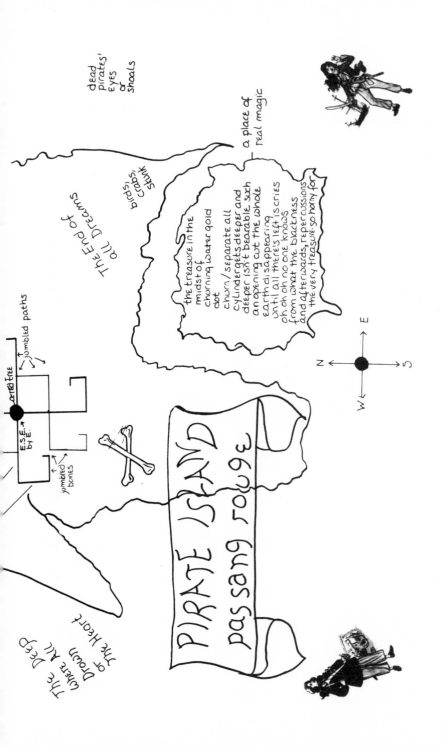